80 Proof Lives

Dr. Tibby!
Thank you for taking such
good care of my children. Read
& be blessed!   *Felicia S.W. Thomas*
                                    10/15/11

a novel

D1598829

Felicia S.W. Thomas

Umani Publishing, llc

Tallahassee, Florida

Amani Publishing, LLC
P. O. Box 12045
Tallahassee, FL 32317
(850) 264-3341

A company based on faith, hope, and love

Visit our website at: **www.Barbarajoewilliams.com**

Email us at: **amanipublishing@aol.com**

ISBN-13: 9780981584775
ISBN-10: 0981584772
LCCN: 2010919043

Cover photo courtesy of: **BigStockPhoto.com**

Cover creation by: **Diane Bass**, TDB811@aol.com

Dedication

This book is dedicated, first and foremost, to my three beautiful children, who believe in me fully, who inspire me endlessly, and who love me unconditionally. I also dedicate this book to my late mother, Marion V. Cottrell, whom I love dearly, whom I miss terribly, and who inspired me in her own way to help me achieve this goal in my life. Finally, I dedicate this book to the late Michael Moody.

Acknowledgement

I thank those who read this novel in its infancy, and helped me nurse it to its present state: Baron Thomas, Yanela Gordon, Lizzie Washington, Valerie Chamberlain, Wendy Casey, and Marlon Nesbeth.

I thank my wonderful editors, whose insight made this novel a better read: Liz Jameson and Dr. Jessica Wallace.

I thank my publisher, Barbara Joe Williams, for taking me under her wing and mentoring me through this process.

Above all, I thank my husband, Baron, for his unwavering belief in this novel. To my sister, Vallie, and my brother, Antonio, thank you for giving me a special kind of strength. Thank you to the rest of my family, my friends and acquaintances, who lit up when I mentioned I would be publishing this novel, and for telling me, "It's about time!"

To my fellow writers in the Tallahassee Authors Network (TAN), and Tallahassee Writers Association (TWA), thank you for your support and the very much needed pat on the back.

/CHAPTER I/

In my hometown, there was nothing for a 15-year-old girl to do but fight, drink, have babies, or some combination of the three. I found out the hard way I couldn't fight. I found out the painful way I couldn't drink. As for having babies, I wasn't exactly sure about how to get started on that one. If anybody in Quincy, Florida, was sure about getting started, it was Miss Lipstick. It was the summer of 1976, and I was put in the unique position of asking her, thanks to my momma.

Miss Lipstick was a legend in every nook and cranny of the city and had a reputation that crossed state lines. She was the queen of the bootleg beer business. She cooked up her own special brand of white lightning in the back yard with the giant tub, fire, and corn from the feed store. She sold it by the Mason jar for five dollars a pop, and bought sealed liquor from the stores for the new generation of drinkers. By all accounts, she had more customers than all the bootleg breweries and liquor stores in Quincy. She collected quite a few customers in her other business, and she reigned supreme in that, too. Because of her vast popularity, Miss Lipstick had eyes and ears in high and low places, extending her reach far and wide into the Quincy community.

In the '60s and '70s, tobacco was king and ruled Quincy with a heavy hand. Anybody old enough to toddle could pick up garbage in the fields; anybody with facial hair could harvest the rows of leaves from sunup to sundown; and anybody with breasts had to endure the foul smelling aroma of cooked tobacco after the stringing process, to cure it.

A branch of the Coca-Cola dynasty called Quincy home. The old money that poured in from the dynasty was evident in the affluent section of the city, which was decorated in brilliant floral colors, courtesy of God's magnificent, artistic hand. The fragrant jasmine flower with its shining leaves bloomed yellow and white, juxtaposed near the honeysuckle fuchsia, which bloomed true to its name. With a backdrop of rich green, well-shaped shrubbery, the beautiful pink ridge flowers and the elegant orange glow vine popped. The final piece of His mastery was the firecracker plant, which lit up gardens with its colorful foliage that blasted up and out in different directions, making that part of Quincy a visual and sensual treat.

The gardens were the perfect complement to the city's grand antebellum residences with the stately columns and pillars; homes that were the pride of its ancestry. Rows of white, genteel, two-story structures with well-constructed Southern porches and finely manicured lawns graced the downtown core along Duval, Love, and King Streets, but the grandeur stopped at the corner of Jefferson and Adams. Bushes and trees grew wild in open lots. The faces of centuries-old buildings of various heights and colors sported signs of age, the crumbling facades revealing cracks filled with browning grass crawling to the roof. Broken sidewalks and streets across town lay abused, abandoned, and neglected.

On a map of Florida, just below the southern border of Georgia, along Highway 90 between Tallahassee and Pensacola, what looks like a series of dots is a series of small towns breaking up the monotony of trees, the endless roads, and the naked landscape. Quincy is the largest of the smallest — a historic, one-industry town and the place of my birth. As far as I know, I was born without much fanfare, no praise, no dancing in the streets. I quietly slipped out of a warm, soft belly on Mother's Day, 1961. I often wondered if I was born on April Fool's Day and the hospital sent me home with the wrong mother. Millie Frye and I generally left each other alone. Her style of parenting was to let me grow with as little interference from her as possible.

Growing up alone with no friends, no other family, and no money, I was left to entertain myself daily with books I borrowed from the library and kept way too long. I hid myself in murder mysteries, romance novels and humorous stories. When Momma screamed for me, she could usually find me deep in the pages of some lavish tale.

Reading so much watered my fertile imagination, and gave me the tools I needed to become a superb dreamer, and a master liar. I was an heiress to a toilet paper fortune and was kept safe by a legion of bodyguards; I was a stowaway on a doomed voyage to India and swashbuckling pirates rescued me from the sinking vessel; I was the youngest and the blackest princess in all the fairest lands, courted by the most handsome princes. Long after my books were closed, my head was still in them.

A freight train rolled by on the tracks behind my home in the projects every other night. Its thunderous roar penetrated my sleep cycle and carried me off to exotic locales. When I was awake, its long, forlorn whistle, invited me to join it on its long distance travels. There were days when hopping a locomotive traveling at prohibitive speeds that could puree my body into a bloody soup du jour was a better choice than staying at home. Alas, I was never brave enough to rise to the challenge, so my body stayed put and my journeys were reserved for my fantasies.

I preferred my fantasies to the real world, anyway. I was beautiful only in my dreams. My mirror, mirror on the wall reflected a mahogany-skinned girl with large brown eyes and thin lips, crooked teeth and a nose wide enough to smell her ears. My short, coarse hair hated me and rebelled whenever I was in public. I kept it in two large dukie braids to contain it, but no hairstyle flattered my round face. I was not too tall, nor too heavy. I was not even so plain as to be too ugly. Momma, on the other hand, could have been beautiful had she tried. Her thick, black hair was a mass of tangled chaos but would fall in silky waves when she combed it. Her green eyes, high yellow skin and elegant cheek bones turned men's heads. Momma claimed she used to have a shape like a figure eight; it was my fault, I guessed, that her profile looked more like an "S." She had looks that could arrest men's hearts, but her bad leg and dark attitude seemed to attract men who were fond of being arrested.

I had no luck whatsoever attracting boys. They either saw through me or treated me like the punch line of a mean-spirited joke. I'd never had a boyfriend and probably never would. I collected crushes like archaeologists collected artifacts. I'd see a cute boy, have an imaginary relationship with him, and then discard him when I saw someone new. I had one longstanding crush that just wouldn't go away. His name was Randy, and he wasn't just a fellow student at my school, he was the star of my show. He was my happily ever after, my ride into the sunset when the credits rolled. Every other crush defaulted to him. Unfortunately, Randy was like the boys who behaved as if I were invisible.

Friday, June 11, was the last day of school. That 3 p.m. dismissal bell took longer and longer to ring the closer it got to the end of the day. When I finally made it home, I celebrated by holing up in my tiny room enjoying the best of Agatha Christie and thanking God ninth grade was officially over. I planned my summer like a nervous bride planned her wedding. I would attend summer school during the day and pitch a tent at the library if I could get away with it.

My room was my sanctuary and I worshipped at the altar of the written page. I gave the sterile white walls personality by covering them with my artistic renditions of the titles of every book I'd ever read. So far, two of four walls were completely covered with everything from *The Cat in the Hat* to *Great Expectations*. A third wall showcased the various certificates I'd earned over the years for academic achievements, and my spelling bee trophies covered the base boards along the same wall. I learned as a very young child that my Momma wasn't even mildly interested in my academic success.

"Mommy, look at my drawing of Big Bird," I remember saying to her as a five-year-old kindergartener. I was so proud of that picture. I stayed in the lines, my colors were pretty, and Mrs. Collins had written "Good Job" on the front.

"I don't have time to be looking at no paper," she said while she lay in the bed, not even turning over to face me. Her indifference shouldn't have phased me. She continued turning me down when I asked her to sing the alphabet song with me, or to watch Sesame Street, or even play patty cake. She outright refused to come to any parent-teacher meetings or do any homework with me.

"You a smart little chick. You don't need my help." She told me that one time too many. At five and a half, I stopped asking her for help and showing her my report cards. At six years of age, I shut down on my mother, closed myself up in an airtight vault and never shared myself with her again.

Momma was determined not to have any proof of me visible anywhere in her space, and everything but my room was her space. The popcorn walls of the apartment were bare, with nary a baby picture of me nor my kindergarten art to adorn them. Every attempt I made to make the place look less like a prison and more like a home was met with open hostility, and sometimes an open hand. So, I kept all my cherished things in my haven. It had enough square footage for my literary art and a closet big enough for a few second-hand fashion don'ts.

To a casual observer, my life might have appeared dull and slightly gray. To me, my unremarkable existence was an explosion of crayons, especially the closer I came to being on my own. Guilty excitement coursed through me like an electric charge when I thought about my impending exit. As of May 14, 1979, I would be eighteen — only three days, eleven months, and two years separated me from my legally-imposed, indentured servitude. I boogied around the room with my imaginary Soul Train partner, then belly-flopped onto my bed and dove happily back into the pursuits of Hercules Poirot. I was reveling in this joy when

Momma's sharp voice cut through it like a jigsaw around four o'clock. Like any other day of the week, she screamed at me, "Girl, get yo' nose outta that book and go get me a beer from Lipstick!"

Momma didn't actually call me "girl." She called me Fla, which rhymes with clay. I cringed every time she hollered my name. "Flaaaa!" she squealed at the highest pitch a human ear could tolerate. Some people thought my name was Florida, like the character Esther Rolle played on *Good Times.* No, I told them, it's pronounced just like it's spelled. So they called me Flaw. I would say no again, it's Fla, with a long "a" and no period. I don't know what possessed the woman to name me after a state. I didn't like telling people my name was Fla Frye.

"Where's the money?" I asked, cutting Hercules Poirot off in mid-sentence.

"You don't need no money. You gettin' it on credit from Lipstick."

Beer was mother's milk to Momma. The first week of a new month, Momma financed her drinking through the courtesy of the Social Security Administration. The rest of the month, she relied on her tab. I probably logged hundreds of miles over the years walking Quincy, buying, begging and borrowing on behalf of Momma's habit. Consequently, the eleven households that sold liquor without the benefit of a license knew me like family. Some of the bootleggers were kind and friendly; others were creepy and crazy. They were forgiving in degrees when Momma's tab went unpaid, so I knew who to tap and when if I came with no money. I knew almost nothing about Miss Lipstick.

I was in the fifth grade the last time Momma and I paid Miss Lipstick a visit. It was two weeks before my birthday. Even that wouldn't have made it an occasion special enough for Momma to make me dress up on a Saturday morning in a hideous, mauve thing with ruffles around my neck and knees, and for her to put on a bra. She liked to let her ample breasts roll around in her T-shirts like two large honey dews in a grocer's burlap bag. She washed her hair, and brushed it. It fell to her shoulders and lay down like an obedient puppy. It was shiny and so pretty. My hair was determined to be obstinate. Every short strand decided to go its own way as I wrestled it into submission to get it into a ponytail holder.

It had to be a visit of significance because Momma only revved up her sixteen-year-old Honda Civic, a rusty sardine can on wheels held together by spit and glue, when the destination served her interests, like going to the doctor or to the Social Security office. We puffed and jerked and spluttered out of the project parking lot and made our way to Miss Lipstick's. We parked at the curb in front of the house and with greater difficulty than usual, Momma unfolded herself out of the little car.

She leaned into the open window and shouted at me. "Don't get out yet!"

I had been struggling with the door, which I normally had to push open with my feet. Her limp was much more pronounced and she leaned quite heavily on her crutch. I watched as she disappeared into the depths of the house. I had no concept of time, so I counted the number of people who walked into the house, then came out staggering. I counted twelve before Momma came storming out. She threw the screen door open so hard it whacked the front of the house, producing a cloud of dust that I could see from the car. She walked fast, dragging her crutch behind her. She folded herself back into the car and sat with her fist jammed in her mouth. Her face was streaked with tears. Even as a ten-year-old child, I recognized naked fear.

"What's the matter, Momma?" I asked, her fear infecting me.

"Shut up!" she barked. "Don't talk to me!"

The aftermath of that visit sent me to bed early that night and us to church the next morning — I, in my mauve, ruffled straitjacket, and Momma very lovely in a pleated blue mini-skirt, sheer white top, and bra. All morning, she was alternately afraid and angry. Even during the service, she fidgeted and pinched me on the shoulder if I moved. I remember the men's appreciative stares, even with Momma on a crutch, and their wives' jealous glares. We were asked to leave as Momma escorted me to the altar during the call to salvation. No one would have known she was drunk if she hadn't worn her skirt backwards and unzipped.

That five-year-old memory plunged me into near hysterics, yet Momma still wanted to send me over there alone. Momma didn't like what Miss Lipstick did for a living, didn't like that she owed Miss Lipstick a lot of money, and didn't like that she was terrified of Miss Lipstick. That didn't stop her, though, from drinking Miss Lipstick's bootleg liquor.

Momma ignored my quick, short breaths, the pleading in my eyes, and the whine in my voice. She dragged her bad leg away from the refrigerator in our tiny kitchen, frustrated that the fridge contained only food. She pulled her crutch behind her, as though it were chained to her wrist. It was old and splintered, weak and dirty. No self-respecting termite would touch it. I suspected she didn't really need the crutch, not when she had a daughter who carried her weight.

I sighed, but not too loudly, as Momma would interpret it as sass. Sass would result in a lot of yelling and cussing. I'd rather be hit.

I grabbed my book and tucked it under my arm. The trek to get the beer would take at least fifteen minutes, one way. Momma wanted it in less than ten minutes, total.

I strolled through the pass, a shortcut behind the projects that residents took to get into town. The pass was a place where the tops of the trees formed a canopy over a raggedy bridge with no railing. The only troubled waters this eroding bridge covered had dried up years ago and it was now just a hideout for teenagers who were making out. I spent so much time down there I knew every blade of grass by name. I sat down under a particularly leafy tree to finish a chapter in the late afternoon sun. Hercules Poirot was noticing a small detail the police had missed when the temperature dropped a degree or two and a familiar churning sensation returned to my stomach. I raised my head slowly and saw Cast Iron Kat towering over me. We were neighbors in the projects. Her real name was Katherine Marie Morehead. With a name like that, she should have been pretty. She should have been a cheerleader, the trophy girlfriend of the captain of the football team. But Cast Iron Kat wasn't pretty. She was stunning.

Cast Iron Kat was tall but big-boned. Her eyes were deep set and light brown, almost hazel. She had full, perky breasts that sat up high under her chin. She wore shorts that showed off long and shapely caramel-colored legs. She had a tiny waist and a round butt. A flawless complexion completed the masterpiece. She was just the kind of girl Randy would go for. But as good as Randy looked, Cast Iron Kat would have made him look better. She was no cheerleader, though, and she belonged to no boy. She was a card-carrying bully with a reputation for pulling girls' shirts off during fights. Cast Iron Kat was known to carry a large book bag that must have contained her arsenal of torture. I thought I was safe since I was two years younger than Cast Iron Kat and did not travel in the same circles. She would poke fun at me when our paths crossed in the projects, but I'd hoped to finish high school without a full on, psychological scarring. Nevertheless, her failure to achieve the minimum standards set by the state of Florida's Department of Education threatened to make her my classmate in the next school term. If she didn't get a passing score in summer school, she'd be experiencing the tenth grade for the third time.

Cast Iron Kat snatched the book out of my hands, looked at it briefly, and then tossed Poirot into the dirt. She casually swung her heavy book bag, leaves and all clinging to its underside, back and forth near my head. Something large and square protruded from the bag.

"Hey, Flop. What you readin'?" Every now and then, not often, we ran into each other in this secluded spot to perform the waltz of the bully. I cowered under my tree, waiting for that thing in her bag to be hurled at me.

"Tell me the name of that book, girl," she insisted.

"It's, ah, Agatha Christie, *The Murder of Roger Ackroyd*. It's real good."

"What's it about?"

"It's about this Belgian detective who . . ." I began but was interrupted.

"Animals in it?" she asked.

"Just the killer," I quipped. I chuckled at my own joke. Cast Iron Kat didn't seem to find it very funny.

"Never mind." She curled her lip. "You gon' be in summer school, ain't you?"

"Yeah."

She glared down at me with one hand on her slim hips, pulsing her bag like a barbell with the other hand.

"Guess, I'll be seein' ya, then." She turned and walked away. I could see there were leaves sticking to her bottom as well as the book bag.

She had never actually hit me. Cast Iron Kat liked to toy with me, like big game did with smaller animals they intended to devour. I blew out my breath in relief when her back disappeared in the distance; only then was it safe to crawl around in the dry grass to get my book. I knew I'd better get on the good foot to get that beer.

If Momma ever found out I was deliberately putting so much time between her and her beer, my life would be in danger. What the heck, it was the only way I could get back at her for sending me alone into sketchy neighborhoods to hydrate her vice. If she wanted to get drunk, which was whenever she was breathing, she'd send me into places where she knew nothing but men up to no good hung out. I wasn't blessed with Cast Iron Kat's good looks, or even a slice of Momma's, but I had the misfortune of being quite narrow in the waist and generous in the hips. Ironically, what God gave me below the waist, He took away above. I was built like a boy from my armpits to my ribs. It didn't seem to matter to the men — they leered at me like I was a grape they wanted to peel. I had to endure the visual mauling because it didn't matter to Momma either — neither rain, heat nor the threat of bodily harm to her only child would stand between her and her liquid lover.

A strong and abiding dread set up shop in my chest. I couldn't go back, and I didn't want to go forward. I stood in that same spot too long weighing my options. I had none, and I couldn't put off going to Miss Lipstick's any longer. Nothing I'd read in any of the adventure novels or my murder mysteries could have prepared me for what I was about to encounter.

/CHAPTER II/

Twenty minutes after I left home, Miss Lipstick's royal blue house with the peeling white paint around the shutters came into view. I fought an overwhelming urge to hyperventilate, vomit or pass out right there in the street. Turning around to go back home without the beer was unthinkable at this point. The apartment landing did not make a comfortable bed.

I coaxed my feet to move, one and then the other. As I got closer, the stench of stale liquor and smoke met me at the sidewalk and escorted me onto a dilapidated porch that sagged under the weight of all the people sitting on it. The porch dwellers I saw were in various stages of filth and inertia. The occasional swatting of a fly alerted me they were alive and the scent of my flight instincts must have given them a jolt. Heads started popping up and hands started reaching out to touch me. I hurried on to the screen door. It was closed, but it might as well have been open, since it had so many holes in it I could see clear through to the backdoor of the shotgun house. Dust plastered my naked arm as I opened the ancient screen door.

Miss Lipstick's home was the local flop house where the drunk and the high slept off her wares. It was many things to many people. It served as a home for the homeless, filled a need for the needy, and provided help for the helpless.

The homeless, the needy and the helpless were present and accounted for. They were all collapsed on Miss Lipstick's furniture and crowded around the entrance. They sat on any upright surface or available spot on the rotting wooden floor.

I observed men and women of all shapes, sizes and colors crawling around her place like insects — in the kitchen, on the porch, on the side of the house. Every single square inch was occupied. Miss Lipstick's place wasn't very big, but it was full.

"What you after here?" a man asked, his voice seeming to come from his enormous feet. He was a big black man sitting in a small white recliner pushed up in a corner that he filled up all by himself. He had a smooth, baby face untouched by the ravages of age, surrounded by a dome of snow white hair. His chin was obscured by a completely white beard and his dark eyes were covered by equally bushy white brows — eyes that seemed to see everything at once. He sat with his long fingers laced together. His left index finger was missing. He chewed on a cigar and talked around it.

"I . . . I'm lookin' for Miss Lipstick."

"OK," he said. "Let me get her." When he lifted himself out of the chair, the floor squeaked and his head nearly scraped the ceiling. He had to pick his way through the maze of bodies on the floor and did so with surprising ease and grace for a man his size. He moved quietly to a banged up wooden door adjacent to the kitchen and thumped lightly on it twice, but it sounded like a cannon ball going off.

"Lipstick. Somebody want you!" he said.

"What's that, Root Charlie?" a voice asked from behind the door.

"Somebody here for you. A li'l gal," Root Charlie said. He went back to his chair, settled back into the crater he'd made in it, and resumed his blank stare.

The door opened and Miss Lipstick made her appearance, as grand as any queen during a ceremonial service. She floated into the room, her arms spread wide, parting the room like the Red Sea and welcoming those who were privileged enough to be in her presence. The handful of women remained seated, but every man stood up as she entered the living room — every man except Root Charlie.

I hadn't actually seen Miss Lipstick during that infamous visit five years earlier, but something about her stirred my memory. Miss Lipstick was an impressive creature. Her red-bone complexion was the perfect canvas to showcase the ugly black moles that traveled in all directions from her brows to her chest, with a slight detour around her wide nose. She was about fifty years old, if you believed Miss Lipstick; seventy, if you believed the lines in her face. The dusty, black wig resting on her head looked like something birds had made a home in. A cigarette was firmly implanted in the corner of her mouth. She was an engaging hostess and held court with her irreverent tongue. As much as she liked to talk, that cigarette never fell out. Her brown eyes were watery, but they managed to light up the room. When she smiled, she displayed all ten of the brown teeth she had left. She wore an oversized, multi-colored housedress that disguised a frail figure. When she laughed, it was the laugh of a lifelong smoker, full of the spasms and coughs of three packs a day. Miss Lipstick's skin, her house, and her perpetual guests reeked of alcohol and tobacco products.

The moles and the smell pushed the memory to the surface of my brain. Momma must have bought beer from Miss Lipstick before I was ten. I had a hazy flashback of being five years old, sitting between Momma and Miss Lipstick, being hugged and kissed. I also remembered a flash of light. I played connect the dots with the moles on her neck and laughed. I dismissed this as a false memory. I didn't think Miss Lipstick knew me like that and she didn't seem to be the kind of woman to display such affection anyway, but it had to have been her. I had no memories of Momma ever touching me in such a maternal way.

The cast of characters who played Miss Lipstick's loyal supporting subjects were varied and included many: old men with faces that depicted an epic in every crease, young men whose lineless faces hadn't started chapter one, and women whose faces told a fairy tale, but whose eyes told the true story. They all stared at me. They started gathering around me, imprisoning me and my book where I stood. I had nowhere to run. I felt like the piece of raw meat a lion tamer might throw to his pack of big, hungry cats. I squeezed my book, wishing Scotty could beam me up into 1940s London to join Hercules.

Miss Lipstick took me by the arm. She squeezed it gingerly as we took a few steps into the kitchen.

"Y'all put your eyes back in your head. This a child. Find something to do." There was authority in Miss Lipstick's voice. She uttered the command and everyone obeyed, immediately.

She stood in front of me, puffing on her cigarette and squinting at me through the smoke. Her eyes gave me the once-over twice. She walked around me, checking me out like I was a new car she wanted to drive. I couldn't tell if she was pleased with what she saw. I silently cursed my mother for sending me over here alone and without a single dime in my pockets. Anybody in the bootleg liquor business knew you paid at the back door, paid no taxes, and paid no attention to what was going on at the front door. However, with no money to pass along, house rules were you had to get the bootleg directly from its source.

"Why you here?" she asked. I thought it was a trick question.

"My momma wants a beer," I answered timidly. I couldn't look directly at her. There was mucus built up in the corner of her eyes and her wig was askew on her head, sliding down to the left over her ear.

A man unsteady on his feet ambled through the kitchen. He stopped in his tracks when he saw me. He pointed a trembling finger in my direction.

"Hey, Lipstick! Don't she look ...! You look just like . . ." His words dribbled down his chin.

Miss Lipstick cleared her throat with great exaggeration.

"... like yo' Momma. That's all. You don't even look like Karla." He waved his hand as if he were erasing the statement from an invisible chalk board.

"Johnny, don't you need to be outside waitin' for yo' son to pick you up?"

Johnny couldn't stand still in one place. He swayed back and forth. "Naw, ma'am. I ain't got my shot yet!"

"You still owe me for the last six. I can't give you no more credit!" Miss Lipstick never took her eyes off my face.

"Come on, Lipstick, give me my egg!" Johnny stuck out his lip and whined. He threw an old fashioned tantrum.

"Root Charlie, get on the job!" Miss Lipstick said, her voice level slightly elevated. The big man in the corner got up silently and in two great strides, stood over Johnny. Johnny was no small man, but he was a light weight compared to Root Charlie. With the five-fingered hand, Root Charlie grabbed Johnny by the scruff of the neck, causing him to howl, and picked him up off the floor. When Root Charlie turned toward the door, Johnny began to beg.

"Lipstick, please! Come on, Lipstick. I'll settle up, I promise! I get my Social Security next week."

Miss Lipstick held up a gnarled hand. "Let him go, Charlie." Root Charlie released Johnny into a pathetic puddle, and then resumed his position in his chair. His facial expression never changed.

"Go on, get yo' egg," Miss Lipstick said to Johnny.

Johnny rubbed his neck vigorously, turning and twisting it to make sure it still worked. He wiped his runny nose with the sleeve of his shirt, smearing most of the snot on his face. He reached for the door of the refrigerator.

"Wash them nasty hands before you put 'em in my 'fridgerator." Johnny obliged quickly. Afterward, he grabbed an egg, a Mason jar half-full of liquid that looked like water, and a small shot glass. He cracked the egg and drank its contents straight out of the shell. I was repulsed.

"Don't look so particular, gal," Miss Lipstick said, laughing at me. "If he don't coat that stomach first, he'll tear it up with that moonshine. It ain't pretty when that happen. You know anything 'bout moonshine?"

I shook my head. "I ain't never seen it being made, but Mr. Willie sell it out the back of his truck and Miss Rutha Mae make it and sell it." I wasn't sure whether I was revealing trade secrets. The whole house erupted in laughter.

"I know Willie and Rutha Mae. They good people, but they ain't got nothing on Lipstick moonshine. Let me tell you something. When you want hot water, you go to them. When you want the best White Lightnin', you come to Lipstick." The whole house agreed with her. Johnny demonstrated his agreement by tossing back the liquid he poured into the shot glass.

"You got what you came for, now get outta my house." Johnny stumbled through the living room, nearly tripping over several pairs of legs crisscrossed on the floor, fumbled with the doorknob, and finally let himself out. Root Charlie stared straight ahead.

Miss Lipstick continued her conversation with me as if the flow had not been broken.

"You turned out pretty good. Ain't seen you in a while, but you grew into a nice figure. Yeah." She pounded me lightly in the chest with the palm of her hand. "Ain't got much up here." She looked down her own dress. "But who am I to talk." She nodded her head and smiled. I didn't think my developmental impairment was so funny, but when Miss Lipstick peered inside her own clothes, her wig fell forward. It caused laughter to bubble at the surface in my gut, but fear held it down. I wasn't ready to be comfortable with this woman yet.

She motioned for me to sit down at what served as her dining room table, an old three-legged card table in the middle of the tiny kitchen. The refrigerator was at my back. She sat in the opposite chair.

"How you doin' in school?" Miss Lipstick asked.

"Good?" I answered as if it were one of the answers on a multiple choice test.

"Just good? You can do better than that. Tell me what you get, A's, B's?"

"I get A's. Some B's."

"That's good." She patted my knee. "Real good." She gazed at me for a minute longer, her eyes roaming all over my face.

"What yo' favorite class? I bet it's English."

The grin that spread across my face answered her question.

"What you like about it?"

I searched my mind. There were so many things.

"Well, I like reading a lot. See." I picked up my mystery book as if I needed proof. Miss Lipstick took it from me and held it way out in front of her. She flipped through a few pages and gave it back to me.

"I like how you get to go places in stories and I like conjugating verbs and stuff."

"Conjugating?" She screwed up her face. "They teaching that in school now? No wonder so many young gals roun' here got babies."

I couldn't stifle the laugh that broke through against my will, and the release felt good. "No, Miss Lipstick. Conjugating is something you do to words. It's just about words."

She spanked the table, making it nearly fall into our laps.

"Oh. Shoot. You just taught me something new. See, you already teaching."

I added a shrug to my shaking shoulders.

"I'm so glad to hear this." She let out a raw, raspy laugh and hid her face behind her wrinkled hands. "That's wonderful, gal." She wiped her eyes. "You like science a little bit, but you don't like math, do you?"

"No, ma'am." I continued to laugh. "I do OK in math, but I like English the best."

"Good. So, you going up to FAM-C when you graduate, or Bethune to take up some kinda English degree?" She got up and walked around to the refrigerator, at my back. I'd almost forgotten why I was there.

"It ain't been Florida A&M College in a long time, Miss Lipstick," I ventured to correct her. "It's Florida A&M University now. They say FAMU."

"I know, gal. It was FAM-C 'til '53 and it always will be. Love that school. That mean you going to FAM*U*?"

"Naw. I'm not going to no college. I'm getting me a job at TG&Y. They always hiring."

"You mean to tell me you givin' up a F-A-M-U for a T-G-and-Y!" Miss Lipstick shrieked. She punctuated each letter of the university and the retail establishment. I felt the cold on my back coming from the refrigerator. She slammed the door closed with such force the whole appliance shook. I hopped up out of the chair and faced her.

Miss Lipstick squawked like a hen. She bobbed her head around and if she'd put a feather in her wig, she could have looked like a hen. The joy had disappeared, replaced by an inexplicable outrage.

"What your Momma say about that?"

I couldn't think of an answer fast enough. "Uh," was all I could squeeze from my throat.

"Come on, gal! What she say?" She was resting her head against the refrigerator.

"She don't say nothing, except she want me to work in a convenience store so I can get her beer all the time."

Miss Lipstick raised her head from the Kenmore and turned to face me. Now her wig was way back off her forehead. Gray cornrows and wisps of black hair peeked out from underneath. Her hands were balled up, her long darkened nails resembling claws. She took a long, controlled drag off her cigarette, which seemed to bring her down a bit, and blew a cloud of smoke in my direction. I thought it would be rude to cough, so I kept it in.

"You can't be nothing important around here!" Miss Lipstick said. She was animated, waving her cigarette hand around in the air.

"But I make A's, Miss Lipstick. I can get a good job here in Quincy." I mentally calculated whether and how fast I could make like a bullet through the front door.

"It ain't enough." Her fingers were trembling. "Quincy ain't a bad place, but it can be when you ignorant. You need to go to college if you want to be somebody great, if you want to travel for real like you do in them stories. What you look like with a brain like yours behind a cash register or slinging burgers?"

Miss Lipstick snatched the door of the Kenmore open again, and grabbed the tall silver can of Colt 45. She slammed it down in front of me, the violence of the move causing me to almost stumble back into the living room.

"You tell yo' momma, she owe me too much money!" Miss Lipstick ended the conversation and retired to the room off the kitchen. I thought I saw a pair of brown feet hanging off the edge of a bed before she slammed the door shut. It probably took me twenty minutes to get to her house — I know it only took twenty seconds to clear out of there.

/CHAPTER III/

"I gotta work for Miss Lipstick?" I asked in disbelief. I was on my knees before her, trying to implore her to use some reason.

"That's what I said," Momma answered.

"But I don't want to spend my summer working for her!"

Momma turned her head slowly, like it was on a ratchet. She zeroed in on me as I kneeled at her feet.

"Don't nobody give a damn about what you want, or what's best for you! You get stuck and you just have to make do!"

"How am I supposed to work for Miss Lipstick and go to summer school, too?" I whined.

"I already told you, Fla! You belong to Lipstick now. She want her money. I don't have it. It's the only way I can settle up with her."

"That's not fair, Momma. It's ludicrous."

"Don't you be using them big words at me," she said, raining my face with spit. "You don't have to go to school anyway. I don't appreciate you asking that principal behind my back. Summer school ain't gonna do you no good, no way. You don't need big words to ring up a register."

"There ain't nothing else to do around here!" I retorted as respectfully as I could. "Principal Lester asked me what I was doing and he said I could come if I wanted to. He said I might be able to help some of the other students."

Momma had tuned me out before I completed my speech, and there was not a hint of tenderness in her face. It was flat and blank, like a movie screen. The blue lights of the TV danced on it, and not even the antics of Fred Sanford could produce movement. If not for the single tear that broke away from the corner of her moist eyes, from the neck up, she could have been a beautiful corpse.

"Momma, what did that lady say to you last night?" I was on the verge of tears myself.

"She ain't no lady," Momma said, her lip curled into itself.

"Then why you sending me over there and you scared of her?"

Momma pushed me off my knees and onto my butt. She pulled herself up from the sofa and limped into the kitchen.

"I ain't scared of that . . . that woman!"

"Why don't we just pay your tab with them checks you get every month? I can eat at school. I can pick pecans to help. How much do you owe her?"

Momma received checks every month from some anonymous source that she wouldn't discuss with me. I didn't care where they came from. Everybody I knew was dirt poor. Those checks made us mud poor, because of the little extra keeping us together. Momma never had a job to my knowledge, but she sure worked overtime making me feel like crap.

"That ain't none of your business!" she shouted. She was fluttering around the kitchen, pulling open cabinets that were empty, spinning around in a circle in the tight space. "You just be a child and stay in your place! You working for her! That's the end of it!"

My alarm was not a figment of my imagination. Momma's stricken countenance was an exact replica of her expression five years earlier. After I had returned home with the beer around 6 p.m., I said nothing about Momma being cut off. I thought I would have at least a couple of days to break it to her, but a couple of hours later, Root Charlie came to the living room door. He asked for Millie and when she appeared, he said, "Lipstick want you." Momma's whole body tensed up. So did mine.

"You want me to go with you, Momma?"

Before she could answer, Root Charlie piped up, "No, just her. I got my car. Let's go."

Momma looked back at me. Her lips were a thin, tight line. Her knuckles were white on the door knob.

"I need to put on a bra," she told Root Charlie, and tried to close the door. She would have been more successful pushing a train in the opposite direction. Root Charlie put a dirty boot in the way and effortlessly pushed the door back with the four-fingered hand.

"No time. Now."

When Momma left, she was limping harder and slower. She was hyperventilating and sweating profusely. A wave of guilt swept over me as the long tail of the deuce and a quarter, which rolled off Buick's assembly line an Electra 225, disappeared out of the parking lot. I was afraid, for the first time in my life, that she might get hurt and would not come back.

Of course she did come back, around midnight. I couldn't sleep, or eat, or watch TV in the meantime. So I read. I finished *The Murder of Roger Ackroyd* and began *Murder on the Orient Express*. I was elbow deep in the questioning of the passengers when Momma walked in the house. Her eyes were bloodshot and swollen. She said nothing to me the rest of the night. She went to her room and slammed the door. All day Saturday, I lay in bed surrounded by my books, transporting myself to more exciting places, only returning occasionally for a generic root beer and a bag of chips. I was also planning a strategic mission to read the entire mystery section of the library that summer. I was such a geek, but I was a happy one, until Momma dropped the bomb on me Saturday evening.

"I still think you said something to that woman. She never cut me off before."

Logic was not on my side. Mercy was not in Momma's vocabulary. I couldn't appeal to her heart because I wasn't sure if it was functioning properly. I rose to my feet, only to find myself in the shadow of the latest stray momma had brought home. She would drive the old Honda to troll the streets and search for his kind. She fed them. She clothed them. She gave them a warm bed to sleep in, then she crawled into bed with them. This one's name was Jerome.

"Flaw, you just do what yo' momma say," Jerome said in a counterfeit parental voice. He was unemployed, uneducated, and under my Momma every chance he got. That beer-guzzling, skirt-chasing, non-bathing sweat stain with eyeballs was the color of asphalt and his odor was that unique combination of six-day-old funk, a twelve-day drinking binge, and onions. It was a pungent uppercut to the nose. Momma had a knack for attracting men like him during her time of the month — when the checks came. Jerome came the first week of June and would not leave.

He had a mind like a series of one-way streets — I could tell where he was coming from and I knew where he was going. I hated the way he looked at me, his beady, glassy eyes burning through my clothes and into my skin. I kept as much distance between him and myself as the tiny apartment would allow. He grinned at me now as he raised his tobacco-stained index and middle fingers to his cracked, puckered lips — his not-so-subtle gesture that he wanted cigarettes. He pulled a wad of dollars from his pocket and motioned for me to come and get them. He jammed the money in my hand, his slimy fingers lingering too long on my palm.

"You know my brand. Marlboro!" he said.

"Momma, it's getting dark out there," I complained.

"It ain't that dark, girl. It's just 6:30," Jerome said.

"Momma?"

"Like Jerome said, it ain't that dark. Go on and hurry back with his stuff," Momma said, trying to impress Jerome.

I fumed the whole way to the store. I wasn't as angry with Jerome as I was with Momma. She made me do things for him. She'd do anything to keep his favor.

As I trudged through the projects at dusk, I ran into many girls not much older than I was who had at least two children. It was the fashionable thing to do to wear babies on their hips like accessories to match their strollers and their baby bags. I witnessed the population of Quincy increase daily — four of my classmates left in the middle of the school year to contribute to the head count. I surmised the girls got pregnant somewhere between ninth and twelfth grade and never made it to graduation. The whole community was witness to their daily hardships. They screamed at their babies at home, cussed out the fathers in the street, and came to me when they needed some type of educational assistance as part of their last ditch effort to snag some evidence they could finish high school, or at least get their GEDs.

"Fla, can you babysit for me since you outta school?" Donquala asked me, pulling two ashy-faced children under the age of three behind her. Donquala was nineteen and still had to complete the ninth grade. She was seven months pregnant with her third child.

"I can't this time," I said, with mixed feelings of guilt and joy. The money was OK but those children needed patience and a highly-paid, professional behavioral specialist — neither of which I could give them. "I have to work this summer."

"Oh, you do?" She was always on the verge of a breakdown. "I'm trying to get my GED and I ain't got nobody to watch the kids for me. Momma be working the late shift."

I gave her my best sympathetic boilerplate response. "If I can do something, I'll let you know."

"Please, Fla. See what you can do." She turned on the children as if she had another face. "Shut up, Quantavious! Shut up!" She waddled off with her brood.

I quickened my pace to the store. The projects were Cast Iron Kat's turf and I wasn't welcome in it, even though I lived there, too. The last thing I wanted was to run into her in the dark. I was momentarily grateful I was being forced to work for Miss Lipstick. I'd have somewhere to go in the afternoons, instead of staying in the house around Jerome and planning my life around Cast Iron Kat's presence. Then, the moment passed. My fear of Miss Lipstick surpassed my fear of Cast Iron Kat, and my dread didn't sway momma in the least. Instead, she was only too pleased to have me out here at night buying Jerome one of the three staples of his diet — cigarettes, alcohol and the number.

"Hey, sweet thang," the dark-skinned, gray-bearded cashier said. I gave him the money for the cigarettes and an insincere smile for the comment. I stomped out of the store. In my fury, I threw the cigarettes on the ground in an area that was all orange clay and started kicking them, pretending they were Jerome. It felt good, like a secret high. The last kick was stronger than I intended, and the pack burst open. Cigarettes were torn apart. No infraction brought me a greater punishment from Momma than for me to neglect Jerome. I could accidentally spill one of her beer cans or just be having a good day. That would subject me to a profanity-laced tirade. To cause any kind of harm to Jerome would push me into the realm of physical punishment.

My brain was running on all cylinders. I looked at my feet to see if any of the cigarettes could be salvaged. While I bent over searching for fragments, inspiration struck. I got down on all fours and made sure my hands and knees were encrusted with clay. Then I ran home.

"Girl, you was gone too long!" Momma accused before I even closed the door. "Where Jerome cigarettes?" They were curled up in each other's arms, facing the TV. I walked around to stand in front of it, to give them the full effect. I pulled out the mangled pieces of cigarettes and crushed them into Jerome's hands.

"What the hell?" he asked, dumbfounded.

"Well, what had happened was I was running to get back home when I fell. See." I pointed to my orange knees and palms. "The cigarettes got broke that way."

I was breathing fast, adrenaline rushing through my body.

They looked at me for a few minutes. Momma's mouth started turning up at the corners, the sign she was about to lay into me.

"It's OK," said Jerome, too understanding. "Ain't no sweat." I needed to take a bath after being in Jerome's presence. Momma needed one, too, for different reasons.

She cuddled up under Jerome where a layer of fat hanging off his upper arm met the fat from his meaty chest. She breathed in his tainted stink like it was pure oxygen. Momma's contented expression made me sick. I walked fast to my room, knowing Jerome's eyes were right behind me. When I thought the coast was clear, I buried my face in the pillow and waited for what I thought was laughter welling up inside me. To my surprise, it was a spring of tears that gushed out of me, and I spent the night sleeping on a drenched pillow.

Momma and Jerome engaged in cheerful banter regarding their shallow social life. They didn't let my little issue — that of working for a woman my own mother was deathly afraid of — curtail their plans for the best party this side of the projects on the following Saturday. Momma wouldn't have the money for the party for another eleven days, but Jerome talked her into spending some of her medicine money for the party. What Jerome wanted, Jerome got.

Momma was well known in the projects for throwing a good shindig, primarily because she supplied all the food, all the liquor, and round-the-clock fun. It didn't matter that I needed books for school or braces for my teeth. It only mattered that her guests were never without Bacardi and Coke in their cups and Spam sandwiches — masquerading as ham — on their plates. Momma thought it was classier to cut the sandwiches into triangles and put a toothpick through them. She figured no one would guess it wasn't ham. After a couple of drinks, they wouldn't care. Her house parties brought out the worst people and the worst in those people. I was only invited to the party after it was over, to clean up. I hated house parties.

I did everything but sleep over at the library the following week. I was on a mission to find a book in there that would swallow me up, a sort of Alisha in Wonderland. It took me thirty minutes to walk to the library, but walking through town made it seem longer.

Every day, I passed throngs of black men standing around on the broken sidewalks, lying down on people's yards, and loitering around businesses. They were the casualties of progress. The tobacco business was on its way out and nothing new was coming into Quincy. Jobs were scarce for the uneducated and those men with no other employable skills became living road kill. Their hopelessness was poisonous to me, the library my antidote. It was my refuge — the only place where I felt safe and welcome.

The two-story colonial brick building was my second home. I loved the old-fashioned bell that hung over the door and announced my arrival. Mrs. McCullough, who always greeted me warmly, was waiting for me inside.

"Good morning, Fla. I knew you'd be the first one here." Every morning of that week, I sat on the steps of the library before it opened for business. Without fail, 9:30 a.m. would find me and Mrs. McCullough the only two people in there, which suited me fabulously. I was there on Saturday like clockwork. I didn't need to wear a "kick me" sign to indicate I was a nerd. It was permanently tattooed on my back.

Mrs. McCullough was a cool, old white lady and a stereotypical librarian. She was five foot two, wore her white cotton candy hair in a tight bun, and had been a librarian for forty years. Sometimes, I asked her a question about her life and I would be embroiled in a tale more fantastic than any I could find between the covers of a book.

"Good morning, Mrs. Mac." I beamed at her. "About the fines . . .," I continued sheepishly.

"Shh," she said, placing a wrinkled finger to her lips. "No talking in the library." She did that every time, and every time, I wanted to kiss her. Besides, I'd probably racked up a good fifty dollars in fines, which I couldn't see myself paying until I got a job. She shooed me off into the stacks and went about her work.

I wandered the aisles of the mystery section, fondling title after title. I had an Agatha Christie fix, but I needed to experiment with something different. I crept over to the smallest section in the library — the black authors section. I'd studied these authors last school term, but my mind had been on one track since the third grade when I discovered Nancy Drew. I sat cross-legged and skimmed the pages of Toni Morrison's *The Bluest Eye*, Zora Neale

Hurston's *Their Eyes Were Watching God*, and Richard Wright's *Native Son*. My appetite for years had been limited to mystery and romance novels. It was on that day I discovered that I had been missing a great feast, and I dined for hours. A handful of diehard patrons like me filtered in and out, but I remained alone in my section.

"Fla," I heard Mrs. Mac's elderly voice call me. "Where are you, dear?"

"In the black authors section!" I yelled so she could find me.

"Oh, you moved from your mysteries. Good for you. You should always expand your horizons." Mrs. Mac congratulated me again when she found me. She moved rather slowly. "You've been back here for the last three hours?"

"Yes," I said, my head still in the *The Bluest Eye*.

"Listen. I brought this huge hoagie from home this morning and I couldn't possibly eat it all. Why don't you take half of it and go into my office. I'm sure you're good and hungry. Reading always makes me hungry." She giggled like a school girl.

"OK," I said, closing the book and jumping up at the same time. She didn't have to offer twice. Mrs. Mac's office was hidden in the back behind the lobby. I put my treasures on her desk, which was neat and organized with the office supplies arranged around the perimeter of the desk. In the middle, Mrs. Mac had laid out a six-inch ham and cheese hoagie; a large, red apple; and a bottle of Pepsi. It was quite a spread and a treat for me. Real food was a delicacy in my world. Most of what the government put in our cabinets needed water to convert it into something edible.

Mrs. Mac had also placed a handful of Hershey's kisses near the sandwich. I looked for napkins inside the large paper bag on her desk chair, and saw another whole hoagie. It wasn't half of one sandwich — there were two whole sandwiches. There was another apple in the bag, too. Hunger dulled my reasoning for a moment, but I finally realized that that kind old lady had made two lunches with me in mind. I didn't recognize the feelings I was having —

grateful, queasy, and ravenous. This was what it felt like to be looked after. God love the woman. I would have to hold onto that feeling. Mrs. Mac joined me about ten minutes later.

"Mrs. Mac," I said, my mouth full of food. "You made two sandwiches."

"Did I?" she asked, pretending to be forgetful. "I'm so used to making two of everything for me and my husband. I just never stopped, even though he's been gone some thirteen years." She patted my hand. "You just enjoy that now."

She made a fuss of going through the bag. She still choked up when she talked about her husband, Samuel. The only thing that made her feel better was to talk about him some more.

"Your husband ran the old tobacco farm out in the country, didn't he, Mrs. Mac?" I knew her response verbatim.

"Yes, he did. A fine job he made of it, too." She took a cautious bite of her sandwich so as not to dislodge her dentures. "I remember him coming home smelling like he'd rolled around in a river of cigarettes. He loved that job."

Mrs. Mac proceeded to educate me about the role tobacco played in our city. "Tobacco provided plenty of jobs for folks around here," Mrs. Mac lamented. "Too bad things are the way they are now. That's why, my dear, I can't wait to see you finish college, God willing. I know you'll do a fine job."

I couldn't look Mrs. Mac in the eye or confess to her that I had no desire to go to college. To curtail the subject matter, I announced it was time to go. I thanked Mrs. Mac excessively after the lunch and assisted her in shelving some books. I checked out five black authors, and one mystery for good measure, to get me through the party and its aftermath. I would need something strong.

"Where you been?" Momma asked as I walked in the door. She struggled with a large box of beer while Jerome blocked the television and the entire wall behind it. "Get over here and help me!"

I put the books down on the table beside the sofa. Jerome reached over and picked up *Native Son.* "Nah-tih-vee Sss on," he said, butchering the title. He glanced up at me. "Good book. Read it in school." Jerome wore his ignorance like a badge of honor.

I helped Momma chill the beer, make the sandwiches and slice the cheese. It didn't surprise me that she used cheese that didn't come from a cow, but was cooked up in some government laboratory that wouldn't melt in a nuclear attack. Momma instructed me to cut off the hard, moldy parts — she thought it smart to spare her guests the agony of food poisoning. By the time the pigs in a blanket were ready, I was doing all the work. Momma and Jerome were enjoying an episode of *Three's Company.* After I swept, mopped, and dusted, Momma felt like a little nap. I rescued my books and headed to my room.

"Need some help with that Flaw?" Jerome asked.

"It's Fla, with a long "a", and no, I don't need your help." I urgently needed to be on the other side of my bedroom door.

"Just trying to help," he said. "You need to let a man treat you right." He feigned a yawn. "Guess I'll go take a nap, too."

Not only was the apartment small, the walls were tissue paper thin. Their napping kept me from enjoying my books. They napped right up until the first guests arrived at 4:30 in the afternoon, and I had to receive the groups of unknown folks who streamed in, barely giving me the time of day, and knocking me about as they made a beeline for the drinks.

I spent the whole night in and out of my room, tending to guests, dodging Jerome's probing hands, and making sure Momma was the queen of the ball. She was beautiful and effervescent. She became alive, as if the party were a generator to her soul. I tried to grab some sleep in the wee hours before the party was over, but some man who had too much to drink kept invading my room.

"Where the bathroom at?" he asked a wall.

"The next room down. The one with the toilet." After the third time, I locked my door. Whether he actually made it to the bathroom or peed in Momma's room, I'd have to clean it up. I'd have to clean it all up. No matter how deeply I buried my head under my pillow under my covers, I could not block out the sounds of that raunchy party. The music was much louder than it had to be. Marvin Gaye performed a private concert in that eight hundred square foot hall. I heard hard-core cursing, people screaming, things breaking, walls thumping, music bumping, and deranged laughter. I could deal with the foul-smelling bathroom, the scraping of food off the walls, and the gathering up of soiled garments, but the residue of that laughter was the worst. No amount of bleaching, scrubbing or garbage dumping would get rid of it. It wasn't happy laughter at all, not glad-to-be alive joyousness. It was uninhibited, full of abandon, as if there were no tomorrow for those people. Momma's laughter rose above all the others. It was sad. I burrowed deeper into the covers, waiting for the laughter to end, which was my cue to get up and start disinfecting the place.

By Momma's overhung, yet sunny demeanor the next morning, the party had been a success. Jerome had left with some of his friends and they had promised to come back for Momma around five to go to a club that evening. She was so giddy with excitement, she was almost approachable. I still cleaned in silence while she fluttered around the place getting ready. Momma chose a red, silk, button-up blouse that clung seductively to her breasts and made her complexion more beautiful. She donned a seldom-worn pair of blue jeans two sizes too big to accommodate the leg brace she would have to wear, and a pair of red hot flats. This occasion didn't call for a bra. She combed and brushed her hair to within an inch of its life, then pinned it up in the back. Curly tendrils dropped softly into her face. Momma didn't need to wear make-up, but when she did, men halted when they saw her.

I was grateful that I would have all that time to myself to enjoy my new literary finds, to watch my favorite shows, and to eat the leftover party fare. At five o'clock, Momma and I laughed together as we watched back-to-back episodes of *Sanford and Son*. At seven o'clock, I was laughing alone watching *M*A*S*H*. At nine o'clock, Momma exchanged her silk blouse for a T-shirt.

"What time is he coming?" I dared to ask.

"He'll be here!" she snapped. An hour later, the hair came down, the jeans came off, and the fridge came open, emptied of every can and bottle that was left from the party. Thirty minutes later, I draped a blanket over her. As I viewed her pitiful figure, I was torn between "I told you so" and "I'm so sorry." I went to bed exhausted from the tug of war.

/CHAPTER IV/

I embraced summer school like a long, lost relative. Principal Lester allowed me to take the course to boost my 3.8 GPA even higher and to prepare me to be a tutor in the next school term. Monday, June 21st, couldn't come soon enough. I may have gotten a total of four winks the night before. I set out my summer school attire early — a pair of jean shorts I'd have to wash out every night, and a colorful array of plain T-shirts. I was willing to bet Cast Iron Kat had a million outfits to choose from, even though there wasn't much to any one of them. She never wore the same thing twice. I envied her, but I couldn't dwell on it for long.

On the first day of summer school, I awoke before the sun peeked over the horizon and was fully dressed two hours before school would begin. Momma and Jerome wouldn't be up before the crack of noon, so I had the quiet of the morning to reflect while I choked down the sandy granules somebody put in a cereal box. After I managed to swallow the last bite, I decided to go on to school.

Carter Jackson High School was on the extreme southern end of the main street that ran along the projects. The air was dry and humid at 7:00 in the morning, but there was purpose in my steps. Nobody but the janitor, Mr. Wilkins, was on the premises. He was my buddy. I was not membership material for any of the cliques, so he let me hang out with him sometimes. I had the privilege of touring the teacher's lounge and the school's back offices after hours. I had the supreme honor of handling his ring of keys, which opened everything from the principal's lair to Pandora's Box.

Mr. Wilkins was a quiet man, like Root Charlie. When he saw me, he gave me a curt nod, and then opened a series of doors that led to the classrooms.

"Good morning, Mr. Wilkins."

"Mornin'. You a little early, ain't ya? Teachers ain't even here yet."

"I like being here by myself." As he walked beside me, his heavy keys jingled.

"Ain't good to be by yourself all the time. Make yourself some friends," he advised.

"I'll try, Mr. Wilkins."

"You want anything from the lounge? I think they got juice in there." He held the classroom door open for me.

"No, sir." I thanked him and settled in the back of Mr. Pierce's English class where I began reading last semester's enormous English literature textbook. It would only be a matter of time before Cast Iron Kat and her flock of blind followers swarmed in. They were probably sitting in the shadow of a trash can dreaming up ways to torture me.

I gave them a lot to work with. I was the only person reading a textbook for recreation in summer school on a Monday morning, and it was no secret to anyone why I was in the class in the first place. I had the saddest, most transparent crush on my teacher, Mr. Pierce.

Malcolm Pierce came to Carter Jackson High in my eighth grade year after he was newly graduated from Florida A&M University with a Bachelors Degree in Education. He did his alma mater proud, but he did his African ancestors even prouder. Mr. Pierce was every bit of six feet tall and had dark chocolate skin that looked smooth to the touch. He had full, sexy lips; straight, white teeth; and a smile almost as blinding as Randy's, except Mr. Pierce had dimples so deep, it seemed his cheeks were trying to meet on the inside of his mouth. Mr. Pierce must have been some kind of athlete because his lean body could not be disguised by jackets, chinos or polos. The man had the face of a movie star and body of a track star. His looks captured the attention of anything female on campus, but the intelligence he bestowed on us captured the respect of all, even his skeptical old colleagues who were students when lessons were taught from stone tablets. The best part — *the very best part* — was the way Mr. Pierce put a title on all his students' names. We were accustomed to "Boy!" in an angry voice or "Girl!" in a sarcastic tone or our first names said in a shrill pitch that was the equivalent of fingernails on a chalkboard. In Mr. Pierce's class, I was Miss Frye. The boys were Mr. Hamilton and such.

During the school year, I performed literary somersaults, like writing thought-provoking essays on Baldwin and Hemingway, just to be favored by one of his smiles. I wrote poetry. I ate chalk dust. I did anything Mr. Pierce asked me to. He fit nicely into the role of a prince.

There were many nights that I dreamt of marrying Randy. On the day shift, especially during class, I dreamt of marrying Mr. Pierce, so I doodled Mrs. Malcolm Pierce or Fla Pierce over and over in all my journals. There were just two problems with my fantasy. There was soon to be a Mrs. Pierce, and I'd heard that she was some shapely, blonde goddess. The only black and white couple I was aware of was Tom and Helen Willis of *The Jeffersons*. I didn't know what I had to do to compete with that. The dilemma didn't stop my gazing into his soulful brown eyes and watching his lips move when he was speaking.

"Y'all, Flop dreamin' 'bout Mr. Pierce again." Cast Iron Kat poked me hard in the shoulder, bringing me out of my trance. Her entourage snickered on cue. They had entered the classroom with their usual noise and nonsense.

"Why you even in here? That man marrying a white girl. What he want with yo' ugly, black behind?" She poked me again. I said nothing.

"Hey, Flop. If you was born in France, would you be a French Frye?" Their laughter was cruel and mocking.

"Why your Momma name you after a state?" She very seldom got to be clever. "Because you was born in Florida?

That mean if you was born in Arr Kansas, your name would be Ass?"

I don't know where she got the idea that the abbreviation for Arkansas was AS instead of Ark. Correcting her wouldn't have made a difference. All around me I could see mouths open, laughing at the same thing she said to me every chance she got. I mimicked this scene as it unfolded, I knew it so well. I always had a witty retort ready, but I could never push it out of my mouth. I dreamt about the clever comebacks that would demolish Cast Iron Kat and make her wish she'd never crossed my path. My self-esteem was an inch high because of the way they chipped away at me. I hated them all. The six of them together didn't possess a full brain.

"You mocking me, girl?" Cast Iron Kat asked.

"I didn't say nothing," I said.

"I saw you. You was making fun of me." It was odd how she thought she had the corner on that market. I rolled my eyes at the irony of the matter.

A chorus of school girl oohs erupted in the room as my eye rolling seemed to have pushed Cast Iron Kat's strange behavior into fifth gear. I braced for the fist she carried around with my name embroidered on it. She stood in front of my desk; the other girls followed suit. Then I heard that deep, velvet voice with a slight southern drawl order, "Y'all take a seat."

"I'm gone get you after school," Cast Iron Kat leaned down and whispered in my ear. "I'm gone make you cry," she threatened.

"Sit down, Miss Morehead," Mr. Pierce said. It was an uneventful class if I didn't take into account that Cast Iron Kat hated my guts. Mr. Pierce explained that we were taking the Mechanics of English and Literature. The courses were combined and concentrated. We'd do a lot in a short period of time. I was up for the challenge. The collective groans from the rest of the class told me I was the only one.

Before the end of class, Mr. Pierce summoned me to his desk. I rolled my eyes again at the kissing noises I heard. They were so immature.

"Yes, my prince," I wanted to say. "Yes, Mr. Pierce," I heard myself say.

"Did you take a look at the college manual I gave you, Miss Frye?" I had not even cracked open that college manual, a fifty page glossy advertisement designed to entice high school graduates to reach for excellence at various institutions of higher learning. At that moment, the manual was excellently leveling my bed. I was too desperately in love with Mr. Pierce to disappoint him.

"I took a look at it. I haven't decided which one yet." The specter of college was terrifying to me.

"Think about it, Miss Frye. I may be a little biased, but FAMU has an excellent English department. You have a future in teaching." His teeth were brilliant, and they were shining on me.

"I want you to think about that Upward Bound program next summer, too. It will give you quite a leg up when you go to college. We'll talk about it some more at the end of the term. OK?" He winked at me. I could have flat lined that day. At any rate, we could talk all he wanted. I wasn't certain I would tell him what he wanted to hear.

According to bully protocol, whenever I had an encounter with Cast Iron Kat, I was required to run home. I asked Mr. Wilkins to keep me posted on the whereabouts of the lovely spawns of Satan, and as soon as he informed me they had an appointment to harass some other unlucky, unpopular girl in the restrooms, I put the wind at my back and hastened to my next destination. Half way there, I impeded my own progress, as I remembered where I was running to.

The first day of summer school, was, coincidentally, my first day of employment at Miss Lipstick's. I approached her domicile heavily, like a convicted murderer facing the sentencing judge. Her home was again thick with people. They started drawing near me, the accident of my youth and sobriety apparently magnetizing. When Miss Lipstick appeared at the door of her bedroom, they went their separate ways.

"Come on in the kitchen," she said harshly. "All you got to do is keep the living room and kitchen clean. You gonna wash some laundry. The washing machine out on the back porch." Miss Lipstick showed me the areas that would be of interest to me. She brought me to the kitchen.

"You want something to eat, I got stuff for you in the cabinet. You want a drink, I got root beer and water. You drink anything else . . .," Miss Lipstick trailed off and let me fill in the blanks.

"Yes, ma'am," I said to her retreating back.

Miss Lipstick informed me I would have to work Mondays, Tuesdays and Thursdays from 2 p.m. to 5 p.m. I supposed it was a light sentence, considering how big a tab Momma could create in just a week. To soften the blow, I decided to get a snack right then. I opened up the cabinet above the countertop next to the sink. In it was a box of Stage Planks and bags of black licorice. When I could find change in the cushions at home, I would run to Miss Duval's and buy Stage Plank cookies and black licorice. I put the licorice between the two large cookies to make the sweetest, crunchiest sandwich. Incidentally, root beer was my favorite drink.

My job orientation was bumpy, at best, and hostile, at worst. Miss Lipstick barely spoke to me. It was like being at home. When she did speak, her tone was sharp and unforgiving.

"Don't drink my liquor," she repeated. "Don't go in my room and don't go in that room out on the back porch. You hear me?" I heard her and so did the population of the flop house. She was speaking to me, but it was a warning to them not to corrupt me. Nobody went against Miss Lipstick's rules.

If I had homework, she allowed me to complete it before performing my duties. I was working on an essay that was due the next day. I hit a brick wall. The words just wouldn't come together. I wanted to stimulate my brain by taking a little walk, but I didn't want to mix with the crowd outside. They unnerved me. They were loud. Good hygiene was not a priority for them, yet they felt it necessary to stand within inches of me to say hello. I felt trapped until I had to leave for my other cage. I folded my arms and put my head down on the table, hoping the next hour would fly by.

Then, I heard the screen door squeak open and close.

"Hey, y'all. Where Lipstick at?" It was a masculine voice, but with a feminine inflection. I lifted my head and saw a strange man standing in the living room, his hands on his hips. He was tall and thin, with a youthful-looking face that was pecan tan, hidden under an old man's scruffy beard. The blue jeans he wore were hanging on him and his yellow, washed out, cotton shirt had seen better days. He was checking me out as I did so to him.

"Who this?" he asked while pointing to me. No one was sober enough to answer, so he introduced himself to me.

"Hey, girlfriend. My name Eugene. Who you?" He extended a hand while his eyes gripped mine.

"I'm, uh, Fla," I finally answered.

"You sure about that?" he asked. His hand fluttered to his chin. "Ooh, you that girl working for Lipstick, ain't you?"

I didn't realize my employment was news worthy, but the creature standing before me was definitely worthy of mention. He had large, tobacco-stained lips and the hand that still held mine had long, elegant fingers which were perfectly manicured. More than one cigarette found a home between those digits. It was his eyes that gave me pause. They were bloodshot behind the brown, either from crying or excessive alcohol consumption, but there was a slight desperation in them. I recognized that desperation. I saw it every time I looked at my Momma.

"Yeah, that's me," I answered.

He jerked his head over toward Miss Lipstick's room. "Lipstick in there?" he asked.

"Yeah, she in there." Suddenly, the sink full of dishes was beckoning me. "I better finish these."

"You do that, heah," Eugene said. He crossed over quickly to Miss Lipstick's door and boldly entered.

"Lipstick," he said. I heard a faint voice say something I couldn't decipher. "You seen him? He been here today?" Again, the faint answer. "You tell him I'm lookin' for him, okay? Bye, girlfriend." He closed the door and spun on his heel. Then, he opened the door again.

"Lipstick, you got some money? You always got money. You know I'll pay you back." He went all the way into the room and came out in a few seconds. The friendly hand he laid in my back had some greenery in it. He leaned into the sink with me.

"See ya, girlfriend. Fla right?" he said.

"Uh huh," I said.

"Well, I'm gonna let you get back to yo' job. I'll be seeing you again." Eugene left, switching his hips more gracefully than I'd seen any woman do. I was sorry he was gone, because I thought he was going to be all the excitement I would see for the rest of the week. I had nothing else to look forward to other than more dirty dishes in a dirty house filled with dirty people.

Cleaning up behind people who found consolation in the arms of a glass lover was really labor-intensive and smelly. I should have been used to it, but I never had to deal with it on that scale. The unique bodily aromas burned my eyes and it was difficult navigating around people who were barely conscious. I spent more time with my hands in putrid dishwater than anything else, washing glasses that were unclean with the residue of hard drinking. It gave me a unique vantage point to observe the comings and goings into that infamous room.

Miss Lipstick was popular, especially with men. No man was ever turned away based on race, creed or color. Black men of every shade, white men tanned and pale, and yellow men, too. The only color that mattered in Miss Lipstick's house was green. Men of means and men who were just scraping by — all were welcome in Miss Lipstick's domain.

A parade of people entered and exited Miss Lipstick's boudoir. I knew a few of the people. I knew of some of the others. Some people who passed through I was utterly shocked to see. The regulars had already warned me that what went on in that room, stayed in that room. I was free to discuss my opinion with them, but the facts resided in those four walls.

Since I didn't have any friends, there was no ear into which I could share the strange stuff that went on in that house.

"Here you go, Lipstick. Just like I said. I'm a man of my word." Johnny made good on his promise to pay Miss Lipstick. "Now, I'll have a little White Lightnin' on credit, if you please, ma'am." Johnny proceeded to avail himself of another egg from the refrigerator.

"No, sir, Johnny," Miss Lipstick said, her hand in his face. "Ain't no more tabs. You want a taste, you pay up front."

Johnny whined. "You been lettin' folks buy on credit for years and years. You know my money slow." He pulled out his pants pockets, showing he indeed had nothing.

"Can't help you." Miss Lipstick was cold and unrelenting. "Move now or go home. Other folks got to get in here."

The word had apparently spread like a virus that Miss Lipstick was no longer extending credit. She wasn't even present to receive most of the money. Her doorway became a turnstile as men and women, sometimes running into each other, came in without greeting anyone and peeled off rolls of bills or dropped heaping balls of cash on the kitchen table. A few people bought liquor when they came, but for the most part, they deposited the money into the Bank of Lipstick and departed. They all gave a slight nod to Root Charlie, still sitting in his corner, and he sometimes returned it. In the few hours that I worked on one particular day, seven people brought in enough money to cover Miss Lipstick's small dining table. I didn't know what her product was, but Miss Lipstick must have been having a fire sale.

Some of those who came and went that summer had money to burn, the skill to heal, and others had the authority to arrest me. I was folding towels at the kitchen table one Thursday afternoon when a battalion of Quincy's finest kicked in Miss Lipstick's door. Four officers in blue uniforms with arrest paraphernalia dangling from their waists barged in with guns drawn and started waving them around in a dramatic fashion. Their presence filled the house and emptied it at the same time. Not a single one of Miss Lipstick's loyal patrons hung around to see what they wanted. Miss Lipstick displayed no fear. Annoyance was painted on her weathered face as she prepared to confront the fuzz. Root Charlie began to rise up like biscuits in the oven. Miss Lipstick shook her head.

"I got this, Charlie." She turned on the officers.

"Y'all gonna fix my front door. What y'all doing here?" she asked, anger creasing her brow.

They answered, "We came to arrest you for selling liquor with no license and for running a 'ho house. Sheriff said to bring you in."

Miss Lipstick didn't flinch. I folded the same towel three times. I contemplated whether I would need to grab *Their Eyes Were Watching God* and make a break for it, but I wasn't convinced the officers wouldn't shoot a child.

"Ain't no whores in this house, unless you looking for your wife," Miss Lipstick quipped without a hint of humor. My eyes stretched wide, afraid I would finally see her in handcuffs.

"You know the drill, Miss Lipstick," a white officer responded. "Sheriff Waller sent us."

"I see. Got to show everybody he doing his job." She motioned for them to follow her into her quarters. After the last officer entered, there was silence. Suddenly, I heard laughter thundering through the walls. Next thing I knew, everybody rolled out, still laughing. When the officers left, the previously departed flooded back in. Miss Lipstick elbowed me in the side.

"You thought Lipstick was gone, didn't you, baby?" She calmly lit a cigarette. "Lipstick know where all the bodies buried, and who buried 'em." She rounded her mouth and blew out a ring of puffs that resembled a skull and cross bones. "And I know who made 'em bodies, too." She winked at me, then walked away laughing like some evil villain on my Saturday morning cartoons, but with spastic coughs interspersed throughout. Those coughs rattled the whole house. They sometimes lasted two minutes or more. Miss Lipstick waved off any concern I attempted to show.

In her scratchy voice, she said, "Lipstick gonna be all right. It's gon' to take more than a few coffin nails to bring Lipstick down." She went off hacking to her room, still chuckling and scratching her side as she sauntered away.

/CHAPTER V/

I learned quickly that what was done and spoken in Miss Lipstick's house, stayed in Miss Lipstick's house. Her home was the holder of secrets, only to be shared by those who were giving them up. After a few shots, several cases of beer and many potent cocktails, the secrets flowed freely. In a very short period of time, I had sized up the people around Miss Lipstick's place peripherally. Just a few days into the job, I got to know who some of them were and the tales of their woe. Leroy Curtis knew the exact date he crawled into the bottle — it was May 18, 1956. That was the day his four-year-old son and father-in-law left to pick up a cab fare, and never returned. Phyllis Littlejohn had nine children, all taken by social services while she tried to beat a drug and alcohol addiction. Pastor Ricky Sullivan was catapulted out of the pulpit because of rumors of sexual misdeeds without proof of any actual misdeeds. As a result, he hadn't been in a church in ten years, but it didn't stop him from preaching. Miss Lipstick's porch became his makeshift pulpit.

"What we do in the dark, will surely come into the light. Can I hear an amen, somebody?" Pastor Ricky chanted, gesturing wildly with the Bible in one hand, and a cold brew in the other. His congregation gave him his amen by raising their own cans and bottles.

"Are you prepared to meet your maker and answer for those things done in darkness?" he challenged. Miss Lipstick listened to this particular sermon through an open window.

"You go to church, Miss Lipstick?" Curiosity got the best of me. I asked her a question I already knew the answer to.

"I got no use for church and God got no use for Lipstick. Know where I'm going. Made my peace long time ago." She cradled the cigarette between two fingers, striking that classic smoker's pose with one arm supporting the arm of the smoking hand. She seemed to ponder what she'd said before closing the window with finality.

I was fascinated by Pastor Ricky, especially. He didn't just smile with his lips — his whole face participated. His eyes twinkled. His nose wrinkled. His ears sat up. When I saw him, a smile seemed to be required — other occasions required outright laughter. Even in late June, he wore a lime green, polyester three-piece suit with the long jacket. Sweat poured off his head, a combination of the sun's effects and the chemical juice from his S-curl. Pastor Ricky was never without his Bible. It was glued to his hand. He met me on Miss Lipstick's porch on Monday afternoon, his Bible in tow. Just seeing him brought a carbonation of giggles to my lips.

"What are you laughing at there, Jasmine?" he asked with that disarming grin.

"You." A giggle escaped. "Why you call me Jasmine?"

"Why *do* you call me Jasmine?" He tilted his head to the side. The sun glinted off his wet hair.

"Ain't that what I said?" I asked, getting impatient.

"Isn't," Pastor Ricky responded.

"Isn't what?" The circular conversation was making me dizzy.

"Is Jasmine not your name?" he asked.

"I wish. My name is Fla with a long 'a'." I was tired of having to explain that name.

He pursed his lips and furrowed his brow. "What is your mother's name?"

"Millie Frye," I answered.

"That is odd. Odd, indeed." He paused half a second. His voice dropped to a whisper. "My dear, your mother's name is not Millie."

"Yes, it is," I said. "Or maybe it's Millicent. I ain't never seen her driver's license or nothing, but I'm pretty sure that's what it is."

Pastor Ricky started rubbing his temples. "Sweetheart, sweetheart. Your grammar skills are atrocious. What are they teaching you in English class?"

"I speak good and I make the highest grades in my class," I said defensively.

"Speaking and writing are two different things," Pastor Ricky said. "You must also practice the art of speaking. Your mother spoke beautifully."

"My momma?" I had never heard Millie Frye utter a complete sentence without some sort of grammatical violation.

"Pastor Ricky!" Miss Lipstick screamed from the window. Like the smoke that followed in her wake, she appeared out of the air.

"What y'all talking about?" she asked.

"About my momma," I piped up. Pastor Ricky looked uneasy.

"You was?" Miss Lipstick lifted one eyebrow. Pastor Ricky cleared his throat.

"The girl deserves to know her history," he said defiantly.

"What she deserve is to be washing my dishes and folding my towels." Miss Lipstick spoke to me, but some kind of silent duel was going on between the two adults. Their eyes waged a wordless war, and both elders stood their ground, not moving. It seemed to last for minutes, but probably only a few seconds. When Pastor Ricky hung his head under Miss Lipstick's iron glare, I knew he was conceding defeat. Miss Lipstick jerked her head toward the house, and he followed her inside.

"You stay out here," Miss Lipstick said to me.

"Pardon me, Jasmine," Pastor Ricky said, tipping an invisible hat. "I have been summoned."

I obeyed to the letter of the law, but not the spirit. I stayed outside on the porch, near the front door, which happened to be open, where my view of the inside of the house was obstructed only by that rusty screen door. A heated conversation took place inside Miss Lipstick's bedroom. I couldn't make out any words, but the tones were ominous. When the door opened suddenly, I flattened myself against the wall between the door frame and the window. Still, pieces of the hot conversation drifted outside to my ears.

"It's a lie," Pastor Ricky said.

"I decide that," Miss Lipstick said. I peered around the corner and saw Miss Lipstick push Pastor Ricky out of her room. He hesitated at the door, his hand reaching for the knob. Root Charlie stretched out his long legs and shifted in his seat. Pastor Ricky beat a hasty retreat, but paused on the porch to stroke my arm.

"What happened in there?" I whispered.

"It was just a little disagreement between grownups," he said noncommittally.

"Was that about me?"

"Jasmine, don't worry about it, sweetheart." He planted a kiss on my forehead. "I have to go."

I could have sworn that argument had something to do with me. I pushed the thought aside and went in. I stepped over three people sleeping in the middle of the floor. They were curled up in my path, causing me to zigzag all over the living room hunting for my elusive prey. I picked up a river of empty glass bottles every single day of my work week. Some of the bottles had to be pried out of unconscious hands.

Mr. Curtis lay slumped over in his corner of the sofa. A half-empty bottle of Christian Brothers rested in a precarious position in his lap. I leaned over to rescue it.

"Don't touch it," Miss Lipstick said.

"Huh?"

"Mr. Curtis wake up out a dead sleep to save that bottle." She leaned in the doorway of her room, the light behind her revealing she was wearing very little under her thin housedress. Her hand was up elegantly, smoking in that calm way of hers.

"What's wrong with them?" I whispered. I was not immune to the distinct aroma a room full of intoxicated people could create. It was strong and overpowering. My nose twitched in protest.

"Crutches, baby," Miss Lipstick said.

"Ma'am?"

"You ain't got enough years under your belt to understand. Someday you will. But let me tell you this way." She filled her lungs with a bottomless drag on her cigarette and then exhaled with a thunderous cough. "You know when somebody break a leg, they need crutches for a while to help them get better." She waved her cigarette hand in the direction of the living room. "All these people, what broke in they lives ain't better yet."

"You got a crutch, Miss Lipstick?"

She seemed to be someplace else for a few minutes. "Everybody got a crutch."

"What's yours?"

"None of your business, little girl." Her sinister tone meant the question and answer period was over, especially since she left me to go back to her room.

I shrugged my shoulders and resumed my duties, stepping lightly into the human minefield. Harold Melvin & the Blue Notes sang the ironic tune from the small radio on the mantle, "Wake Up Everybody."

I found a can of beer under the sofa that was infested with roaches. I dropped it in disgust, its contents crawling in all directions, including over Miss Lipstick's sleeping houseguests. Unbeknownst to me, Miss Lipstick was watching. She startled me when she called me over to her in that "you in trouble" voice.

"Come here, gal. Don't be looking at people like that."

"Like what?"

"You look at these folks and all you see is a bunch of drunks, winos and what not." She pointed at me with her smoking hand and her voice was raised. "You don't know what these people been through to get where they at. They didn't just wake up one morning and decide they were gonna drink they life away. Most of them were honest, hard working people. Jobs is scarce. They can't even depend on tobacco no more. Them jobs gone. It takes some real bad stuff to make a person do what they do to get through the day. Remember them crutches? You just see the ones who drink they crutch. Folks hide they pain in many ways."

She must have seen the question in my face. She continued.

"I bet you don't even know Pastor Ricky used to be a English teacher. A Ph.D."

"I could tell he was some kind of teacher," I said.

"Uh, huh. Then he started preaching," Miss Lipstick went on. "Things was going good for him for a while. Then, he made a mistake. We all make mistakes, but them church folks don't give nobody a second chance. They broke him." She shook her head.

"You sound like you care about him," I said.

"I do. I love that man. He helped me through some hard times."

"Then why you mad at him? What did he do wrong?"

"I'm not mad, gal," Miss Lipstick said softly. "I just expect certain things from people. That's just how it is. Don't mean I love Pastor Ricky no less." She swept her arm around the room. "I love all of 'em. They need somebody in they corner."

She paused to catch her breath and then coughed badly. She couldn't speak for a second or two.

"I'm not fussing at you or nothing, but I'm just trying to tell you I don't like to see people being judged for something they can't help." She left me standing there, again, puzzled. After my verbal whipping, I felt like going home to hide out in my books. I had to be feeling low if I wanted to go home.

I picked up the last paper cup and was walking out the door at quitting time. I bumped right into Phyllis, a new arrival and a tornado of fabulousness. She blew in and did what Harold could not — the souls on the floor began to stir.

"Phyllis, what's the word, what's the word?" one man asked.

"It's a word you ain't heard," she sang. She let out an infectious laugh.

"Wake up, y'all. Why everybody sleepin'? It's time to party." She clapped her hands, threw them in the air and began dancing by herself.

"It's a party now you back. We ain't seen you 'round here in about a year. Where you been, girl?"

"Doin' my thang! You know me!" She threw her head back and let out another big, hearty laugh. Her deep, throaty voice was easy on the ears, her laughs, short bursts of happy energy.

I was still trying to leave when Phyllis grabbed me in a bear hug. She was a little thing, smaller than me, but I felt swallowed in her embrace.

"Where you going, gorgeous? It ain't a party without you." Phyllis wasn't beautiful like Cast Iron Kat. She just missed that designation because of the deep pits, adult acne and the half inch wide scar that started above her right ear, looped under her chin and ended just below her left ear. She caught me staring at it.

"You lookin' at my other smile?"

"I wasn't looking," I lied.

"You can't help looking. Wanna know how I got it?" I wasn't sure if I did. It was pretty gruesome.

"Some dude liked my smile so much, he wanted me to have two. This second one here put me in the hospital for three months." Phyllis whipped out her original smile as she described this horrific injury. "He almost got my carrot artery."

"You mean your carotid artery?" Instead of being appalled, I was reeled into her spirit. She was like a Technicolor rainbow — short, red hair, sparkling green eyes, butter-colored skin. She was tiny and cute. I just wanted to put her in the crook of my arm, pat her on the head and say, "It's all right. It's all right."

"I know what it's called, beautiful. I'm just playing with you. Lighten up, girl," Phyllis said, smiling the entire time. I loved her instantly, especially the casual way she handed out affection — a neck squeeze, a face pinch, and fully-committed hugs. I didn't realize how much I craved it.

"Don't you look cute today! You got a boyfriend yet?" Phyllis asked.

"Who? Me? Boys don't like me." I tried to throw it away.

"Yes, they do. They just too scared to say so. Look at you. Pretty brown skin like Karla's. I bet you smart like her, too. What's two plus two?" Merriment spilled from Phyllis' every pore. She wrapped skinny arms around me that were scarred like railroad tracks from her wrists to her elbow.

"Look here, don't go anywhere." She made a beeline for the back porch, where there was a little room that emitted a funny-smelling smoke whenever anyone opened the door. Miss Lipstick forbade me to put my toe near that room. I was to only wash and dry clothes on the back porch. Phyllis returned five minutes later with a drink in her hand.

"Why you looking so sad, girl?" she asked. She polished off the drink and put the glass down on a side table.

"I'm not sad," I answered. "I'm just wondering why people keep saying I look like Karla. And my momma is a redbone. Who is Karla?"

"Huh?"

"You said I have brown skin like Karla." The room seemed to have quieted to a whisper. Even Root Charlie paused half a breath.

"Oh, I misspoke, honey. Don't mind me. Liquor'll do that to you." Phyllis shifted her glance to Miss Lipstick's door, and an unspoken conversation seemed to take place between her and the others in the room. She waved them off vigorously as she led me to the porch.

"You heading home?" she asked.

"Yeah," I answered, a bit unnerved since twice today my identity or that of my mother had been mistaken.

"You sure there ain't no boys somewhere?" She peered into my face. If my forehead had been a movie screen, she'd have seen my two leading men, Mr. Pierce and Randy, fighting a duel to decide who would win my hand.

"All righty then." She held me near her on the steps of the front porch. Being close to her was wonderful. Her scent was that of vanilla musk mixed with that funny-smelling smoke from the back porch. "Let me tell you a secret." Phyllis leaned in as if she was about to reveal classified information, but she didn't lower her voice. "If you ever do find somebody you like, don't wear your heart on your sleeve. That way, people can't pick it off and stomp on it." Her hands started to tremble.

"OK." I was skeptical I would ever have the chance to utilize this advice.

"For real, sugar. You just need a thicker skin. Karla was sweet and kind and a little wild at first, but I tell you, she didn't take nothing from nobody."

"Karla?"

Phyllis clapped her hand over her mouth. "I meant, Millie. Excuse me, baby. My head in the clouds."

There were so many thoughts tumbling around in my mind vying for attention, I walked home with my head down. I hoped I'd get the chance to talk to Pastor Ricky again, to find out why he called me Jasmine and to ask him why he needed a crutch. After Miss Lipstick "didn't fuss at me" about the crutches, I wondered if I had judged other people too hastily. I also needed to find out who this Karla was. What would Hercules Poirot do?

/CHAPTER VI/

Summer school had been in session for ten days and I was already tired of dodging Cast Iron Kat's anger. Four days a week for seven weeks, I would have to contend with it. At the mere sight of Carter Jackson High School, I became crestfallen. School was supposed to be my escape from home, and my books were my escape from life. I was reading more to Miss Lipstick's customers than for myself. I began to feel that there was no escape for me.

Cast Iron Kat made it her mission to see just how far she could push me. The more I got right in class, and the more she got wrong, the harder the shoves in the hallway, and the longer the laughs in the lunchroom. I had learned a long time ago to hold my pee until I got to Miss Lipstick's. I carried an extra pair of panties for emergencies. Mr. Pierce wasn't making it any better. He heaped so many compliments upon me that they were becoming too heavy to bear. I never thought I'd see the day that hearing my name coming out of his mouth wouldn't send me on a natural high. With a forked tongue, Mr. Pierce sang my praises and criticized Cast Iron Kat. It was a volatile mixture that spelled nothing but disaster for me.

"Miss Morehead, you are doomed to repeat the tenth grade if you don't get Miss Frye to help you pass this class.

This is your last chance." Mr. Pierce was exasperated. Cast Iron Kat had earned another failing grade on a quiz.

I took myself out of the equation by falling into a trance during the discussion about the essay we were supposed to write to commemorate the recent Bicentennial. The Fourth of July fell on a Sunday that year. I had written the essay the day Mr. Pierce assigned it, but touched it up a bit on Monday, since it was a school holiday. The library was closed and there was nothing else to do but delve into my thoughts. My number one query the day before, and again in that moment, was this Karla person. I turned over and over in my mind who this woman could be, and I was coming up empty. When I woke up from my trance, I found Mr. Pierce pointing at me, but standing menacingly over Cast Iron Kat. Whenever he mentioned my name, I felt Kat's eyes go through me like a dagger. I would certainly be running that day.

"Yes sir," Cast Iron Kat mumbled.

"Don't be too proud to ask for help," Mr. Pierce continued. "We're all going to need help from somebody at some point. Don't let your pride stand in the way of your success." Mr. Pierce directed that last statement at me.

When the final bell rang, I lingered in the classroom. I wanted to give Cast Iron Kat's explosive temper time to diffuse.

"Is there a problem, Miss Frye?" Mr. Pierce asked.

"No." I tried to sound nonchalant while I stacked and restacked my literature textbook, Agatha Christie and my folders, but even I didn't buy it.

"Listen, Fla." Mr. Pierce used my first name and he approached me slowly. I lived this moment a thousand times in my dreams. In that boundless dimension, he would be preparing to kneel before me to ask for my hand. This time, it was a distraction. "Do you carry these books like this every day? Don't you have a book bag?"

"No, but it's OK. It's not that many."

"That literature textbook alone weighs a ton, plus the three and four books I see you carrying all the time. That's way too much." When he walked away, I saw that the view from the back was just as good as the one from the front.

He reached under his desk and pulled out a black canvas book bag.

"Do you want this book bag, Miss Frye?" He held it out to me. He was supposed to be on his knees.

"I do." I reached out to take the empty bag. I slipped it on my finger and then slid it up over my arm. I noticed it was emblazoned with Florida A&M University's Rattler logo and the words "Upward Bound."

"That's from the Upward Bound program. It would be great for you, Miss Frye. You should seriously consider it." Mr. Pierce's eyes were glistening.

"I'll think about it, Mr. Pierce. What do I have to do?"

"All I need is your mother's consent and a copy of your birth certificate." He laughed. "We have to prove you are who you say you are."

The birth certificate would be no problem. Getting Momma's consent was a different matter. Mr. Pierce might have to ask for that in person.

After I put the books in my new book bag, I left the classroom, tiptoed down the hallway and out the double doors. Four of Cast Iron Kat's minions ambushed me outside. Cast Iron Kat was not among them. They pushed me up against the brick wall as if I were in a police lineup and they surrounded me. Their eyes raked me over, inspecting every inch of me for something to degrade me about. They whispered to each other during this exercise while they pointed to different parts of my body. They found something to satisfy their thirst for humiliation.

"Hey, Fla. Where you get them Buster Browns?" Myra asked. My Goodwill sneakers were black at the toe and heel, and white in the middle. They were comfortable and they were all I had.

"Yeah," Dominique chimed in. "Buster Brown, Buster Brown, let me see your shoes get down," she chanted. Her friends thought it was brilliant. They high-fived Dominique and joined her in the mean-spirited jingle. As ridiculous as it was, it still cut me to the quick. They wore the latest, trendiest clothes while I was lucky if I found anything in the thrift shops that fit. If I found anything that fit and matched, it was a bonanza. I imagined myself as a giant wall to deflect the hurt, but it still penetrated.

"And what about that bag?" asked Clovis. "Did your man give it to you? Did you have to kiss him?" She made kissy noises and poked at the bag.

"A man? Kiss Fla?" asked Myra. "That ain't never gonna happen." Her stinky, hot breath was inches from my face. "Ain't nobody ever gonna love you. You too ugly."

Salty tears stung the back of my eyes, but I refused to shed them. A storm of hatred broiled inside of me.

"Hey, y'all leave her to me," I heard Cast Iron Kat say. I was going to pick up my new bag, which was now heavy with books and the chunks of my self-esteem, but it would probably end up on the ground again. "Y'all go on and wait for me out front."

As many words as I knew, I couldn't find one to describe how afraid I really was. Cast Iron Kat had her bag and now my heavy bag was at her disposal. I stared at her out of the corner of my eyes, and held my breath, afraid my inhaling fresh air would anger her. When she reached down to pick up my bag, I covered my head, hoping the brain damage wouldn't be too severe and that someone would respond to my screams.

"Here, girl!" Cast Iron Kat said, shoving the bag hard into my chest.

"Yeah, Kat. Jack her butt up," I heard one of the other girls say. Cast Iron Kat gave her a thumbs up, then turned her attention back to me.

"You so stupid," she whispered. "When I'm ready for you, you'll know it. Now get outta here."

I grasped the bag tightly, in case she changed her mind and decided to bean me with it. I figured it was okay to exhale since the signal I was reading was that I would live another day. Cast Iron Kat walked away from me, not looking back. I watched her, though, as I walked in the other direction, thanking God profusely for this narrow escape.

Mother Nature spared us nothing with regard to the heat and humidity of July. The sun's full fury could be felt first thing in the morning. The little air conditioner in the window of our apartment was no match for the heat waves penetrating the walls. Momma frequently limped around the house in her torn T-shirt and panties uniform, and Jerome chose to go disgustingly topless. I, on the other hand, dressed like winter in Maine to put as much cloth as possible between my flesh and Jerome's scathing stare. Momma and Jerome's threadbare relationship was still hanging in there despite the fact that money was low. He refused to work. The man couldn't keep a job if it was poured on him, but he did freeload better than anybody Momma had ever brought home.

Jerome had also become bolder in his passes at me. He didn't even care if Momma saw him. Momma didn't seem to care at all as long as Jerome's hands were on her somehow, either tenderly or roughly. There were many days when I'd come home and they'd be in the midst of a typical date — drinking like fish, fighting like dogs, and making up like rabbits. There was nowhere to hide from them: the sights, the sounds, the smells. They would have been more comfortable in a barnyard.

I found some solace in my room, and tried to crawl into several different books, but there was no one book that could pull me up out of my funk. I would have happily endured the odors of Miss Lipstick's house, but she'd prohibited me from coming that week. The Fourth of July celebration at her house tended to be a weeklong affair, and she didn't think I'd be safe in that environment. It surely couldn't have been worse than what I was subjected to in my own home.

I went to sleep to escape. After school on Thursday, I lay down and mercifully slept through the night, but I didn't dream. The train came by and called for me, as usual, but I was still too burdened and couldn't move. On Friday morning, my burden was a little lighter because of my decision to go to Miss Lipstick's house, even though she told me not to come over. I was famished and prayed Momma had at least bought some cereal and milk. She did, and I ate quickly so I could leave as soon as possible. I didn't want to disturb Momma's and Jerome's hibernation, so I tried to close the door quietly. Nevertheless, the great beast was awakened.

"Flah, come here a minute." Jerome called me from Momma's bed. I backtracked slowly toward her bedroom door. I saw that Momma lay next to Jerome, but she wasn't asleep.

"What!" I was not going inside that room.

From the door, I could see that Jerome was shirtless and in need of a bra more than Momma. His enormous, rotund gut hung down way past his hips. He brought his arms up over his head, revealing a thicket of nappy hair in his armpits, and flexed the flab around his arms, as if he thought that was enticing to me. I willed my breakfast to go back down my throat.

"Come over here. Don't be scared of Jerome."

"What you want? I got to get to Miss Lipstick!" I would take my chances that she wouldn't send me back home.

"Sit over here, next to me. I won't bite." He moved over in the bed, the covers nearly falling away to show me something I had no desire to see. As I turned to leave, Momma rolled over and began stroking his arm.

"You gonna do what I tell you, little girl. I promise you that!" Jerome said.

I slammed the door as hard as I could, hoping he would interpret it as an obscene expression I wasn't courageous enough to utter. Then again, that's what he wanted.

I ran down the stairs at full speed and rounded the stairwell on the ground floor. The downstairs neighbor, an elderly lady named Miss Lila, was usually away visiting her sick sister in Cairo, Georgia. Today, she was in residence and chatting away at the door with a young girl whom I didn't see until it was too late. I bumped right into Cast Iron Kat, knocking her down hard. I was so stunned, I couldn't even apologize. I simply added octane to my blood and took off toward Miss Lipstick's like a bat out of you-know-where. Cast Iron Kat's words caught up with me, though. She was gonna get me.

I started leaving a stash of books at Miss Lipstick's house so I had plenty of material to choose from. I spent so much time reading after the chores were done that Mr.

Curtis and a few others asked me to come back and read something to them. This was a good day to fulfill my promise. It gave me a little charge. I was at the corner and down the street from Miss Lipstick's house, walking at a clipped pace and looking at my feet when I heard a voice behind me.

"Hey, Jasmine. Wait up, sweetheart." I turned around and saw Pastor Ricky. It had been approximately twenty-four days since I saw him last. I practically threw myself into his arms to reassure myself I was not encountering an apparition. Pastor Ricky held on to me as if he missed me, too. A smile immediately sprang to my face when I looked into his, my cares temporarily laid aside. Pastor Ricky wore one of his popsicle suits that should have melted in the heat. I hoped he didn't see the worry hiding behind my smile. Between Jerome and Cast Iron Kat, I wore anguish like a mask. If he did see anything, he said nothing about it. Pastor Ricky looped his lemon-clad arm through mine.

"I was thinking the other day, about you." As we walked, he nodded his head a lot, causing his curls to bounce and drop hair juice behind us like bread crumbs. His Bible swung at his side.

"Were you thinking about telling me why you call me Jasmine?" That name was so much prettier than mine. I had to know its origin.

"Yes," Pastor Ricky said, but no explanation followed.

"OK." I waited patiently for about three seconds. "Now?"

"Yes." He stopped me and angled my body to face him. "I will tell you." I waited. Still, he said nothing about the name. He was a pastor, at least he used to be, and my elder. Was I allowed to blow up at him? I didn't get a chance to answer my own question. Pastor Ricky's eyes suddenly glazed over. He lifted his head and was looking intently at something behind me.

"Hey, Pastor," I heard the masculine, sing-songy voice say. "I been looking for you. Where you been?"

I turned around and saw Eugene sashaying toward us in khaki capris, a long, orange shirt and flip flops.

"Oh, hey, girlfriend. I didn't know that was you," he said to me. "How you doin'?"

"Good, Eugene." An awkward silence ensued. I rocked back and forth on my heels; Pastor Ricky rubbed his neck; and Eugene struck a pose with both his hands on his hips. The art of small talk would have come in handy.

"So, Pastor, you got some money?" Eugene asked, still posing. Pastor Ricky shrugged his shoulders, then went fishing in the left pocket of his bright yellow pants. He pulled up a few bills neatly folded together.

"This is all I have," Pastor Ricky said. "I can give you . . ."

Eugene snatched the money from his hand. "All of it. Thank you, Pastor. See ya, girlfriend," Eugene said, already walking past us. My mouth was open. Pastor Ricky closed it.

"That's so unladylike," he admonished me.

"But . . . but . . ." It was difficult to form a coherent sentence. "Pastor Ricky . . .," I started in an irritated tone.

"What do you know about your father?" Pastor Ricky asked, adeptly changing the subject to one that was guaranteed to redirect my focus.

"My father?" I'd forgotten I had one.

"Every girl should know her father." A distant look crossed over Pastor Ricky's eyes. "It's important for her to know where she came from. Would you like to meet your father?"

"My father? I have a father? A real father?" It was too much to hope for.

"My dear Jasmine, everyone does." Pastor Ricky sounded amused.

"Momma never talks about him. Gosh. I don't know." I paced the sidewalk, wondering if my dreams would be any match for reality. "Oh, my God."

Pastor Ricky snapped his fingers a couple of times. "Jasmine, are you with me?"

"I don't want a father."

"Pardon me?" Pastor Ricky's curls stopped bouncing.

"I want a daddy. I always dreamed of having a daddy."

"Then we'll go meet your daddy today. Right now." He swiveled his head in all directions.

"Shh." He pursed his lips and nodded his head toward Miss Lipstick's house.

It was fun, pretending it was a conspiracy. I had a feeling though, that the shelf life of a secret outside of Miss Lipstick's house was very short, unless it was her secret.

/CHAPTER VII/

It wasn't quite noon when we began our journey. Pastor Ricky was only too eager to accompany me to meet this man. I was more nervous than I ever remember being. What if my dreams of a father paled in comparison to reality? What if he rejected me? What if he wanted me? My heart thumped a rhythmic message, telling me I was finally going to meet the fantasy I'd created. In my dreams, my daddy was tall with strong shoulders and large hands. He hoisted me up on those shoulders, keeping me safe from things below. He was attentive and very generous. He bought me clothes and books and a big house. He ate lumpy oatmeal with me in the mornings and took me horseback riding in the afternoon. He was overly protective of me, towering over the kids who made fun of me and stepping on them like ants. He would squash Cast Iron Kat. This wonderful, invincible man, the ten-year concoction of a lonely little girl, was finally going to have a face.

"When we get in his office, I'll do all the talking," announced Pastor Ricky.

"Why do you get to do the talking? He's my daddy, ain't he?"

"Isn't he. I want to know where his head is, where he's been all these years. I want to cross-examine him first. You know, catch him in a lie." Pastor Ricky rubbed his hands over his Bible, and then ran them through his hair. He wiped his hands on his suit, the wetness and the oil leaving an ugly stain on his right breast pocket.

According to Pastor Ricky, my daddy was a bean counter for the man, the city hall man. He had a title and an office in the headquarters for the City of Quincy.

When we arrived, city hall was bustling with activity. Its exterior was getting a face lift, like so many of the buildings west of the downtown core needed. Construction materials lay about haphazardly in piles in a designated corner of the parking lot. Toward the rear of the building, the employee parking lot was full. People filed in and out, paying utility bills, changing phone numbers, and complaining about trash service. The white secretary with the permed blonde curls at the front desk looked overwhelmed. She had a phone to her ear and a small crush of people flanking her desk, all wanting different things and her undivided attention. She barely looked up when we asked for my daddy's location. She had to be distracted — every single person in that crowd cut their eyes at Pastor Ricky. He got some interesting looks from white people.

"Second floor, third door to the left," she threw at us. She turned her focus back to the elderly white man who was waving a blue piece of paper under her nose.

As each step brought me closer to my daddy, my flight instincts grew stronger. I felt Pastor Ricky pulling me up the stairs. When we reached the top step, my foot froze in mid-air.

"Don't chicken out now," said Pastor Ricky. "Come on, Jasmine. We've been waiting too long for this. Come on."

"I don't know. What if he don't want me? Doesn't want me?" I corrected myself, already on my best behavior.

"We'll deal with it. If you don't do this now, you'll always regret it." We paused outside my father's door. The name plate read, "Calvin Walters — Jr. Accountant." I ran my fingers over the lettering, and then nervously turned the knob.

"Who's there? Can I help you?" the gravelly voice asked.

We entered an adequately appointed room not much bigger than a standard office cubicle. There were no book shelves to hold the three short rows of books stacked behind the man sitting at the desk. His walls were crowded with certificates for jobs well done, and college diplomas issued to Calvin A. Walters by Florida A&M University and Florida State University in 1963 and 1965, respectively. A broad-shouldered man of about thirty-five sat behind a miniature desk in the tiny space. He was dressed smartly in a white shirt, blue and white striped tie and I assumed the light blue pants that matched the light blue jacket hanging on the back of the chair. He was extraordinarily handsome — textbook father material.

Before I could speak, Pastor Ricky jumped in.

"Yes, you sure can help. You can help your daughter here." Pastor Ricky leaned way over the desk, his hair drops pelting documents that looked important.

The good-looking, round face looking up at me was mine. He had a wide forehead and a widow's peak formed by that hair I fought with so hard. He had the same wide nose and thin lips that were pressed into a tight line. I was looking at myself, older, masculine, a dead ringer in skin tone. I was hypnotized by the man until he uttered the words, "She never said you were mine." In that moment, Calvin Walters bore no resemblance to the father of my dreams.

"Man, you crazy. Look at her. You looking in a mirror." Pastor Ricky slipped into his native vernacular when he got angry. His normally pleasant features were distorted by his anger. "What you talking 'bout, she never told you she was yours?" He thumped the desk hard and began pacing, his face creased by a ferocious-looking frown. He sat down abruptly and thumbed through his Bible.

"What it say in here." He jabbed his finger in a passage. "What it say here? Honor your father and your mother! How she gonna honor you?"

"It also says, does it not, that men shall not be lovers of themselves and that one shall not be drunk with wine of the spirits," my father threw back at him. "You don't get to pick and choose God's word. You live by all of it or none of it, you hypocrite." His voice was strained, but calm and his face, immobile.

Pastor Ricky didn't bat an eye. "We ain't talking about me, Cal. We talking about your child. She didn't get to pick and choose her parents. You ran for the job and, dammit, you been elected!" Pastor Ricky's chest was heaving high.

"I don't know what you talking about, Ricky!"

I wasn't expecting my father to throw his arms around me and welcome his long lost daughter into his heart, but I wasn't prepared for an outright rejection. Pastor Ricky's ranting became a dull, annoying sound in my ear.

"You know you was the only one she was dating. When she turned up pregnant, it had to cross your mind. Hell. Nobody told you. You a fool!"

My daddy sat back, the color draining from his face. He looked at me with my eyes and drew in the brows we had in common. Pastor Ricky's manner grew increasingly volatile. My father was still calm, as Pastor Ricky's behavior made a small space seem even smaller.

"Are you saying I'm not your daughter?" I managed to ask above a whisper.

The response he gave was not loving, paternal or even friendly. It was the verbal equivalent of swatting a gnat. He fixed his eyes to the left of my head and said, "Nobody showed me any proof."

That fueled another burst of anger in Pastor Ricky.

"You want proof?" Pastor Ricky said. I was beginning to suspect that he had juiced himself up before this meeting. "I got an idea. How 'bout a blood test, right here, right now? I prick the little girl's finger, then I take some blood from the side of yo' neck." He produced a pocket knife from deep within a hiding place in his suit.

Mr. Walters picked up the phone and punched in a couple of numbers with the long fingers he passed on to me. "Get me security. This is Walters."

While Pastor Ricky was threatening violence and Walters was calling the cops, I was paralyzed. When I heard the switch blade whipping open, the feeling returned in my limbs. It was time to separate Pastor Ricky from this situation.

"Pastor Ricky, you got your Bible?" I asked him, trying to redirect his focus. I didn't do it as well as he could.

"I know. He needs the hand of the Lord on him. I'm just gonna lay my hands on him." Pastor Ricky clenched and unclenched his fists. His Bible was on the desk. He knocked it over when he lunged at the man.

"Pastor Ricky!" I screamed. "Don't. Please don't!" Pastor Ricky was a man possessed. He grabbed a handful of Mr. Walter's shirt and jacked him up.

"Get off me, man!" Mr. Walters said, his face turning red and his eyes bulging. Pastor Ricky had him hemmed up in a corner of that small office. "Call the police, girl!"

"Pastor Ricky, stop!" I screamed again. Pastor Ricky brandished the knife and held it dangerously close to Calvin Walter's throat.

"Tell her she your daughter!" Pastor Ricky demanded. Calvin Walter's eyes were locked on the blade. "Tell her!" he yelled louder.

"You don't have to do this!" I cried.

"Yes, I do, Jasmine. Now listen. This man got something to say to you." I heard feet rushing up to the door. "Turn that lock, won't you," he said casually. I quickly flipped the lock and tucked myself away in the farthest corner I could find. I covered my eyes.

"We don't have all day! Say it! Say it! Say it!" Pastor Ricky kept repeating. Someone began knocking furiously on the door.

"Mr. Walters, you all right in there?" a man's voice asked. "It's security."

"Say it," Pastor Ricky pushed him. I heard keys rattling on the other side of the door. Pastor Ricky started to dig the knife in the side of Calvin Walter's neck.

"There's a crazy man in here with a knife at my throat! Get the cops!" Calvin Walters shouted.

"Yeah, get the cops. Then we can have a whole party up in here to hear what you got to say." Pastor Ricky was not afraid.

"All right!" Calvin Walters relented. "She's my daughter," he said softly. I always wanted to hear my father claim me as his daughter, but not during a confession extracted at knife point. I wished he would just take it back.

"What else?" Pastor Ricky asked.

"What do you mean what else? That's what you wanted me to say and I said it," Calvin Walters said through gritted teeth. The door opened and was thrown back. Two slight, white police officers with weapons in hand followed by three security guards armed with night sticks and flash lights stormed into the room.

One of the police officers barked an order. "Get away from him, sir. Now!"

"Don't shoot him!" I screamed. Pastor Ricky dropped the knife and put his hands up in surrender. The police officers accosted him and immediately put him in handcuffs. The noise had drawn other city employees out of their offices. They crowded outside the door.

"We have no problem here, do we, gentlemen?" Pastor Ricky caught the attention of Calvin Walters, who was busy readjusting his shirt and tie. His eyes darted nervously toward his co-workers. "Unless Mr. Walters wants to explain why we're here."

"What did happen in here, sir?" asked the officer who did not have Pastor Ricky in custody. The office was in an upheaval. Papers and books covered the floor. The desk chair was turned over. There was no room for anyone to move. A tiny trickle of blood dripped from Mr. Walter's neck, which he seemed not to notice. "Are you hurt? You want to press charges?"

Mr. Walters batted at the dust on his pants. His eyes rested briefly on me, still hanging out in the corner, and then came back to Pastor Ricky.

"Tell him who I am," Pastor Ricky huffed. "Tell him who she is. Go on," he goaded.

"He's nobody," Mr. Walters finally said. "Get him out of here, and take the girl, too. I don't want to press charges."

"Are you sure, sir? This man has committed a crime. We can take him in anyway."

"I'm sure," Mr. Walters said. "Everything's fine. You all can go back to your offices. I'm okay and I can handle things." They left with their necks still craned toward his office.

The officers were reluctant to let Pastor Ricky go. Mr. Walters pleaded with them to release him. They finally took the handcuffs off. After they did, Pastor Ricky reached down in the corner and pulled me up.

"I ain't leavin' til they all know who she is, Mr. High and Mighty," Pastor Ricky said.

"If they ask me again about pressing charges, I may say something different," said Calvin Walters.

"No," I said, finding my voice. "We need to go. Please!" I tugged on Pastor Ricky's arm with what strength I had left.

"I ain't gonna let him do you like that. How you gonna treat a little girl like that? She didn't ask to be here. And she is your little girl. You know it. She know it. The whole world know it." Pastor Ricky's tone was mocking. "What kinda' man you is, all dressed up in yo' white shirt and striped tie, running numbers for the man, thinking you somebody important. Ain't nothing more important than a man being a daddy to his little girl. I want you to know something. It's your loss."

The officers and the guards were still present. They looked confused. "What are we doing here, sir?" the younger guard inquired. Mr. Walters jerked his head toward the door. "I got this, Bill. Thank y'all for coming." The officers and the guards left, shaking their heads. The big man in the small office turned up his chair, picked up some of the papers he'd been working on and shook out the wrinkles from his blue jacket. He sat down and said nothing else to us. He picked up his pen again, and held it poised over the papers on his desk. Pastor Ricky gave me an "it's going to be all right" smile. He picked up his Bible, bowed to Mr. Walters and led me out of the office.

"Mimi didn't tell me she was pregnant," he yelled as we closed the door behind us, as if it justified his behavior and absolved him of the guilt I hoped would plague him for the rest of his life.

The trip down the stairs took less time than the trip up. In the lobby, I breathed for the first time.

"Excuse that display of ignorance in there." Pastor Ricky straightened out his suit. "That man always did push my buttons." He regained his composure. "You all right, Jasmine?"

I simply shook my head. Calvin Walters wasn't worthy of the energy required to produce a tear.

"Don't let what just happened in there change you at all," Pastor Ricky admonished me.

"How was it supposed to change me?" I asked, feeling only emptiness.

"Who do you think you are, Jasmine?" Pastor Ricky asked.

"I'm nobody. I feel like a nobody. People treat me like a nobody." I shrugged my shoulders and failed to meet Pastor Ricky's eyes. He lifted my chin.

"I'm going to say this so that you understand me perfectly. You ain't a nobody. Do you hear me? You are a person of every consequence. You are somebody worth loving. And you have to be the first person to do it. It doesn't matter what he thinks. Do you hear me?"

The entire city hall lobby heard him. I nodded yes and threaded my arms through his. I let him hold me. I felt something wet hitting the part in my hair. I looked up to see if it was his hair. I was surprised to see his tears.

"Why are you crying, Pastor Ricky?" We walked outside through the full parking lot.

"Hey. Check this out." He bent over and picked up a loose brick covered with plaster from the construction pile. "Let's find his car and open it with this big key." Pastor Ricky was frantic and seemed serious about the deed.

"We can't do that. We'll go to jail," I said, trying to calm him down.

"You meet some real nice people in prison. I used to have a prison ministry. Met some good people in bad circumstances." I was worried that the tether between Pastor Ricky and his sense of what was good and what was not, had finally snapped.

"No, Pastor Ricky. You supposed to be a man of God. You're supposed to be teaching me the right way." I couldn't help smiling at our role reversal. I got the feeling that everything would be all right, despite my lousy father. Pastor Ricky would do just fine as a surrogate daddy, and at that moment, he loved me enough for two parents.

Pastor Ricky rubbed his eyes vigorously.

"You okay?" I asked.

"I'm going to run back inside to get some tissue for my eyes. They burn sometimes." Pastor Ricky darted off toward the back of the building, although I remembered the restrooms being near the entrance. He wasn't gone long, and returned without the tissue.

"Where's the tissue, Pastor Ricky?" I interrogated him.

"I changed my mind," he said.

"But your eyes. Are they still burning?" I continued.

"They're fine," he snapped.

"Pastor Ricky, you didn't . . .?" I tried to ask.

"I'm sorry, Jasmine. You didn't deserve that," Pastor Ricky said. "Listen, I haven't always been saved," he confessed. "I could have been in prison, not just visiting prisoners. In another time, I might have taken this brick and opened up your father's head. But the Good Lord gave me another chance. I use my skills for good now. Won't it do you good to get back at that stuck up you know what? Nobody hurts you like that. Nobody."

I was amazed at the intensity of his feeling. His hands were shaking at his side. Something white was stuck to his palms. I filed away that piece of information and decided to ask some questions that were rolling around in my head. "Back in my...that man's office, it sounded like you were saying I was your little girl."

"Did it? I probably was. You're real special to me, Jasmine. You remind me of somebody." Pastor Ricky's smile could not overcome the sadness in his eyes.

"Let's get some ice cream." He was good at changing the subject. We walked arm-in-arm through the city. "You know what a sundae is without the cherry?" Pastor Ricky asked.

"No. What?" I felt a genuine smile coming back.

"A Saturdae. With an "e". Get it?" He showed me all his teeth in an open-mouth grin.

"You are so funny." I gave his arm a little squeeze and he reciprocated.

Pastor Ricky and I toured downtown Quincy as if neither of us had been born there. We walked past a dollar store and a convenience store where attendants pumped the gas for customers. We breezed by a family-owned grocery store, a mom-and-pop pharmacy and a hamburger joint where Pastor Ricky paid for the ice cream. The creamy butter pecan soft serve was the perfect foil to the hot, muggy day.

I stopped in my tracks. "Pastor Ricky, who is Mimi? He said something about Mimi."

"Mimi? Mimi and I were good friends," Pastor Ricky said.

"You knew my momma before I was born? She was your friend? What happened? Tell me about her." Questions were gushing out of me like a fountain. I knew next to nothing about Millie Frye. I had lived with the woman for almost sixteen years, and she was a complete stranger to me.

"Is Mimi her nickname?" Ice cream melted down my arm as I waited for Pastor Ricky to share his information with me.

"Slow down, Jasmine. Let a man breathe." He casually licked the circumference of his chocolate covered cone like a lemon-colored lizard. He needed more prompting.

"I like Mimi. It kind of makes her seem like a nicer person, more alive, you know."

Pastor Ricky took a deep breath. "I know. We'll talk about her another day."

"Another day? Why not today?" I trained on him what I hoped were sad, puppy dog eyes.

"Another day, Jasmine," he said with finality.

"You promise?"

He put his hand on his Bible. "I promise." We toasted this promise, his chocolate ice cream to my butter pecan. The ice cream was delicious and cold, but it didn't counteract my embarrassment or the humiliation. I had woken up that morning believing I had a perfect father. I would go to sleep that night knowing that my existence was a hypothesis to this man — something that had to be proved to a high degree of certainty before he would attach his name to me. I regretted ever releasing Calvin Walters from my fantasies. Now that he was loose in the real world, I prayed I wouldn't inherit his brand of ignorance.

/CHAPTER VIII/

A parade of uniforms through Miss Lipstick's house was not an uncommon occurrence. When officers materialized in uniform, they were there on official business. When they were out of uniform, they were customers. Some days, the lines blurred. Miss Lipstick clued me in that the customers from the back porch could get so rowdy while officers were on site that the officers would be derelict of duty if they didn't escort them out. Handling the high was not a Root Charlie assignment. The officers would allow the high, happy and the helpless to sit in the back seat, handcuffed, to assist them in coming down off their high. The only other alternative was to arrest them, and it would be difficult for the officer to explain how he happened to be at Miss Lipstick's, out of uniform, in his government-issued vehicle, while a violation of law was occurring. I was sorely disappointed to see Phyllis become a routine visitor to that room, but I never saw her taken out in handcuffs. She breezed by me sometimes, though, as if she didn't know me.

Mr. Curtis never went into that room. He parked himself every day on the deep end of Miss Lipstick's well-worn sofa. Everyone knew that was Mr. Curtis' spot. They left him alone to drink his Christian Brothers weekdays from nine to five, Saturdays and Sundays, from nine to two. It was the closest he'd ever come to anything Christian.

It was a quiet Monday afternoon, and very hot and dry outside. Alcohol and heat don't mix, so Miss Lipstick sent the regulars out in search of water. Mr. Curtis sat in his spot in all seasons, his watery eyes swimming in a pool of grief. He turned the bottle vertical, dousing himself with the contents that ran down his scratchy bearded chin and soaked his shirt. Root Charlie sat in his corner, not smiling or drinking. If not for the chewing of his cigar, I wouldn't have guessed he was anything but a big, black statue.

"I got your favorite story, Mr. Curtis," I said softly. He blinked furiously as he rotated his body toward the sound of my voice.

"Read it to me, baby," he slurred. "You sound just like Karla when you read."

"Who is Karla, Mr. Curtis?" I prodded gently, hoping to catch him before he slipped away. I was too late. He smiled a little as I read how a little boy never grew up and lived in another world. I read and used voices for the different characters. He nodded and smiled at my one-woman show.

"Mr. Curtis, who is Karla?" I tried again.

"Lipstick baby," he answered out of his fog.

"You mean Miss Lipstick has a daughter?"

"She did." His head bobbed uncontrollably.

"Tell me more about her. What was she like?" This was more intriguing than any trap Captain Hook could invent.

He took a long, deep breath. His answer was interrupted by a uniform that cast a long shadow into the living room.

"I'll get Miss Lipstick," I announced. If the handcuffs were out, he was visiting Miss Lipstick. If they weren't, he was there for one of Miss Lipstick's customers. The officer stretched a long blue arm and a large, dark-skinned hand across the room and touched me on the shoulder.

"That won't be necessary," he whispered. "I'm here for him." I followed his nod over to Mr. Curtis.

"Why? Mr. Curtis don't bother nobody." I glanced at Root Charlie for help. He didn't move.

"This is grown up business, little lady. Nothing for you to concern yourself with." He turned to Mr. Curtis and reached down to grab his arm. Mr. Curtis looked up and recognition dawned in his weary eyes.

"What you want with me?"

"Just a little matter of probation, Mr. Curtis. Let's not make this difficult."

"Probation? I'm through with my papers. What y'all want with me?" Mr. Curtis was not getting up and the officer was beginning to pull a little harder.

"Come on now, Mr. Curtis." The officer's voice lost its polite edge.

"I ain't going nowhere," said Mr. Curtis.

"Don't make me pull out the handcuffs!" The officer bent down and grabbed Mr. Curtis under his arms to lift him up. The officer was big and solid. After he got Mr. Curtis to his feet, he found himself staring up at Mr. Curtis from the floor. As frail and feeble as Mr. Curtis was, he showed remarkable strength and agility in flinging a much younger and much stronger man to the floor.

"Don't put your hands on me!" he screamed. Mr. Curtis started staggering around the room.

"What's this commotion in my damn house!" Miss Lipstick appeared at my side. I watched the whole scene, *Peter Pan* clasped to my chest, from the other side of the sofa. In one swift motion, Miss Lipstick grabbed my arm and pulled me toward the kitchen while she advanced into the living room. A switch flipped on somewhere in Root Charlie and the giant of a man started shifting his feet. The officer obviously felt Root Charlie's energy because his hand began sliding down toward his weapon. Miss Lipstick held up a finger, and Root Charlie stilled.

"Larry, what you doing on my floor?" she addressed the officer.

"Lipstick, I don't want no trouble. I got orders here to bring Leroy Curtis in about a probation matter. I'm just here doing my job." The officer picked himself up, the red of embarrassment glowing under his dark skin. He pulled out a folded letter from his back pocket. "It says here, as of today's date, July 12, 1976, Leroy Curtis failed to complete his probation. That's why I'm here now to take him in."

"I told you I ain't going nowhere. They want to take me, Lipstick, just like they took my boy! They took my boy!" Mr. Curtis revealed a wound that was open and allowed to fester for 20 years. It was raw rage and grief. He began stumbling around, his eyes and nose running. Weird, raspy noises were coming from his mouth. A dark spot materialized around his zipper and a trickle of water appeared at the cuff of his pants.

"They took my boy." He pounded the wall with fists full of arthritis. Wood chips and dust peppered the floor around him. The pain in his cries pierced my 15-year-old soul. "They stole my boy and did something to him! What did y'all do with my boy? I want him back. Make them give me my boy, Lipstick!"

I was blinded by tears. My heart wanted to wrap itself around Mr. Curtis and sponge up some of his misery. I could not imagine bottling up that kind of pain for two decades. It was in that moment, I understood.

"Larry, you come back here later to do your job, you hear me?" Miss Lipstick was looking at Mr. Curtis, but addressing the officer.

"Lipstick, I got to do my duty. I can't be losing stuff and pushing things under the rug for you no mo'. My boss already looking at me crazy," Officer Larry said.

"I'll handle your boss," she snapped. "You done here for the day. Now go on." The officer hesitated for a long time, but eventually tipped his cap and left like a good little boy.

"Look at you, Leroy. Sit down," she ordered him. He was so wound up, she had to physically push him down. Considering Miss Lipstick was pretty weak and Mr. Curtis was strengthened in his grief, it was an awesome testament to her will. She stooped down to his eye level, placing her hands on his shoulders.

"Baby, when you lose a child, it tears up your heart like nothing. You can't bring 'em back, so you got to move on. If you spend your life beating yourself up about what you could have done differently, you ain't never gonna have no peace. Cry for your boy, Lee-Roy, then bury him, here." She pointed to her temple. "Pull yourself out of his grave and find something to live the rest of your life for."

Miss Lipstick said her piece and returned to her haven. She wouldn't let me see her face. With tears still streaming down mine, I watched Mr. Curtis. It took a minute for him to realize she was gone. I wondered if anything got through to him in his state. I walked over to him and sat down. The dark spot in his pants had grown and he developed a new smell. I ignored those things and laid my head on his shoulder. I was surprised when he patted my hand. He stood up slowly, looked at himself, and walked out the door. It was about 4:45 p.m. Mr. Curtis had left his bottle of Christian Brothers behind, still a quarter full.

"Mr. Curtis." I held up the bottle. I had mistakenly picked up bottles before that I thought were empty. They had one or two drops worth of intoxication left. It was like sticking my hand in a rabid dog's mouth. Mr. Curtis veered neither to the left nor to the right that day.

I was left spent on the couch. Phyllis walked through the front door and joined me.

"Shame what they did to that man." She pulled me in to her. "You OK, gorgeous?"

"You saw all that?"

"Naw, honey. For one, the fuzz and Phyllis don't mix too good." Phyllis counted down on her fingers. "For number two, when I see Mr. Curtis leave this house with no Brothers, I know it got something to do with his boy."

We were both surprised to hear labored sounds of weeping and coughing coming from Miss Lipstick's room. I approached the door and knocked lightly.

"Just go home, baby," Miss Lipstick said, her voice weak. On cue, Phyllis came over to me, took me by the shoulders and led me to the sofa on the porch. A letter was hanging out of her back pocket.

"I don't understand. I just wanted to help her the way she helped Mr. Curtis. It's not like she lost a child."

Phyllis grunted and couldn't sit still on the sofa.

"Miss Lipstick been through a lot, baby. A lot." She squirmed in her seat.

"Like what?" I asked.

"She lost a lot of weight, for one thing. You should have seen her back in the day." Phyllis roared with laughter.

"Miss Lipstick had hips she could loan to somebody like me."

"Really? She wasn't always so little like she is now?" I perked up at this news.

"Baby, Miss Lipstick was something. Men lined up for Lipstick." Phyllis said it with pride.

"Looks like they still do," I observed wryly.

"She a good person." She stroked my chin with fingers that trembled slightly. "Always remember that. She would give anybody the shirt off her back. Give 'em a job, help 'em earn extra money, get 'em off drugs." Phyllis stood up suddenly and walked to the far side of the porch. The letter stayed behind.

The letter was an official one from the Department of Health and Rehabilitative Services. It was dated July 1 and was addressed to Miss Phyllis Littlejohn. Mr. Edward Cooper told her, in three lines, her request to obtain the custody of her minor child, Vishay Milton, age 9, had been denied. The last drug test administered determined Miss Littlejohn had cannabis in her system. It was the position of the department that Miss Littlejohn remained unfit to care for the minor, who would remain in the custody of the State of Florida.

I didn't realize my gasp was audible. Phyllis whirled around, saw the letter in my hand and snatched it away. She tore it viciously into confetti and battled her eyes to keep them from betraying the vibration in her lips.

"I'm sorry, Phyllis," I said, my head down.

Phyllis swooped me up in her arms. "No, Miss Dark and Lovely. I'm the one sorry. It was my own fault. I should have done more for my babies. I screwed up. You ain't done nothing wrong."

"What did you have to do?" I pumped her for information. She seemed willing to share with me.

Phyllis absentmindedly pulled her fingers through that tight weave on my head, except she made it feel like silk.

"I had to do a lot of stuff, baby, but it still wasn't enough. I gave up some things. Some hard things. I stayed good for a long time. Almost a year. I was so close." She scratched my scalp with her long nails and it felt good.

"You did that for your children? Is that what mommas are supposed to do?" A mother making sacrifices for her children was a foreign concept to me.

"A momma's supposed to move mountains for her children. I was so excited, I was crazy. When you about to get something you been wanting a long time, you lose your mind a little bit." Her nails dug deeper into my head. She loosened my braids and began parting my hair with ease. It seemed the most natural thing in the world for me to lie down in her lap.

"Do they teach classes or something on how to be a momma?"

Phyllis' trademark laugh rang out softly. "No baby. They probably should, though. Loving is easy. Raising is the hard part. Y'all don't come with an instruction manual when you born." She braided every hair on my head, even those in that stubborn region on the nape of the neck, the kitchen. I think she braided up a little of my neck, too. Lying in her lap, being pampered like a princess, I wanted it to last forever.

"Phyllis, do you ever see your children?" I asked.

"I see them all the time. They so grown now. They did pretty good without me." Her affliction hung around her head like a broken halo. I couldn't allow Phyllis to believe she was a bad mother.

"What's in that back room, Phyllis?"

Phyllis was meticulous in her braiding. Her fingers flew around my head. She was so close, I could feel her warm breath on my scalp.

"Just stuff to put up your arm, put up your nose, or put in your mouth to make your heart beat slower or faster, depending on your mood, so it don't hurt so much when it break."

"If you stop going back there, maybe you'll get your little girl back."

Phyllis' fingers paused. "I wish it was that easy, baby."

"So, if things get too hard for me, can I come back there? Sometimes, stuff gets real hard for me and I need to . . ."

Phyllis grabbed my chin and turned it hard toward her. She wore a scowl I'd never seen before.

"Uh, uh. Don't even think about it," she said. "You get hooked on education. Make your momma proud."

"Phyllis." I felt the need to return the affection she gave me without hesitation. "HRS is wrong. You are a good momma."

She leaned down and kissed my forehead. Her façade fell apart in the wake of the torrent.

/CHAPTER IX/

It was growing more difficult to concentrate in class. The large, dark bags under my eyes were the evidence of my staying awake as long as possible to ensure no uninvited guests entered my room during the night. The Fourth of July was eleven days previous, but on that Thursday, I looked like fireworks had gone off in my face.

In class, my head was like a bowling ball I was trying to balance on a straw. I caught myself a few times before it went slamming into the desk.

"Miss Frye, am I boring you?" Mr. Pierce asked. My tired eyes adjusted enough to focus on the handsome brown face that was inches from mine.

"No ma'am. I meant, no sir." The class snickered. Then Cast Iron Kat piped up.

"You ain't never boring to Fla, Mr. Pierce. That girl would kiss . . .,"

"That's enough, Miss Morehead!" he scolded her. "Are you getting enough sleep?" He asked me. "What's going on with you?"

"Nothing," I answered. A whole lot of stuff wanted to come through that nothing and explode in his face. Then, I wanted him to pick me up and hold me.

"Everything's okay, then?" If he didn't see it, he didn't want to see it.

"Yes, sir."

"Well, then, if everything's okay, Miss Frye, explain this." He placed a piece of paper on my desk. A big, red "C" was circled in the middle of it. It had my name on it, but I didn't remember writing it.

"That is not your best work, Miss Frye," Mr. Pierce said derisively. "In fact, I didn't even recognize it at first. I don't expect such shoddy work from you."

I could almost hear Cast Iron Kat's thoughts. She didn't like that. After knocking her down the way I did, she would probably show me no mercy when she was ready for me.

"I'll do better," I promised. Mr. Pierce made a surprise move by picking up my hand and squeezing it. It woke me all the way up. I wondered if he could feel my heart beating through my sweaty, trembling palm. In that micro-second of time, there was only Mr. Pierce and me in the room. His brown eyes penetrated mine, right through to the back of my eyeballs. His lips were moving, beginning to spread across his perfect teeth in the grandest smile. I felt myself lifting up out of my seat. He was saying something about marriage. Oh my God, what was he saying?

"I've moved my wedding date up to this December. Since it's going to be in Tallahassee instead of Virginia, you're all invited to come," Mr. Pierce said. Thunderous applause followed this announcement and amongst the joyous sounds, I heard grating laughter. Mr. Pierce's hand suddenly became too hot to hold and I snatched it away. I began rubbing it hard against the denim in my jeans, trying to scrape the skin off where'd he touched me. How could he? How dare he? Did he really think I would even go to his wedding?

Mr. Pierce returned to his desk, where the other students drowned him in congratulatory wishes. Mercifully for me, the bell rang and I stole the opportunity to slink out unnoticed. I had no such luck. Cast Iron Kat's girls were on my heels. This would be the day I'd bawl like a baby if they said anything to me. I was already on the precipice of a breakdown.

"Where you going?" said Myra, as she stood in front of me. "You ain't said nothing to Mr. Pierce about his wedding. That's rude."

I expected Cast Iron Kat to chip in and turn the knife deeper in my back. She stood behind Myra with an unreadable expression on her face. I did not want that girl to see me cry, but the storm clouds were gathering inside me.

"You know Fla in love with Mr. Pierce," she said. "We could mess her up right now."

"Yeah," said Myra. She was itching to get her hands on me.

"But my momma said you don't kick a dog when it's down, so let's leave the teacher's pet alone."

Myra and I gasped in unison. Cast Iron Kat guided her away from me and left me with a sliver of dignity. I was down one knight in shining armor since Mr. Pierce bit the dust. The body count of men who had abandoned me recently was growing high and too fast. While I made my way to Miss Lipstick's house, I wondered what was wrong with me.

At Miss Lipstick's, the place was too quiet. There was no inane chattering and no extremely loud conversations in the volume that only two drunks could hear each other. I was immediately drawn to the enormous hole left behind in the chair where Root Charlie normally sat. If Root Charlie was missing, he was probably somewhere doing Miss Lipstick's bidding.

I knocked once at Miss Lipstick's door and waited for that familiar voice to answer. I knocked again and still no answer came.

"Miss Lipstick, I'm here," I said to the door.

"You gone have to say it louder'n that," Johnny said, his disheveled appearance and jerky movements indicating he'd already had his shots. "She ain't here. She at the horse-pital."

My hand flew to my throat in alarm. "Is she okay?"

"I don't know," said Johnny and stumbled away.

I realized who I was asking. Johnny wouldn't know if he was okay. As usual, a sink full of dishes was waiting for me.

I just couldn't face them today. I sat down at the kitchen table and covered my face with my hands.

"Psst. Hey." The sound of a voice came from the back porch.

"Hey, girlfriend." Someone poked me in the shoulder, so I removed my hands and found myself beholding Eugene.

"What's wrong with you?" He swatted my arm lightly.

"Men," I said.

"Girl, I know what you mean," he said with a neck roll. "Tell Eugene about it. What he do?"

"I don't really want to talk about it, Eugene. It's just too hard."

"I know how you feel. Tell you what. I know what'll make you feel better." His waxed eyebrows danced a little jig before he opened the refrigerator and pulled out a can of Pepsi. He went to the forbidden room off the porch and returned with a half-empty, pear-shaped bottle containing a clear liquid. After rinsing out one of the shot glasses from the sink, he filled it two-thirds high with the Pepsi, and the remaining third with the clear liquid. I reached for it before Eugene was done pouring.

"Hold on, girlfriend," Eugene said, stopping my hand in midair. "You ain't drinking this in Lipstick house. Come on." He took the same hand and pulled me outside, past the forbidden room to the crumbling steps that had separated from the back porch.

"Nobody come out here unless they got to throw up." Eugene assisted me into a seated position. I was anxious. "I think we okay. Here."

My hand shook so hard Eugene would not relinquish the glass completely. When he did, I still spilled some on my clothes.

"Take it easy, girl," Eugene advised. "Just bring it to your mouth."

In slow motion, the glass with the dark liquid concoction inched toward my mouth. I wrapped my lips around the edge of the glass and tipped it over. There wasn't enough in my mouth to swallow when the scream behind me caused me to spill the rest of the drink in my lap and drop the glass on the steps.

"What you think you doing!"

My blood froze. If Miss Lipstick caught me drinking her liquor, I didn't know what she'd do to me. Thank God it was only Phyllis.

"Eugene, you can't be giving her none of that! Did you flip to the other side of your mind or something?" Phyllis harangued as she wagged her finger in Eugene's face.

"A little taste ain't gonna hurt her. Shoot!" Eugene responded.

"But a little taste will hurt you. You know if Lipstick was here, she would gut you like a fish over this girl."

Eugene laughed, but Phyllis was not smiling. Eugene could have rested his elbow on her head, but her anger brought out the claws.

"Get outta here now," she ordered him.

Eugene sucked his teeth. "Girl, you so crazy." He took Phyllis' advice, though, and made himself scarce. Phyllis sat down next to me and hugged her knees. I waited for my scolding.

"I don't know how Lipstick find out about all the stuff she know, but she won't hear about this from me. Go home and clean yourself up before Lipstick see you like this." She bumped her knees against mine and then left me out there by myself, smelling ripe in the sun.

My downward spiral continued. I didn't bother to go back through the house. I didn't want to be reminded of where that spiral could end. I felt like such a failure — I couldn't even get drunk right.

I dragged myself toward home, but decided to spend a little time at the pass. I was without a book, so I had no buffer against the negative thoughts that consumed me. I hid in a cut under the bridge so no one would see me. I needed to be in the dark. I wanted to stay in the dark. I deserved to be alone. However, I wasn't going to be alone. I heard footsteps on the raggedy bridge over my head. I looked up through the missing slats and saw a boy — a good-looking boy. He wore a T-shirt that accentuated his well-defined biceps and sagging jeans. He was trying to wrap those biceps around a girl who was putting him off. I couldn't see the girl's face.

"Come on, girl," he said in a very smooth, soft voice.

"I thought we was just gonna talk," the girl said.

"We can talk later. Come down here under the bridge. It's a good place."

That was my signal to bolt. There was no way I could get out without being seen, so I crawled out of my hiding place and was met by none other than Cast Iron Kat.

Why was this girl always showing up at my lowest moments? Kat trained her eyes on me and my legs turned to cement. My voice deserted me. I didn't think the boy would help me even if I asked, he was drooling so heavily over Cast Iron Kat. She approached me and grabbed my shirt in both hands. If she was going to rip my shirt off, I begged with my eyes, please send the good-looking boy away. I would be mortified. She could just bury me right there under the bridge.

"Why you always where I am?" Cast Iron Kat's nose touched my nose.

"I didn't know you would be here," I responded in a small voice.

"You always in my way," she said. "Don't think I forgot you knocked me down and be making fun of me in class."

"No, I don't."

"Yes, you do." Over her shoulder, Cast Iron Kat yelled to the boy, "Michael, I'll meet up with you another time. I got to show this girl I mean business."

Michael was distressed. "You can do that another time, Kat. You and me s'posed to get together."

"Naw, she been asking for it. I'll see you later." Cast Iron Kat pulled me by my shirt and my legs moved involuntarily. We went up the embankment, across the little brook and up the hill to the back side of the projects. Michael was yelling that it wasn't fair and something else not so kind about Kat. I know she heard him because I saw her wince. When we reached the first level of the projects, she brought me back to her nose. This time, I winced.

"You lucky this time, girl." Cast Iron Kat said. "I'm gonna beat you real bad the next time I see you," she promised. "Now, go home." She shoved me away from her and ran in the direction of her apartment.

Cast Iron Kat said I was lucky. Her sarcasm was lost on me. She lived a charmed life. Everybody wanted to be around her. All the boys liked her. Nobody was putting their hands on her without her permission. Lucky, indeed.

My mouth was opened so wide and for so long, I'm sure I caught several flies. Then, I remembered Pastor Ricky's admonition. It was not ladylike to stand in the middle of the street with my mouth open. I looked toward my apartment, and winced again.

/CHAPTER X/

Momma was beside herself over that malevolent, feeble-minded, knuckle-dragger she called a man. On more than one occasion, Jerome had pushed her around and cursed her while we sat at the table trying to eat our powdered eggs and reconstituted orange juice. The abuse was bad, but watching Momma take it was unbearable.

Jerome was fond of backhanding Momma. He flung his hand out like a boomerang and popped her in the face. It was a horrible sound. The imprint of the back of his hand was visible on her light skin. Sometimes, he drew blood and Momma said not a word to him. She screamed at me, though. It was a well-orchestrated mess and a dismal round of foolishness. For my part, I squelched the desire to throw up all over both of them — not because it wasn't the right thing to do, but because those fake eggs were rough going down the first time. I kept my mouth closed and tried to think of something good — like one day visiting Calvin Walters at his grave. Although he'd never laid a hand on me, my spirit was just as bruised as momma's face. He had hurt me — the man who was supposed to protect me and love me. Instead, he abandoned me and left me worse off than before I knew him. Our disastrous introduction had occurred more than eight days before, but it seemed like an eternity had passed.

We all ate in silence for several more minutes. When Momma stood up to clean Jerome's area and put his plate on the small bar behind her, he blew a gasket for reasons only known to him.

"You cripple!" Jerome kicked Momma's crutch away from her and she dropped hard to the floor, where she lay there whimpering. I had to leave. I needed a change of scenery.

"Sit down, Flaw!" he ordered me. Momma lay pitifully on the floor. I searched for something motherly in her. Do I have to listen to this guy? I wanted to ask. When she said nothing, I scrambled out of there. Before I reached the door, he yelled at me.

"Come back here, girl!" He followed me, trying to put his hands on me. I wiggled out of his grasp.

"Mimi, make him stop!" I pleaded.

"What did you call me?" She looked at me sharply. "Where did you hear that name?" she asked as she pulled herself up, grabbing onto the table for support.

"That's your nickname, isn't it?"

"Don't you ever call me that again!" she rebuked me. She screamed at me as loudly as she would call my name. Jerome was still buzzing around me like an engorged mosquito.

"Ain't nobody hurting you, girl. Give Jerome some sugar."

Momma refused to stop him. I maneuvered out of all eight of Jerome's nasty limbs and finally made it out of the house.

"You better tell that girl to obey me!" he said to Momma as I slammed the door behind me.

I had started going to Miss Lipstick's on Fridays and Saturdays because being at home was suffocating. I couldn't go to Miss Lipstick's in that condition. She would see right through me and I didn't know how she'd react. Besides, she might also know by now that I almost drank her liquor. Miss Lipstick was an enigma to me. She was rough on the outside, but I sensed a softness somewhere, deep, deep, inside her. I knew that she cared about me in a strange way. At any rate, I longed for someone, anyone, to put their arms around me. I wanted to matter to someone. I was as cold and empty inside as it was hot and oppressive outside. I was so distraught, I didn't care if I was entering Cast Iron Kat's terrain. If she found me and made good on her threats, at least the physical pain would remind me that I was alive.

With my arms folded, my head parallel to the ground, I walked around aimlessly with only the disturbing thoughts of my mother to keep me company. Momma's behavior didn't bother me as much as it used to; our relationship was as estranged as ever. I was still dismayed to be riding shotgun in the old Honda when she took the car out more and more running errands for Jerome and picking him up from strange places. He was always at somebody else's house — his momma's house, his friend's house or his neighbor's house. Some of those friends and neighbors were women, but Momma only cared that he was coming back to her house.

"Momma, I need to study tonight for my test tomorrow. Mr. Pierce gives us tests every Thursday," I complained on one of those jaunts. It was late in the day and I was hungry, too.

"Shut up, girl," was Momma's patent response. "It wouldn't kill ya to get a "F" every now and then. You gonna make me miss this house." Jerome had her coming to the most decrepit neighborhoods in Quincy and she brought me along as some sort of protection. The neighborhoods were without street lights, paved roads, or reasonably habitable homes. The poor little Honda bounced and screeched along as it dipped into potholes, careened near ditches, and rose up over large rocks jutting from the earth.

Momma finally found the house in a maze of dirt clouds far off the main drag and blew the horn. The screen door that was hanging by a thread on a nearly condemned block house banged open and Jerome waddled outside. He held on to the rotted porch post for assistance. Only a roll of the dice could keep that structure from caving in on Jerome's watch. He leaned into the car on the passenger's side, nearly tipping it over. He traced a lazy circle on my arm.

"Hey, y'all late," he said. I snatched my arm out of the window.

"Get in, baby," Momma sang to him. "Fla, get in the back," she barked at me.

"No, no. She can stay up there." He opened the back door and climbed in. The car uttered a symphony of groans. Momma cut her eyes at me.

Momma and Jerome made small talk on the ride back. Their elementary conversation was replete with vulgarities they thought I couldn't figure out. I sat ramrod still, knowing Jerome was behind me and not beneath trying to cop a feel.

The Honda began spluttering as we neared the railroad tracks. It was never in great shape, but Jerome's punishing weight was more than it could tolerate. On cue, the car stopped on the railroad tracks. As if out of a movie, a train whistled in the distance. Jerome started crying like a two-year-old to get him out of the car. I thought he was being melodramatic until a black dot formed in the horizon. The train was much closer than I realized.

In my fantasies, a handsome stranger effortlessly wrenches the door off its hinges, lifts me out of the car and places me safely away from the danger. Then he just pushes the car off the tracks, his well-defined muscles bulging. In reality, there were no strangers around and Momma and fat Jerome gawked at me while I struggled with the door that wouldn't open without violence. Momma opened her door and moved quickly around the front of the car. She reached for the door handle and let Jerome out. I continued to fight with the door while they tried to judge how far away the train was. The door wouldn't budge, so I slid over to the driver's seat, pumped the gas a few times, and turned the key in the ignition. Fortunately, I had enough experience driving Momma home when she was legally drunk in ten states to know my way around her car.

"Fla, get yo' stupid self outta there! How this gon' make me look if you get hit!" Momma's concern for me was so touching.

The engine stuttered and stalled. I pumped the gas again. The train was getting bigger. Neither Momma nor

Jerome gave a thought to pushing the car. They stood well back from the tracks. Momma was trying to push Jerome toward the car, but he was shaking his meaty head no.

"Fla!" Momma screamed.

At my next attempt to crank up the car, the engine bucked and rebelled and was reluctant to turn over, but it did finally. The train was rapidly approaching, and by now, its whistle was blasting a frantic warning, but I managed to coax the car off the tracks in the nick of time. Momma got in and pushed me over, and Jerome resumed his spot in the back seat.

"I hope you didn't mess up my car," Momma scolded me. Not, "I'm glad you're safe, baby." Not, "This car doesn't mean anything to me." Not even, "Girl, you all right! That was a crazy but brave thing you just did."

She and Jerome continued their conversation. The train whizzed by at break-neck speed when we were just a few yards past the tracks. I sent it a mental postcard to please come back for me, and then I inhaled the sobs that threatened to burst from me.

I discovered that I had walked a good distance away from home, toward the downtown area near city hall. The proximity to that building, my near death experience, and a parental lack of concern for my safety, caused my thoughts to return to Calvin Walters. That whole chapter in my life was like a scab I couldn't stop picking and the hurt inside me festered like an open sore. I wanted not to hurt so much. I wanted to be numb like everybody else at Miss Lipstick's, to not care about tomorrow. I wanted a drink, but it was a deadly sin for me in Miss Lipstick's house. She wouldn't even allow me to sip the many cocktails I'd been offered. In fact, Root Charlie roughly escorted a couple of young guys out before they could share their rum and Coke with me. I was afraid for Eugene and myself if she ever got wind of that failed attempt. I believed I would die of thirst before anybody would even offer me a glass of water.

A couple of hours later, I felt it was safe to go back home. I heard nothing inside, and was relieved to find that Momma and Jerome had vacated the premises. I went to the refrigerator and opened it. It was stripped of all alcohol.

I wouldn't be experimenting with drinking that weekend. I foraged the cupboards to find enough food to hold me through the rest of the weekend. I locked myself in my room. My books and food were all the sustenance I needed.

Friday morning rolled around. Since I had become a fixture on Fridays, I was put to work. An overabundance of soiled towels and glasses was waiting for my attention. The party debris I had to round up left me wondering what kind of Bicentennial celebration they'd had at Miss Lipstick's. It was apparently still going on thirteen days later. Paper cups, empty bottles, and crushed aluminum cans littered the living room floor like a waste dump. The cigarette butts, egg shells and the extra tall pile of sheets suggested mayhem and debauchery. I understood why Miss Lipstick wouldn't allow me in the Zip Code during the week of the party.

"That must have been some party, Miss Lipstick," I said. She sat in the kitchen looking worn out. Root Charlie was in place. The floor was relatively clear of people, but a couple of party goers were still sleeping it off on Miss Lipstick's sofa, encroaching on Mr. Curtis' spot.

"Yeah, it was something. Couldn't no child be here." I dragged a large, black garbage bag behind me, filling it up in no time. After I dumped it on the back porch, Miss Lipstick called me to her.

"Gal, here. Something for you." Miss Lipstick had a shoe box in her lap.

"What's that?"

"Open it and see." A sly grin spread across her face and years melted away. I opened the box and found a treasure trove. There was a small pair of diamond studded earrings, a black and yellow AC/DC transistor radio, and an Ellery Queen mystery magazine. Also in the box was a small silver watch with cartoon hands. I slipped it on right away, and it fit perfectly. It was Christmas in July, and for me, Christmas for the first time in years. The last time I received a Christmas gift, it was probably diapers. I jumped up and down for joy and created such a racket, it should have awakened the dead, but the drunken party goers didn't stir. Root Charlie didn't move a muscle. I draped my arms around Miss Lipstick's neck and squeezed.

"Thank you, thank you, Miss Lipstick!" I sang. She shooed me away, as if the affection made her uncomfortable.

"Enjoy it, baby. I'm going to bed." I sat at the table fiddling with the knobs and antenna of the transistor radio, trying to figure out how to make it work. I put on the earrings, too. They made me feel like a princess. The little drawer in my dresser at home had plenty of plastic and stick on ear wear, but not a single pair of the genuine article. Now, it would. Around 4:30 p.m., according to my new watch, while thoroughly enthralled in the short mysteries, I heard the puny horn of Momma's Honda.

"Flaaaa!" Momma screamed. She didn't get out of the car to come inside to get me. It was easier to break the sound barrier.

"Flaaaa!" Momma leaned into the horn mercilessly.

"Gal, come see what yo' momma want!" An anonymous porch dweller finally achieved consciousness. I came outside to the driver's side, to see what fire Momma needed me to put out.

"Get in the car!" she hollered.

"But I'm not finished . . .," I whined. I thought about the gifts I was leaving behind as I went outside to the car. I was really thinking about the gifts I was leaving behind.

"I said get in the car!" I obliged. I looked at her sideways. She was crying and her eye was black, again.

"Where are we going?" I asked. She drove up two blocks, turned left, and then right on none other than Colored Street. Colored Street was where down and out black people in Quincy hung out when they couldn't get a spot at Miss Lipstick's house. A wave of depression united the group of people, men and women alike, who patronized the few businesses on Colored Street. What went down on Colored Street was legendary — fights, murders, cheating. If you wanted to know what was going on, good, bad or otherwise, in any black person's life in Quincy, you came to Colored Street. Momma pulled up behind a row of parked cars on the crowded street and stopped. I suddenly became fascinated by my own hands, afraid of what she was about to tell me.

"Go in Charlie's and look for Jerome!" she said angrily.

"Huh?"

"You heard me. Go in there and find him!"

"I don't want to go in there." I pleaded with her to no avail.

"You go in there or you don't come home!" Her angry words were accompanied by spit that coated my face. Not coming home, I could deal with that.

"And you ain't going to Lipstick's!" I begrudgingly got out of the car. There were throngs of people on Colored Street looking for available and willing company. Men were picking up women. Women were picking up men. Men were picking up men. I hoped nobody was in the market for a slightly used, 15-year-old girl.

I wrapped my arms around myself tightly as I weaved my way up the sidewalk. I looked back one more time to give Momma one last chance to tell me to come back. Instead, she was waving me on and cussing out the driver behind her who had the audacity to want to drive on the street.

I stepped in the door of Charlie's Place. All Charlie's had to offer were three junkyard quality pool tables, a long bar, and some formerly chic stools with the stuffing busting through. The lighting was very dim, its source coming from a single red Budweiser lamp hanging over the middle pool table. The thick layer of dust and the crumbling walls added to the ambience. The minute I stepped in, all movement ceased. Stevie Wonder even stopped singing "Very Superstitious." My eyes swept the room but I didn't see Jerome. I turned to leave, only to find the threshold blocked by an enormous black body.

"You lookin' for somebody, jailbait?" I looked up into a dark face with a nappy beard and a lone tooth. He slid a sweaty arm with a snake tattooed on it around my shoulder and I recoiled.

"Get yo' hands offa her," I heard a wonderfully angelic voice say in a vernacular that was familiar. My unwanted admirer and I looked around, and we came face to face with Pastor Ricky.

"What you gon' do about it, preacher man?" the man challenged.

"Me, I'm just gonna pray. I cain't speak for nobody else. If this gets back to Lipstick, you know what's gonna happen to you." Pastor Ricky confronted the man in a wide-legged stance, with a pool cue in one hand and a dingy cup of suds in the other. He was decked out in a bold, green-plaid ensemble with a giant collar.

"She belong to Lipstick?" I could hear the fear singe this huge man's voice.

"Sho' do," said Pastor Ricky, nodding his head vigorously.

My admirer removed his arm and left the establishment. I ran up to Pastor Ricky and held him close.

"Where have you been, Pastor Ricky? I miss you." I hadn't seen him since our little adventure to city hall.

"I've been around. Got busy. You're okay, Jasmine," he assured me. "Nobody's gonna bother you in here." He walked me over to the pool table. His Bible rested on the corner. "What pretty earrings. They really light up this room. Take them off."

"What?"

"Take them off. Those are real diamonds," he whispered. "This is not the place to wear something that nice." I removed the earrings and jammed them in my pockets.

"What are you doing here anyway?" Pastor Ricky asked. "This is no place for children, especially a girl."

"Momma told me to come in here and look for her boyfriend." I was still shaking.

"In here?" He shook his head.

"Pastor Ricky, what are you doing in here?" I asked, turning the tables. "This is no place for a preacher, either. Remember?"

"Baby, I'm witnessing to these folks." He raised his cup to a room full of laughter. "We all need Jesus, don't we?" He was rewarded with cheers from his inebriated amen corner.

"Y'all save my spot." Pastor Ricky put down his pool cue and left his Bible. "Come on, Jasmine."

Pastor Ricky held me close to his side as he walked me to the back of Charlie's Place. Charlie's was not an independent building, but one connected to the other buildings on the street, like a ghetto mall. Charlie's supplied pool and liquor, the next place served more liquor, and yet another provided food. There was a barbershop and other little shops that were open for business. A person could be groomed, fed, entertained, and find a little loving on Colored Street. Everything was conveniently located in one place and it was open seven days a week. There were hundreds of people in those buildings looking to get over the week — wall-to-wall flesh of every shade on the black color spectrum.

Pastor Ricky guided me toward the food joint. Between the liquor and the food was a dance hall with strobe lights in effect. Hot, sweaty bodies were already bumping and grinding to the soulful sounds of Johnny Taylor's "Disco Lady," in the poorly air-conditioned space. We had to walk through a mustachioed man and a tall, thin woman who seemed oblivious to anybody else in the place. My mouth was still open when the glorious smell of burgers and fries entered it and exited through my nose.

"Hey, Omar. Give me a Saturday night special. And put it on my tab." Pastor Ricky sat me down at a small round table with a tattered white tablecloth. The only decorations were clogged salt and pepper shakers. Omar must have been a bodybuilder in a former life. He was bald and had muscles bulging through his greasy T-shirt.

"You ain't got no tab, Pastor. You ain't paid yo' bill in ten years," Omar said, his mammoth muscles contracting.

"Then put it on Lipstick's tab," Pastor Ricky said, without missing a beat.

Omar shot Pastor Ricky a look that would have laid him out in his green-plaid suit. But he turned his back and I heard meat sizzling on the grill.

"I would have the swimps and finch fries, but I'm not hungry." I chortled at this greasy spoon pronunciation of shrimp and french fries.

"Stay here, Jasmine," Pastor Ricky continued. "Omar'll take care of you. I'll be right back." Pastor Ricky tipped his imaginary hat and made his way into the dance joint.

I looked around at the place that housed the food. It was decorated in dull gray colors with splashes of yellow and red on the walls that didn't look like paint or condiments. There were cobwebs occupying every corner. Pieces of the ceiling were missing. The floor looked like a week's worth of food was caked on it. The menu must have been excellent to keep folks coming back here.

I was able to confirm this theory when Omar set before me with a bit of attitude, the largest hamburger I'd ever seen in my entire life. It was bigger than my whole head and would probably take me until I was thirty to digest it. The meat dwarfed the buns. Mayonnaise, mustard and ketchup dripped down the side of it. The lettuce, tomatoes, and pickles spanned the entire circumference of the burger. The fries were long and greasy and salty — just the way fries should be. Omar brought me a root beer brimming with ice.

"You think you can handle a Omar burger, little girl?" He looked pleased with himself.

"I'm gonna try," I said, my eyes as wide as the burger. "Hey, Omar," I whispered.

"What you want?" he growled.

"Can I have a beer?" I wanted to test him.

"I'm too fond of my neck, little girl." He wiped down his counter and went about his business. "You enjoy that what I put in front of you, and don't eat another one as long as you live."

I didn't think I could. I attacked the burger, burying my face in its juiciness. Big chunks of beef and bread and vegetable slid down my chin and into my lap. As I looked around for a napkin, Omar brought me a mountain of them.

I made it halfway through the burger when my stomach cried "uncle." I was chewing the last bite carefully so as not to strangle myself when I turned my head toward the dance joint and began to watch. The same man and woman were dancing in close proximity to each other. The psychedelic effect of the strobe lights made it look like they were making one dance move a second. The song had changed and Aretha Franklin's robust and mesmerizing voice demanded that the movements slow down as she sang, "Giving Him Something He Can Feel." The severity of the dances tapered off and I caught snapshots of an ample behind, a gyrating pelvis, and a tensing of back muscles. A plaid-green suit appeared in the middle of them, dancing just as provocatively. At first, Pastor Ricky seemed to be dancing in the woman's circle. As I looked closer, his hips were swaying more in the man's direction.

Another man materialized out of the smoke-filled air and took up a good bit of Pastor Ricky's personal space. I rubbed my eyes hard. The man was Eugene, dressed to the nines in skintight jeans and a loud paisley shirt. Pastor Ricky seemed not to notice him because he was looking at the floor, his hands beating up the air. Flash. Hands descending. Flash. Hands at the chest. Flash. Hands around Eugene's waist.

I whipped my head back to my burger and gulped down what was in my mouth. I didn't know what to think or feel at that moment. I looked around the food joint to see if anybody else had seen what I had seen. The only other people in there were a man hunched over the table, drooling in his sleep, and another couple slobbering into each other's mouths.

After what seemed like an eternity, Pastor Ricky appeared at my table.

"Good, ain't it, Jasmine?" he asked cheerfully.

"Mm, hm," I said, pretending I still had a mouth full of food.

"Come here," Pastor Ricky said, beckoning me to follow him. He pulled me into the middle of the dance crowd. I could feel the heat around my neck like a bowtie.

"Have you ever danced with a boy, Jasmine?" We stood stark still, totally incongruent to everyone else. Jutting elbows and gyrating behinds were invading my space.

"No. I never danced with anybody." Pastor Ricky took my hands in his and held them tightly. His hands were dripping wet. Perspiration and S curl spray poured off his head and down his neck, making him glisten under the lights. A potent cocktail I could not name bathed his breath.

Pastor Ricky pulled me so close to him that my head rested in his chest. We began to sway, to the left, to the right, against the grain of "Boogie Wonderland." Pastor Ricky's heart, though, kept the beat of the up-tempo music. I could feel it against my cheek. *Thump, thump*, it said. *Thump, thump*, I heard. *Thump, thump*, it beat for me.

He rested his head atop mine, locking my head in place. He held me like a drowning man holding onto a life raft. I was frightened. I was in unfamiliar surroundings, in an unfamiliar situation. I was appalled by his masculine touch, but I found it comforting at the same time. It wasn't entirely sexual, but it wasn't platonic either. It was somewhere in between. It was familial.

"Pastor Ricky, I'm ready to go," I said softly.

"Shh," he quieted me. "Not yet. I'm dancing at your wedding."

I couldn't look up and I had no idea how much time had passed. I thought about Momma, how furious she'd be.

"Pastor Ricky. My momma." I said.

"She'll be alright. Let me have this, Jasmine. Just a few more minutes."

A few more minutes I gave him. When he was ready, he looked at his arm for a nonexistent watch. "OK, I say we are done here. Let's go."

My mouth was dry. A question hovered over my lips.

"Pastor Ricky?"

"Yes, Jasmine." He looked deep into my eyes. I never realized how really handsome Pastor Ricky was. He was smiling, but again, the smile didn't reach his beautiful hazel eyes.

"I'm in a lot of trouble." I couldn't form the words to ask the question that had already been answered.

"No, you ain't," he said.

"Aren't. Pastor Ricky?" I tried again.

"Yes, Jasmine?" he answered.

"Why do you keep calling me Jasmine?"

"Because Jasmine is the prettiest flower that ever bloomed." Finally, I got an explanation but not one I was expecting. "It blooms yellow and white here in Florida, and it's the sweetest-smelling flower. But there's nothing more beautiful than Jasmine, in black. It only exists in the most beautiful places." He stroked my face. "Like here." He pointed to his chest and his voice cracked. "And in my heart. I carry a black Jasmine with me every day of my life."

"You think I'm pretty?"

"Jasmine, you are the most beautiful girl in the world," Pastor Ricky said.

I couldn't swallow around the lump in my throat. "I love you, Pastor Ricky." The words just came tumbling out.

Tears sprang to his eyes. "I love you, too, my angel," he choked out. He hugged me tightly, for a long time. He gave me a big sloppy kiss on the side of my face. He looked near exhaustion.

We walked outside into the thick, humid night air. It was nearing dusk, and the population of Colored Street had increased exponentially in the last hour and a half. Momma limped quickly down the sidewalk to meet us. She was livid. She could move pretty good when she was fueled.

"Where you been all this time?" she demanded.

"I was helping her look for your man, Millie." The lie just slid off Pastor Ricky's tongue. "We looked everywhere. The pool hall. The juke joint. Even the men's toilet. He ain't in there. Anywhere else you want this child to look?"

Momma looked like somebody kicked her in the belly with a steel-toed boot.

"I—I just wanted her to stick her head in. She didn't have to go all the way in." Her redbone features were turning a deep crimson.

"There's an officer on the corner. We can ask him to help your little girl find your man in this here juke joint."

"No, I'm taking my baby home. It's past her bedtime." That phrase rang hollow in everybody's ears.

Pastor Ricky gave me a big wink as Momma walked me around to the passenger side of the car and tried to open the door for me. She struggled with it. I gave it my special yank and it came right open.

This was a new development, to say the least. I was beautiful, like a flower, to somebody. I was more like a weed to my own momma. I stared at her profile as she drove home frantically, the bruising around her eye and the swelling in her cheeks an appalling sight. Momma turned her head slightly toward me. I saw that Jerome had given her a matching pair of black eyes.

"Don't look at me like that," she said, startling me.

"Like what?" I asked.

"Jerome love me. He'll be back. It's your fault he gone."

That unladylike expression fell on me. "What did I do? I do everything you tell me to do for him, Momma."

"You ain't nice enough to him. You be disrespectful. You a hateful child." I couldn't believe she was saying such things.

"You want me to be nice to somebody who beats on you and calls you names? How does that make me a hateful person?" She gave me the back of her head. Her hands gripped the steering wheel until her knuckles turned white.

"Jerome love me. You just don't want me to have nobody," she fussed. "Let me tell you something, girl. When Jerome come back, he ain't leavin' me again. I'm giving him everything he want!"

/CHAPTER XI/

The rest of the evening was long and tortured. The only signs of life in that apartment came from the television. Momma told me I couldn't go to Miss Lipstick's or the library, because she knew I was happy in those places. I had already decided to disobey her. On Saturday morning, I would simply wait for her to pass out and just leave. When morning came, I only had to wait ten minutes from the time she shuffled out of bed to get to the refrigerator.

I was so glad rebellion kicked in when it did. Saturday, July 17, 1976, at approximately 6:53 p.m. and 22 seconds, is permanently date-stamped in my brain. I know that because I looked at my watch. The crowd at Miss Lipstick's, during their moments of lucidity, described the kind of books they wanted me to read to them, and I delivered. They were like sponges, soaking up the eloquence of Alex Haley's and Zora Neale Hurston's pens. That Saturday, they were in the mood for something sweet, romantic and black. My scouring of the library's black section yielded a dearth of romance novels, but I did find some to fit the bill. I read slowly, so they didn't miss a word. I explained passages carefully, to increase their understanding. I reread sections they enjoyed the most, which was the entire book, so I spent most of the day reading. It was entertaining for them, but it also met some indescribable need in me.

I was sitting beside Mr. Curtis on the old sofa, bringing down the curtain on the romance between the main characters, when, at that precise hour, Randy Robinson pierced the veil of my dreams and stepped out into my reality. There he was, a living, breathing, three-dimensional persona, standing in the doorway of Miss Lipstick's home, cutting off the circulation to my head. He was so delicious to look at, everyone wanted to touch him, especially me.

I would see him occasionally when I walked around town. It was always such a treat to gaze upon him. There were involuntary stirrings in my body that only Randy could evoke. Since Mr. Pierce had betrothed himself to another woman, there was no chance he'd ever be my prince. But I had Randy, and oh, what a dashing figure he cut. It was his clear, mocha-colored skin, the tight, spiraled curls on his perfect head, and his athletic body that made me seek him out at the end-of-the-year school dance last May.

I wanted to strut my stuff in a new dress just for him, but Momma wouldn't give me the money. So, for three weeks, I picked up pecans, washed dishes for neighbors, and did classmate's homework. I sold myself out for $20.49. It was just enough to buy a pretty yellow sundress with splashes of pink in it, and some yellow jelly shoes.

On the day of the dance, I fussed and fought the short hair Mother Africa had raked her hands through. My fashion sense was very limited and every style I attempted looked like a mini-bomb went off on my head. The braids didn't cut it, so I decided to take drastic and dangerous action. I gave myself a home permanent. I'd never had my hair permed before, but I had to look perfect.

"Why would you put lye and other harsh chemicals in your hair that could leave you bald and scarred for life?" I asked myself. To that, I answered, "My God, because he's worth the risk."

I ran to the dollar store to buy some costume jewelry and the cheapest perm I could find — some no name brand that promised to make me look like a Nubian goddess. My goals were not so lofty. I scanned the directions and then tossed them aside. I said a little prayer, and went for it.

When it felt like a colony of ants was marching across my scalp, it was time to wash out the chemicals. An hour later, my hair still clung to my head and not too much was at my feet. I blow dried it, curled it, and gave it the Farrah flip, which was still popular with black girls. I put on the rest of my ensemble — the dress, the jellies, some fake diamond earrings, and scrutinized myself. My mirror said I looked good. Momma said I didn't. I wanted to believe my mirror. Anyway, the lights would be low in the gym.

I could have spotted Randy in a crowd of a million. He wasn't even dressed properly, as if he had decided to come at the last minute. He was wearing a black T-shirt with "Up Yours" written on the back, torn blue jeans, and dirty sneakers. He was exquisite.

I took my place on the wall with the other flat-chested, unpopular girls — one other short black girl, two dowdy-looking white girls with long, stringy, brown hair, and a new Asian girl — a cultural palette of losers.

Randy tossed a smile at some girl over in my vicinity, but I caught it, and treasured it. My heart just melted into my toes.

I didn't have the pleasure of dancing with him, but it seemed like every other girl did. I wished I were all of them. The DJ put on the Bee Gees' "More Than a Woman," followed by the Spinners' "Could It Be I'm Falling in Love." He was playing the soundtrack to my heart. I loved those songs. I drifted off to a warm and exotic island where Randy and I relaxed on a sandy white beach, holding hands.

"Hey, girl, you gonna dance with me, know what I'm saying!" Randy demanded of Belinda, the most popular girl in school.

"You wanna dance with me, it's gonna cost you," she retorted with much attitude.

"I ain't gonna pay you for no dance, know what I'm saying. Stop playing, girl. Come here." Those were the words I'd longed to hear from him. He would say it, and I would come. If he were talking to me, I'd have floated across the room.

"See ya," Belinda said, and started to walk away. He looked after her, obviously liking what he saw. She wore a short, red, "come-get-me" type dress that looked like she sprayed it on. Her hair was upswept in a grown-up do, something that had seen a professional's attention. I absentmindedly touched my scalp. It was beginning to scab over where I'd left the perm in too long. Please don't dance with her, my heart pleaded.

"Wait, wait. Let me see what I got." I felt sick, watching him dig in his pockets for money for the privilege of dancing with her. Why didn't he know that I would have danced with him all night, for free? His searching turned up a quarter, and he held it up like it was a rare gold coin, his smile lighting up the dimly-lit gym.

"That's all you got?" Belinda said with disdain.

"That's it." I had a $1.27 left over and it was balled up in my fist. Should I give it to him to dance with a girl who would make him happy, or should I offer to pay him for a dance, which would make me happy? Suddenly, I felt something like a two by four slam into my back. I had glided into the path of a couple doing an extreme version of the funky chicken. I fell, face first into the gym floor, my meager change escaping my hand and scattering all over the floor. I looked around and saw Cast Iron Kat. She had all thirty-two teeth on display.

"Hey, Randy! Here some money. When you done with Belinda, dance with Fla. She want to dance with you all night long," she sang.

I was mortified. My dress was also a dollar store find and the paper thin material ripped up the side from the minimal impact of my knee hitting the floor. I pulled myself up to my feet with no help from anyone when I saw Randy approach. Was he going to see if I was all right, be true to my dreams of him as my prince, my knight in raggedy jeans? He reached out and picked up the dollar that landed by my foot.

"I'm gonna borrow this. Pay you back later, know what I'm saying. Hey, Belinda!" He winked at me and ran off, leaving me wishing I were dead. I rushed out with half the gym laughing at me. Tears blinded my path that night. I don't know how I made it home.

A voice brought me back to the present. "My old man wanted me to drop this off to ya, Miss Lipstick," he said. I stared at him, wishing he didn't look so good. A fresh hurt and humiliation welled up inside me while I stood there facing him, Wild West style.

"All right. Give it here." Miss Lipstick reached out a bony hand and grasped the money. She never counted anything at the moment it was given to her. The unwritten, unspoken rule was, you don't cheat Miss Lipstick. "You can go now." She showed him the door with a cigarette trail, which he began to follow.

"Hold up, handsome." There was an extra bounce in Phyllis' step. "Which way you going home?" She gave me a wink. Oh, God, Phyllis, don't! my eyes pleaded.

"Huh?" Randy wasn't expecting the question. "I live over off Seventh Street." I couldn't take my begging eyes off him.

"You know this young lady right here, don't you? Don't y'all go to the same school?" Phyllis stood behind me with her hands on my shoulders.

Randy looked at me briefly. I wanted to run into a wall or sink into one of the holes in the floor.

"Her?"

"Yeah, her," said Phyllis. Her tone was defensive. My face was red. Randy was halfway out the door.

"Wait, wait." Phyllis touched him on the shoulder to keep him from leaving.

Miss Lipstick watched with amusement. "Phyllis, what you doing?"

"Gorgeous here going home and handsome can walk her. That's all I'm saying." Phyllis threw up her hands as if her intentions should have been clear to everybody. My face burned hot.

Miss Lipstick dismissed the arrangement out of hand. "Phyllis, let that boy go home. It ain't even time for her to leave."

"Lipstick, let the young people go home," Phyllis said out of the corner of her mouth. Miss Lipstick sucked her lips. Phyllis collected my book, which she pushed into my arms, and my transistor radio, which she jammed into my hand.

"You ready to go home, ain't you, gorgeous?" Phyllis said to me.

My voice cracked and scraped my throat. "Not really."

"I gotta go. My old man looking for me," said Randy.

"You going the same way. Just walk her as far as you can." Phyllis shoved me right up into Randy's face. "Y'all go on outside and work it out."

"We don't have to do that." I found my voice, but it was as weak as my knees. "We don't even live in the same direction. I got to get home, too." I was so flustered I was tripping all over myself to keep this from happening.

"Fine. It's settled. Y'all go on now. Don't let dark catch you," said Phyllis.

My attempt at being demure and alluring must have come off as a deer-in-the-headlights look because Randy took my arm and pulled me outside.

"Well," he said, once we were out of range of prying adults.

"Well what?" I came out of my dream-like state and confronted the pain. "You don't have to walk me anywhere. Bye!" I repossessed my arm and my faculties and started in the direction of home. I picked up my pace when I heard matching footsteps. I quickened to a brisk run and almost broke out into a sprint when he started yelling for me to stop.

"Hey, wait, girl! Why you running?" Oh, Lord. Randy was talking to me, and only me. I screeched to a halt.

"I already told you, you don't have to walk me nowhere. If you scared of Miss Lipstick, I'll just tell her you walked me home." I wanted to give him an out, but I hoped against hope that he wouldn't take it.

Randy looked down at his feet. "I ain't scared of Lipstick. And I kinda wanna walk you home."

My heart missed a few hundred beats. We were nowhere near a hospital or an ambulance, but I had a feeling I was going to need those paddles.

"Really? Kinda? You're lying. You don't even like me." I started walking again. He got around me and blocked my path.

"Would you stop moving, girl? Dang!" he said, his frustration evident. "I ain't used to no girl trying to run away from me."

I slowed my pace, but I didn't stop. I was still wounded from the gym encounter. He embarrassed me more than the fall. He was so good-looking. I'd forgive him anything, and I wasn't ready to forgive him yet.

"You don't even know who I am, do you?" I asked.

"Yeah, I do. We go to the same school. I be seeing you around," he said.

"What's my name, then?"

"Girl, it's . . ., it's something," he attempted.

Close enough for me. "It's Fla."

He snapped his fingers. "Yeah, that's it. I knew it was something crazy."

I took a deep breath. I was going to have to choose my battles. At least I had his undivided attention for a while.

"Oh, I know. You that real smart girl. Always readin' and stuff. I don't usually hang with smart girls," he said, as if it were a compliment.

"What's the matter with smart girls?" I asked, on the verge of being upset.

"Nothing," he answered. "They just ain't that . . .,"

"Pretty? Smart girls aren't pretty? Is that it?" Now, I was angry.

"Naw, that ain't it."

"You ..." Randy searched his brain for the right words. "You pretty enough, see what I'm saying. I just cain't be with no smart girl 'cause, well, you ain't my speed. See what I'm sayin'?"

I didn't know what he was saying, but I really wanted to. I didn't know where to go from there. This was the most intimate conversation I'd ever had with a boy, and it was with the boy of my dreams. The more he talked though, the more I realized my chances of having any kind of relationship with him were diminishing. From him, I experienced a special kind of rejection.

"So, if I was dumb, you might like me?"

"That's not it. What I'm trying to say . . . I don't know what I'm trying to say." His obvious struggle to say the right thing made me give him some slack. "If you're gonna be with me, you got to give it up, see what I'm sayin'." I was desperately trying to see.

"Give what up?"

"I knew it. I knew it. Them boys owe me. I knew it." Randy walked around in a circle, beating the air with his fist.

"You knew what?" I began withdrawing the leniency I was prepared to give him.

"You a virgin, ain't you? I knew it."

"So what if I am?" I felt dejected. "You can't like virgins, either?"

"No, girl. It's just that, a girl like you can't be with somebody like me unless you willing not to be a virgin no more. See what I'm saying?" I finally saw what he was saying. He was so smooth and his words slid off a velvet tongue. I swallowed hard. I had read the *Life Cycle* series and watched actors insinuate the act on television, but even the thought of committing the act itself terrified me. It was a high price to pay for his company. A lot of boys liked Cast Iron Kat. I wondered if she could afford the attention. At that thought, I had to shake my head. She was the last person I wanted in my head. It crossed my mind that she may have been this close to Randy. "Do I have to?" I asked, shaking my head.

Randy shrugged his shoulders. "You want to be with me?" Randy couldn't have asked a more loaded question.

"Yes, I want to be with you. Real bad. Randy, there ain't nobody I want to be with more than you in this whole world," I squeaked out. It was hard to speak with my heart in my throat. My hands wanted to reach out and stroke his face, but I was scared. He might disappear.

"See. That's what people do when they want to be with somebody." He smiled and it was all I could do to stay upright.

"Uh, huh. You, you're the best. Ever." Phyllis told me not to put my heart on my sleeve, and here I was, smearing it all over my body like peanut butter.

He took a step closer to me. "Let's try something out first." He then put his arm around my waist and pulled me in to him. He brought his head down and parted his lips. I didn't know what I was supposed to do. I flipped through my mental rolodex of TV shows and began imitating the kissing scenes. I tilted my head to the left, opened my mouth wide and stuck out my tongue.

Randy opened his eyes and frowned. "You 'bout to lick me?"

"Oh. You weren't going to kiss me?" My cheeks burned a deep crimson.

"You never kissed anybody before?" I shook my head and tried to squirm out of his hold. He gripped my waist tighter.

"Let me show you. Come here."

He put both of his hands on either side of my face, and brought his perfect face to mine. I dropped the book and the radio. To this day, I swear I don't know how it switched on, but it did and another of my favorites, Minnie Ripperton's "Loving You," was playing. The song read my feelings. I locked my knees to avoid falling and ruining this perfect moment.

The thing I had wanted from him for so long was about to happen. Randy's beautiful, full lips met my thin, quivering ones. His lips tasted like sweet blackberries, just as I'd imagined. What I didn't imagine was that he would kiss me so hard. He crushed my lips back against my teeth. Then, he stuck his tongue in my mouth, igniting my gag reflex. I had to pull away from him. Where was the kiss I had dreamt of, that was perfectly choreographed? It was supposed to be the one where he kissed me deeply and sweetly. The one in which I found myself returning his kiss as passionately as he was. Randy then grabbed me and hugged me. The hug was better. It was warm. It didn't feel just real — it was surreal. It touched me at my core. I wrapped my arms around his neck and held on. He folded me up in his embrace and I believed our hearts beat in tune with the music, in tune with each other. I could stand there in that spot forever, even with light rain droplets falling on us. Randy pulled away from me this time and stared at me, as if he was waiting for some kind of approval. I think the grin that spread across my face was what he was looking for. How could I tell him that kiss was a horrible let-down? He bent down to pick up my book and my magic radio, took my hand and walked me all the way to my door.

I prepared myself for a goodnight hug. I couldn't bear another kiss. I still couldn't believe I was holding Randy's hand and he was looking at me as if he was happy to be with me. In that moment, I was the happiest girl on the face of the earth. Then my moment was stolen from me. The door jerked open and we were flooded with light from inside the apartment. Jerome stepped in the doorway, his fat shadow covering both Randy and me.

"Get your hands off her, boy," Jerome demanded. He glared at Randy, and then looked at me as if I'd betrayed him.

"Who you, man?" Randy asked indignantly. He dropped my hand unceremoniously.

"Get away from her," Jerome repeated as he reached past Randy to grab at me. Randy didn't move and pushed Jerome's hand away.

"You don't tell me what to do, old man!" Randy said angrily.

"You don't know who you messing with, boy!" Jerome yelled. He grabbed a handful of Randy's shirt and tried hoisting him off the ground. Jerome's strength did not match his girth and he trembled as he struggled to lift the very lean Randy off the ground. Randy picked Jerome's fingers off his shirt, one by one, and pushed him away. Jerome toppled over with a thud into the apartment. Momma appeared from somewhere and added her own piece to the fight.

"You better get away from that boy with yo' fast tail. He only want one thing from you. Get in here!" Momma shouted. I was nowhere near the frey. I stood back in amazement at this boy and man tussling in the doorway, the wrong one fighting over me. The commotion brought curious neighbors outside, but apparently, the disturbance wasn't worthy of police intervention. They watched us like we were in a prime time television show.

"We didn't do anything!" I wailed.

"Get in here, Fla!" she yelled. Meanwhile, Jerome had scrambled to his feet and tried to make another go at Randy. Jerome was uncoordinated and appeared cartoonish as he tried to fight Randy. He doubled over every time Randy brushed up against his gut. It would have been funny if it weren't so ridiculous. Randy ended the comedy by putting his full weight behind his strong arms, toppling Jerome over off his feet. He hit the floor with a sickening splat.

"Man, you crazy!" Randy side-stepped him easily. Half of Jerome's body was on the landing, the other half in the apartment. He couldn't get to Randy, so he grabbed me around the ankle.

"You can't have what's mine!" Jerome said to Randy while he was looking up at me.

"Get outta here, boy!" Momma screamed at Randy, threatening him with the crutch she retrieved from behind the door.

"Momma, leave him alone!" I cried.

"Shut up, girl! Get in here like I told you with your stupid self!" She was leaning over Jerome, tending to his bruised behind and ego.

I wanted to stomp his face. Momma's eyes dared me to. I wanted Randy to take me and carry me out of there.

"I don't belong to you! Let me go!" I pulled my ankle out of his grasp with minimal effort. Jerome really was nothing but a huge gelatinous blob.

"You belong to me, though, and you don't talk to him like that," Momma scolded me. "Now get your fast behind in this house or I'm gonna call the police out here!"

It was the ultimate threat. Nobody in the projects wanted to see the cops. It was like spraying Raid in a roach infested corner. Everybody went scrambling, trying to get out of the way, even if they'd done nothing wrong. Randy apparently didn't want that. He threw up his hands and walked away. He left me.

Not ten minutes before, I hovered over the earth. Now, I had been brought crashing down to it. I lay on my bed and pulled a romance novel from underneath it. I read to nurse my wounds, but it wasn't helping. I slept in fits and starts, dreaming of the prince who rode off without me, and the fire-breathing dragon that my momma let back into the house.

/CHAPTER XII/

Pastor Ricky's absence was as noticeable as a ladder with a missing rung. I longed for his sermons. I wished for the unconventional grammar lessons. I yearned for the laughs. I pined for my friend.

"I haven't seen Pastor Ricky since the beginning of the month, Miss Lipstick. Do you know where he is?" I was toweling dry about a hundred glasses, some formerly jelly jars, mayonnaise jars and pickle jars. In their new life, they held all manner of wine coolers and hard liquors — all the cures for life's ailments. Miss Lipstick sat at the kitchen table, which was leaning to the left. She sat there casually counting out balled up piles of cash. There were crumpled tens, twenties and lots of ones. Her cigarette was never far from her hand. It was a rare occasion that we were in the house alone, with the exception of Root Charlie.

"Pastor Ricky ain't welcome in my house no more." She methodically straightened out each bill, turned it face up and placed it in its proper category.

"Ma'am?"

"You heard me, gal." Miss Lipstick's voice had picked up a menacing tone, but was still steady.

"What did he do? I thought you liked Pastor Ricky."

"Ain't got nothing to do with liking him. Got to do with what he did, behind my back." She stopped counting and looked up at me. "You know what I'm talking about, don't you, gal?"

I plumbed my mind trying to recall any event that happened before that enchanting walk home with Randy. I remembered the juke joint last week and going to city hall to see ... Ooh, that must have been it.

"Don't play with me, child. You went to see your daddy!"

I looked down at my feet. I felt bad but I didn't know why. "Yes, ma'am. He didn't want me though."

Her hands stayed again. "If you wanted to know about your daddy, you could've asked me. Could've saved you some heartache."

I didn't believe her, but I couldn't say so. Miss Lipstick had yet to give me a straight answer about anything. She would have made an excellent politician.

"You knew he didn't want me?" It hurt to say but I had to know.

"I didn't want you to find out this way, baby. That sorry excuse for a man ain't nothing but a yard bird in a nice suit. He didn't even come to the hospital when you was born. Every dog'll have its day. You want to know something, ask me."

Miss Lipstick was good at being tight-lipped. Since she was giving me an inch, I would take it.

"You were there when I was born?" Perhaps now, I would get some of the long awaited information about Momma. "Tell me about it." I was wrist deep in a jelly jar, my mind's pistons firing away.

For the first time since I'd started working for her, Miss Lipstick behaved nervously, uneasy. She stopped counting and picked up her cigarette. Her fingers shook as if she was having her own personal earthquake. "Lots of crying. All I can remember." She went back to counting.

I had managed to open a vault and now it shut tight again. "OK. But I can still ask you anything?"

"Just about," she said, her tone cryptic.

"Who is Karla? Everybody keeps acting like it's some big secret." I stopped washing the jelly jar.

Miss Lipstick suddenly launched into a coughing fit that sent her cigarette flying to the floor. I jumped up and quickly stamped it out, then thumped Miss Lipstick lightly on the back. If I hit her any harder, it seemed my whole hand would go straight through her. She pulled herself up weakly and waved me off to allow the cough to run its course. It was a horrible sound, a long, dry heave, as if she couldn't get air into her lungs. At the same time, she was spitting up clumps of phlegm and some kind of black substance, the equivalent of a human hairball. It was hard to look at but I forced myself not to look away. I was terrified.

"Miss Lipstick, you all right? Do I need to call a doctor or the ambulance?" It was frightening to watch her and be helpless.

While she was yet bent over hawking up a lung, she rotated her wrists furiously, like helicopter propellers. Root Charlie noiselessly came to her side and examined her. He didn't touch her, but combed her body with his x-ray vision.

"She all right," he diagnosed her in that incredibly deep voice. "Ain't nothing to do." The coughing finally subsided, and she was able to speak again.

"Don't ask me about Karla," she said between long heaves.

"You just said I could ask you anything, Miss Lipstick!" I forgot who I was talking to.

"Don't sass me, little girl." There was a hardness in her voice. "You ain't too big to put over my knee." She pushed the stacks of money toward me and some rubber bands she pulled out of her pocket. "I'll call Dr. Sally later. Wrap this money for me after you dry yo' hands. I can't go to the bank myself, so you have to deposit this. Don't count it. Just put it in this envelope and take it to Quincy State. "Here." She dug into her pockets once more. "For you." She tossed a couple of crisp, folded twenty dollar bills in my direction, and then hobbled to her bed. There would be no more discussion about Karla today. I was truly disappointed, but the money was a welcome distraction. I finished the jelly jars and dried my hands, the whole while pondering Miss Lipstick's reluctance to talk about Karla. I wrapped the money, and there was quite a bit of it. I put it all in an envelope, grabbed *Fire Next Time,* and hit the road to the bank.

Quincy State was the oldest bank in Quincy and almost everybody with a pulse and a job had an account there. It was in an old, beige brick building near the downtown core. The two-story exterior was crumbling and it cried out for a facelift. Through the glass double doors, I saw into the small lobby. It was plain, with linoleum floors and wood accents. There were a handful of people at the counters and a couple of people sitting in chairs along the wall. In the middle of the lobby, a stuffy looking young white guy with glasses that covered his whole face sat at an enormous wooden desk flanked by two large potted palms. I entered quietly, immediately caressed by the cool air inside. I joined the people sitting in the chairs.

While I waited, I fondled the heavy envelope and wondered how much was inside. It felt like a lot, but I had no frame of reference. I must have fiddled with it too much, as the crinkling of the paper in this super-quiet environment invited looks of annoyance. The envelope wasn't sealed — I'd merely closed the clasp. I think I put twenty stacks of bills in that envelope, easily. I wouldn't be able to do the math because I didn't know how many bills were in each stack. I had been too preoccupied to notice.

What would I do with all that money, if it was mine? *Were* mine, I corrected myself, thinking of Pastor Ricky. What wouldn't I do? I'd sail around the world. I'd buy a bookstore and a two-story house with four bedrooms and two bathrooms. I'd buy Pastor Ricky some new suits. I was in stage three of my daydream when I became aware of a pair of light blue eyes on me. I saw my reflection in his over-sized spectacles and snapped to.

"May I help you, Miss?"

I scoured my surroundings, looking for this "Miss" he was talking about. No white person had ever referred to me as "Miss."

"I'm talking to you." His name tag said he was Matt Szynciewski. After I butchered it three times, he told me to call him Mr. Matt. He may have been Mr. Matt, but those large glasses could not be ignored. Big Glasses was all of twenty-five and crouched down to my level, his hands resting on his thighs. I just knew he wanted to pat me on the head and throw me a bone.

"Ah, yes. I'm here to make a deposit."

"That's an awfully big envelope for such a little girl." I wanted to swat him in the face with that big envelope. I was not a three-year-old.

"I need to make a deposit for Miss Lipstick."

The goofy expression disappeared instantly. He stood up and walk-ran at a clipped pace to a corridor somewhere behind his desk. The people sitting next to me looked at me and I looked at them.

Big Glasses came back in a couple of minutes and I followed him into the bowels of the bank. We walked down a maze of silent hallways with offices on either side. The walls were covered with one certificate after another, extolling the excellence of this particular bank. We passed several offices before we dead-ended at a door with a gold plate on it that simply stated "bank manager." I wondered if we were in the right place. The bank was so deceptively large that maybe Big Glasses got lost. He rapped twice and opened the door. He gestured for me to go in. I gestured "in there?" He gestured "yes" and shoved me in, closing the door soundly behind me.

The bank manager sat facing away in a shiny, brown leather chair with a high back, so I couldn't see who I was meeting. He was on the phone and didn't bother to lower his voice.

"Yes, I'll take care of it." There was a long pause. "We'll see. When there's enough, I'll tell you enough. Certainly. Take care."

The great chair began to swivel around, and I came face to face with one of those men of means who were never turned away from Miss Lipstick's door.

The bank manager was a white man of about fifty with big, round, baby blue eyes that peeked out of a pear-shaped head. His cheeks glowed as if he'd applied rouge to them. His neck was bursting from his collar and the hands that he held together on his desk were equally large. In accord with the enormity of his Santa-like physique, his manner was very pleasant. He addressed me as if I really owned a toilet paper fortune, instead of the two twenty-dollar bills in my pocket. He had a southern drawl, like Mr. Pierce, but with a shade of rural country dialect, as if he'd grown up in some little farming town with two names and no traffic light.

"Miss Frye, I believe it is?" he said.

I didn't tell anybody my name. How did he know it?

As if to answer my bewildered expression, he leaned back and had a hearty laugh at my expense.

"I was expecting you, Miss Frye. Don't be so alarmed. Now, let's have a look-see at what you brought me today."

I handed the envelope over. I remained quiet during the transaction, not knowing what to say to this man, feeling I was out of my league. I didn't have many occasions to conduct business with white men who were bank managers. He turned his back to me as he emptied the envelope. I had a chance to take in the cavernous room. It was just the sort of office I'd expect a bank manager to have. It was large and comfortable, with the same wooden accents as the bank lobby. The desk, which looked like the grandfather of Big Glasses' desk, was covered with papers, pens, gem clips, and banking brochures. His desk calendar revealed that this day, Monday, July 19, 1976, was a full day for him. My eyes followed the river of office supplies to the name plate partially hidden by a stack of documents. I was scared to disturb anything, but the last name looked familiar. As quietly as I could, I leaned over and pulled the name plate over a smidge. It read Jackson Richards. That name tickled my brain, and I knew I wouldn't rest until I could scratch that itch.

Jackson Richards' fat fingers started pecking away at the computer in front of him. The computer was big and clunky, beige and square. The electronic contraption ate up three-quarters of the table it was sitting on. Neon green words blinked furiously on a black screen. Computers were an oddity to me. They were the wave of the future my teachers proclaimed. At Carter Jackson High, only the principal had one.

I could see that he was typing numbers and letters into the account of a Beatrice Miller. She was earning three percent interest on fifteen thousand dollars.

"Miss Frye," Jackson Richards said suddenly, causing me to jump in my chair.

"Yes," I answered, fearing I had been caught doing something wrong. The man must have had eyes in the back of his head.

"I'm giving you two deposit slips today in this here envelope. You are to put this envelope in Miss Lipstick's hands. No one else is to open this envelope. You understand?"

Of course I understood. I was indignant. How simple did he think I was? Envelope. Hand.

"Yes, I understand," I answered softly, hoping he would pick up on the hint of attitude. He gave me the envelope but held on to it. Was he about to tell me to breathe in, then out?

"Miss Frye. There's one more thing." Mr. Richards reached into a drawer in his desk and pulled out another envelope. He passed it to me.

"Since you're here, might as well give this to you now." He slid the envelope over to me.

"What is it? Can I open it? It's for me?"

He suppressed a chuckle. "An envelope. Yes and yes."

I wanted to rip open that envelope like Christmas morning. Not that I had much experience getting presents on Christmas morning but I heard that's what you're supposed to do. I carefully lifted the flap of the envelope and removed its contents. It was a $400 money order payable to Millie Frye. Apparently, Jackson Richards was Santa Claus.

I was more than a little puzzled. "This is for my momma?"

"That is for you, for your care." His expression told me I was a simple child.

"Ah, so you're the one who's been sending Momma those checks every month. I thought I recognized your name."

He nodded his head. "For nigh on 15 years now. You are 15?" I nodded my head.

"Did she hit the lottery or something? Momma never had a job that I know of."

"This is from an account that was set up for you on the day you were born. I want you to know something. You are very special to this lady, in more ways than you can possibly imagine."

"What lady? My Momma?" My being special to her was news to me. All of this was news to me. I couldn't remember the last time I had new clothes from a department store, or a new book bag, or even dental care, and Momma had been receiving $400 every month for me — specifically for me. It explained where she got the money to buy all that beer, but it didn't explain away everything. I felt my ears getting hot.

"Sir?" Mr. Richards had just said something.

"I said I can't go into that right now. One day, you'll understand." He began leafing through a thick document.

I was really getting tired of people making these cryptic comments to me, and then saying they couldn't explain it or couldn't tell me anymore. It was frustrating. But at least I knew about the money now.

"Oh, Mr. Richards," I said. He'd gone back to his typing.

"Yes, ma'am?" He seemed interested in what I had to say.

"Three percent of $15,000 is $450.00, not $400.00. You have $400.00 up there." I wanted to be helpful. I didn't know anything about banking, but I didn't want anyone cheated out of anything.

Mr. Richards frowned. I thought he might rebuke me for reviewing someone's private information. Instead, he looked at the screen closely then leaned way back in his chair.

"Miss Frye, I do believe you are correct." Mr. Richards fixed the error right then. "You are very quick on your feet and very smart, young lady."

"Thank you," I said, trying to sound modest.

"No, ma'am. Don't take it lightly." He fixed his gaze on me. "This lady's been investing in toilet paper stock for years and she would have been shorted. Our policy at Quincy State is to take care of every customer as if they were our only customer. Any time you want to go into finance, look me up. I mean it." He offered his hand to me, which engulfed mine. His hand was soft, warm and dry, but he shook mine firmly. I hate limp noodle handshakes.

"You take care, now," Mr. Richards said.

I walked outside the bank, feeling good about myself for catching the mistake. My curious nature took over and I played devil's advocate with myself over whether to open that envelope. Mr. Richards probably put something on the seal that would alert Miss Lipstick that it had been tampered with. The last thing I wanted to do was come between Miss Lipstick and her money, even if it was just a piece of paper that said how much she had. I was having this conversation with myself when, in my peripheral vision, I caught sight of an old man dressed in a bright yellow suit. I had strict orders to get this envelope to Miss Lipstick, so there would be no dallying. If I saw Pastor Ricky in the near future, I'd tell him some old man was wearing one of his suits. I kept walking without breaking my stride.

"Jasmine. You just gonna walk by me? I'm hurt," the man said.

The clothes were certainly those of Pastor Ricky's, but the grammar was not the King's English.

"Pastor Ricky?" I was still not sure because the man was pale and much smaller than the Pastor Ricky I knew, who was tall and robust.

"It's me, Jasmine." He opened his arms and I fell into them easily. The familiar scent of him, the S-curl spray and a case of beer confirmed that it was Pastor Ricky.

"Pastor Ricky, where have you been? I missed you." I held onto him tightly.

"I miss you, too, Jasmine. You don't know how much." He didn't bother to smile. Now his eyes and demeanor matched. His hair was falling out in places and he seemed a little disoriented.

"What's the matter, Pastor Ricky?" I asked, still holding on.

"I'm just tired, sweetheart. I need to take care of some things before I go see my daddy." Pastor Ricky returned my embrace, but it was like a vice grip.

This was exciting news. Pastor Ricky never talked about his family.

"Since you took me to see my daddy, I'll go with you to see yours."

He could barely part his lips.

"No, Jasmine. But you can come to church with me this Sunday. I'd really like you to be there."

I guess the things he needed to take care of had to do with the church. If my presence there would bring him some measure of comfort, I was more than happy to accompany him.

"Yeah. I'd love to go with you." Pastor Ricky didn't correct me.

Those two twenty-dollar bills were burning a hole in my pocket. I'd never possessed that much money at one time that was actually mine. I felt rich. I tucked the envelopes between pages of my book and directed my feet to the library. I calculated enough time to make a mad dash over there before Miss Lipstick would start to miss me. I wanted to be a good patron and repay Mrs. Mac's kindness by paying my library fines.

The bell announced my arrival. Mrs. Mac was behind the front desk stamping dates into books that a white, male patron was checking out. She looked up and smiled at me. When the man left, I pulled out my forty dollars and put it on the desk as if it were a hundred dollars.

"I can pay my fines today, Mrs. Mac," I was happy to finally say.

"What fines, Miss Fla?" Mrs. Mac seemed genuinely confused.

"The fines I owe. For all the books I kept a long time." I explained in short sentences to jog her memory. "I still have some of them."

"I don't recollect you owing this library anything." She took up the money and cupped it in my hand.

"But, Mrs. Mac," I protested. This woman must take my money.

"But Miss Fla, your money's no good here. Period." Mrs. Mac only got stern with me when I would check out so many books I couldn't see over the top of the stack. "I'll tell you what. If you help this young lady in the back find what she's looking for, I'll owe you." Mrs. Mac winked.

"Oh," I said, the dim bulb in my head finally flickering on to its full wattage. "Mrs. Mac, you're the best."

I meandered toward the rear of the library, stopping along the way to peruse the library's newest acquisitions. I tucked away in my memory several titles I would have to review up close.

The girl Mrs. Mac wanted me to help must have been new in town or new to reading. The Gadsden County Public Library was small and not complex. Although Mrs. Mac followed the Dewey Decimal System, she placed large placards over each shelf so the reader could easily find what she was looking for. Anybody who spent just five minutes within the confines of that glorious institution could find the most obscure title — anybody but Cast Iron Kat.

I was astonished to discover her in the shelves amidst everything animal, with a cloud of confusion over head. She had pulled off almost an entire wall of books, including encyclopedias and other reference materials. Books were open and scattered all over the table behind her. There were books at her sandaled feet. Cast Iron Kat wore a black, pleated mini-skirt, and short-sleeved checkerboard blouse. Her long, voluminous hair was pulled back into a neat ponytail. She looked as if she would have been more comfortable striking a provocative pose between the pages of a girlie magazine, rather than prowling through the pages of animal books. My own shorts, formerly jeans I performed meatball surgery on, my thrift store, tie dye T-shirt, and the cornrowed madness on my head made me feel instantly inferior. We stared at each other. Although she was on my home turf, I felt I had no special advantage.

The first words out of Cast Iron Kat's mouth were tinged with hostility.

"I should've known this where you be hanging out all the time. Surprised to see me in here?" She rolled her eyes and neck for effect. "Yes, I read. Hard to believe, ain't it?" She stepped on a couple of books as she backed out of the aisles.

"You better not tell nobody you saw me in here." She tossed books around furiously. Where that dang book?"

A strange mixture of contempt and pity simmered inside me and my language skills failed me.

"This how you do so good in school, ain't it? 'Cause you read a lot? Why you staring at me? 'Kat cain't read. Kat too dumb.' That's what you thinking, ain't it? That lady said she was gonna show me where that book on lizards was. What's her name?" Kat's frustrations were boiling over into belligerence. She had too many square weapons at her disposal and I was directly in the line of fire. To my left, on the shelf full of a series about every animal that walked the earth, near lemurs and lions, I found the book on lizards. I tried handing it to Kat but she snatched it from me before I released it. I stumbled forward and fell into her. How dare she? How dare Kat steal my one and only refuge in this world? Didn't she have everything already? All the beauty. All the boys. Why couldn't she leave me the hell alone!

I regained my balance and left. I didn't even say goodbye to Mrs. McCullough.

/CHAPTER XIII/

Mr. Pierce was fond of testing us on Tuesdays, and Wednesdays and Thursdays. Anxiety levels were through the schoolhouse roof. Panic was evident in Cast Iron Kat and her nitwit sorority sisters because they whispered back and forth amongst themselves while they flipped through the textbook over and over. I was anxious for a different reason. Cast Iron Kat had spared me several times already. If she didn't rise to the challenge of passing this test, I feared her resentment would spill over in my direction. She'd been promising to beat me like I stole something since summer school started and our library encounter threw kerosene on smoldering embers. With only a couple of weeks of summer school left, her academic future was hanging in the balance and it was almost impossible for her to turn things around at this stage. I was sure to be blamed for this.

Our knowledge of the great writers of the twentieth century and their works were on trial, and I was aiming to be convicted. When Mr. Pierce placed that one sheet of paper on my desk, I experienced happiness and dread simultaneously. Mr. Pierce had designed what he called a cheat proof exam — no multiple-choice questions, no fill in the blanks, no answer that could be readily gleaned from a textbook. We had to have read Angelou, Baldwin, E.L.

Doctorow, Faulkner, Hemingway, and Updike. We had to write our answers in essay form, at which I excelled. If there was going to be any cheating, it would have to be blatant. Mr. Pierce was so certain no one could, or would cheat, he announced he would leave the classroom to run an errand about ten minutes after the test had begun. The honor system was in effect. I daresay a good three-fourths of the class found that concept foreign, not to mention stupid. The other one-fourth was scared to death of cheating, or rather, the consequences of being caught. I was a solid member of the one-fourth. I didn't want to cheat. I didn't need to cheat. Although I no longer had a crush on Mr. Pierce, I still didn't want to disappoint him.

Cast Iron Kat, on the other hand, had no such reservations. She boldly left her seat and stood before me, her Amazon hands on both sides of my desk. No words were exchanged. I continued to write. Her impatient sigh said "show me your paper." I brought my arm over the top of the paper, telling her "no can do." She grabbed my wrist with such strength, I thought it would snap off in her hand. With the other hand, Cast Iron Kat stole my paper.

"Let's see if you really that smart or if Mr. Pierce just be helping you." She turned to the rest of the class. "Hush y'all. Listen to this." She cleared her throat dramatically and began to read.

"'Every writer enters into an unspoken contract to contribute to the erection of a solid literary foundation.'" Cast Iron Kat chuckled at the word "erection" and continued. "'Writers of the past set up that foundation. Every writer since, whether great or small, famous or unknown, has added a brick here, a nail there, to weave a structural tapestry of words that forms our present day literary heritage.'"

That's where I'd stopped writing when Cast Iron Kat took my paper. Although she struggled with a few words, she read the piece pretty well. The room was quiet. I had been hunched over in my seat, my heart surging from this deeply personal violation. When Cast Iron Kat's eyes met mine, I straightened up in my seat, the pain in my wrist forgotten momentarily. Something transpired between us.

There she stood when Mr. Pierce found her, with my limb still mangled in her grasp. She released me as if she had received a blast of heat from a blowtorch. Cast Iron Kat couldn't deny she was cheating — she couldn't have been more red-handed if she had dipped her hand in a bucket of paint.

"Miss Morehead!" Mr. Pierce growled. His handsome face darkened with fury. "This is outrageous!"

The classroom snickered. Mr. Pierce lashed out at them with a nonverbal gesture that cut the laughing in mid-breath. He turned his full attention to Cast Iron Kat.

"I have had it up to here, young lady. Sit down!" Kat was still standing in front of my desk. He grabbed her by the arm and assisted her roughly into the seat at his desk. He paced angrily back and forth in front of his desk, and then focused the full potency of his fury in Kat's direction.

"Miss Morehead. I don't know what else I can do to help you. You insist on being a mediocre student, at best. I give you every opportunity to improve yourself and you throw it away."

Cast Iron Kat looked mortified. Her lovely features were downcast and her lower lip hung closer to her chest. My lip began to hang when Mr. Pierce made his way to my desk.

"You wanted to cheat. At least you did that right. You couldn't have cheated off a better student than Miss Frye here. She's got intelligence. She's got ambition. She's going somewhere." I couldn't bear to look at Cast Iron Kat. But I felt the heat of her hatred flowing toward me. Mr. Pierce whipped around and jabbed his finger in the air.

"You, on the other hand, are content with failure. What can you be around here without an education? Do you know how the world will perceive you? Simply ignorant and lazy." Mr. Pierce was pacing the classroom like a caged animal. "Listen to me, all of you! Your imaginations don't have to quit at the city limits. You can be so much more. I can see that you all have the potential. You just have to keep trying! You cannot give up!" He wiped his mouth with his sleeve and took a deep breath.

"Miss Morehead, I've said it once and I'll say it again. You have just been scraping by in here. Summer school is over on August fifth. That's two and a half weeks from now. Needless to say, you've failed this test. If you fail the next two, you are finished! There will be no more social promotions. There will be no more promotions, period." He wagged his finger in her face while he delivered his venomous lecture. Cast Iron Kat's pretty face swelled up. I thought I would relish such a display — Cast Iron Kat receiving her so well-deserved comeuppance. My joy should have been amplified by such a public humiliation. But I was strangely upset, strangely appalled at Mr. Pierce's aggressive behavior. Since he broke my heart by accelerating his wedding date, I found his praise something of a double-edge sword. On one side, I was titillated by his thought that I might go somewhere beyond Quincy's city limits. On the other, I thought he was using me as bait to goad Cast Iron Kat even further. He had to be aware of that girl's animosity toward me. At any rate, judging by her hard stare, I knew I was no longer being toyed with — she would devour me that day.

Mr. Pierce released us early. He was disgusted with us, he'd said. I walked by his desk with Cast Iron Kat's soldiers close behind me.

"I'd like to see you for a moment, Miss Frye," Mr. Pierce said. He rubbed his tired eyes. "Fla, I want to know right now. What do you think of the colleges? Which one do you like best?" He dropped the title on my name and the inflection in his tone told me he meant business.

"The big one," I hedged. I didn't want to have this conversation. That manual was still collecting dust under my bed.

"What big one?" Mr. Pierce asked. There was no more praise in his voice, just irritation.

"You know. The big one in Tallahassee." I knew it was lame.

He formed his hands in a gesture of prayer. "You haven't even looked at it, have you? Fla, I don't understand. You're a brilliant student. You can go places. This city doesn't have to be your quicksand." He took a deep, cleansing breath, as if he needed to keep himself from putting his hands around my throat. "What about Upward Bound? Have you given any thought to that?"

I did not look at him. I shifted from one foot to the other, staring at the world map above his head.

"I don't know, Mr. Pierce. I don't know about college. I know about Quincy."

"Is it money? I can help you get scholarships." After the way he decimated poor Cast Iron Kat, I began to wonder what was in it for him to see me off to college. I didn't trust those sexy brown eyes as much as I used to.

"If you're not going to take this seriously, would you please return the manual?" he asked. As I walked away, only slightly upset that he'd given up on me, he called me back briefly.

"You're throwing away a bright future. Not many kids like you get a chance like this." He moved over to the window and looked out over the school lawn.

I regretted that he was disappointed in me, but I had greater concerns. I wouldn't have a future if Cast Iron Kat had anything to do with it. She had her soldiers waiting for me outside the classroom. They enclosed me in a tight little circle and we walked, military style, toward the courtyard in the middle of the school, known as the Bruise Ring. That's where all the fights took place and where the onlookers had a clear view of the black and blue.

To say I was scared wasn't saying enough. I needed a transfer to a new school. More than I feared the slaps, the kicks and the punches, I feared the prospect of losing my shirt. I had not developed much in the last few months.

Other kids began gathering around the Bruise Ring. I knew there would be a lot of boys, because they just like to see chick-on-chick violence and might catch sight of a boobie or two. But the number of girls, besides Cast Iron Kat's clique, surprised me. I didn't know so many girls wanted to see me get my behind handed to me. For the life of me, I couldn't figure out what I'd done to them. While these thoughts, and others pertaining to escape, ran through my head, I was delivered unceremoniously into the middle of the Bruise Ring. Cast Iron Kat usually made a grand entrance. I wished she'd come on and get it over with.

My wish was granted. Cast Iron Kat approached me rapidly and pushed me in the chest with both hands.

"Think you better than me, don't you, teacher's pet!" she spat. She was no longer beautiful, but full of contempt and raw hatred.

"What did I do to you? I can't help it if I'm smarter than you." If ever there was a time to speak up for myself, this was it. I had nothing to lose, but my shirt and a couple of days of school to heal from my injuries.

"You ain't better than me." We danced around the ring, trading verbal punches. Cast Iron Kat would throw in a swipe every other word, but my raggedy instincts kicked in and I ducked. The insults continued, much to the dismay of the swarming crowd. We had reached the point where the appetizers were finished and it was time for the main course.

"I ain't playing with you no more. Come on. Fight me!" Cast Iron Kat challenged. She had her fists up, her boxer's stance pitch perfect, and my blood in her sights. I was a full inch shorter than this girl, probably twenty pounds lighter, and her anger gave her the strength of two bodybuilders. The terror inside me paralyzed my limbs. I would have conceded defeat, but that wouldn't stop Cast Iron Kat from tenderizing me in front of a bloodthirsty audience. My physicality was not going to get me out of this pickle, so my mouth had to do the work until the teachers showed up, which would be at the same time the paramedics arrived. I couldn't count on anybody to save me. It was time to put on my mask of false bravado.

"I'm not gonna fight you. If beating me up's gonna make you feel smarter, then go ahead. I may be black and blue tomorrow, but I'll still be smart and you'll still be dumb."

She came charging at me like a bull blinded by a red cloak. I managed to dodge her, but someone pushed me back in.

"Who you callin' dumb!" she screamed. "I ain't dumb!"

"That's what your girls call you. They say you're dumb and fast because you're around a whole lot of men all the time." I watched her facial expression metamorphose from resentment to bewilderment. Cast Iron Kat stopped in her tracks and dropped her hands. She looked around in the crowd for the girls who were supposed to have her back.

"Y'all be sayin' that behind my back? Who said that?" Her eyes traveled from one face to the other. They all shrank back into the crowd, as if they wanted to be swallowed by it.

"Who said that 'bout me? Fla?" she addressed me, her voice a plea. She didn't call me Flop. This told me the betrayal was complete. I would have gladly dropped a dime on one of her friends, but I couldn't, simply because I had made it up. I had no way of knowing that her "friends" had previously echoed my fabricated allegations. A disheartened Cast Iron Kat left the ring lower than any human being should ever be. There would be no fight, so the crowd dispersed. I should have run, but I didn't.

It took me longer than usual to report for work. The guilt I carried felt like a forty-pound bag of potatoes. I tried to convince myself that Cast Iron Kat deserved it. She had no right to be beautiful and cruel. My conscience wouldn't let that fly.

The flow of traffic through Miss Lipstick's house had gradually decreased. People traveling in and out of the house reduced a skyscraping stack of liquor boxes on the back porch to a half-empty single story. I washed discolored sheets and stiff towels and eyed one of the partially open boxes. Brown bottles with long necks and label bowties were placed in neat rows. I picked up a bottle and traced my finger along its curves, its round bottom, and its metal cap.

"What you doing, gal!"

I nearly dropped the bottle at the sound of Miss Lipstick's voice.

"I was just looking at it," I lied.

"I don't like the way you looking at it. Put it back." She snatched the bottle from me and dropped it into the box where it clanked hard against another bottle. "A lot of drinking starts with just a look." She examined my face.

"What's ailing you?" She led me back into the kitchen.

I sat down at the table and rested my face in my palm.

"What is it now?" Miss Lipstick asked impatiently. "That boy? I knew he wasn't no good."

"No, Miss Lipstick. It's this girl at school. She keeps messing with me, but . . ." I tried to make sense of my conflicting emotions.

"You know how to fight?" Miss Lipstick asked.

"No. Not really. I never had to," I said.

"It'll come to you when you need it. I can show you a few things . . .," she offered.

"She won't be messing with me anymore, I think." I couldn't put a name to the feelings that were plaguing me, but I wanted them to go away.

"I don't get you." Miss Lipstick massaged her temples.

"Well. She used to mess with me. All the time. I think it's because I'm smart and she's . . ." I searched for a kind euphemism. "She's not as smart. But today, the teacher made her feel real bad and I thought it would make me feel real good. But it didn't."

"I see," Miss Lipstick said.

"She's so mean and always making fun of me. I wish I didn't feel so bad about it." My stomach was in knots.

"You talking about that good-looking chick what live over there near you?" Miss Lipstick tapped my sore wrist. "I know her and her old daddy."

"Yeah, that's her. It ain't fair. She is *so* pretty and the way she dresses, she can have any boy she wants. Why does she have to bother me?"

I noticed that Miss Lipstick wasn't smoking. She was out of her wig and just wearing her natural hair. There was a lot less gray, a lot less hair. Her face looked wan, her body looked skeletal. Old age was a bully, too.

"First of all, if you stopped looking at how she dress and look at her heart, you might see she just like you on the inside. You never thought that what you got might be more important than what she got? Maybe she wants what you got."

"She wants to be ugly and unpopular? She can have it." The very idea struck me as incredible.

Miss Lipstick jerked back like a cat doused by sprinklers. "Don't you ever call yourself ugly. Never! You the most beautiful thing on this here God's green earth. Do you hear me!"

"Yes, ma'am," I replied.

"I'm talking about your smarts, baby. Looks'll only get you so far. You got what it takes to do something important. That girl can see that and she want that. She got a beautiful face, but baby, you got a beautiful brain." Miss Lipstick grasped my hands. "You got to reach out to her and share what you got. You got to want to help her more than you want things to be easy for you. She just don't know how to ask."

"I have to reach out to her? After she's been picking on me forever? That's not fair."

"Baby, life's not fair!" She dropped my hands. "It's never been fair. It's never gonna be fair. You have to use what you got and do your best with it. I'm tired of hearing you say it's not fair." Miss Lipstick was angry, but her actions belied her emotions. She rose up slowly from the chair, wincing as she did. I put my hand on her arm to offer some leverage, but she brushed it away. Root Charlie, his face as immobile as ever, looked at me and shook his head slowly.

/CHAPTER XIV/

I spent the next two days agonizing over Miss Lipstick and Cast Iron Kat. Miss Lipstick was none too thrilled with me and Cast Iron Kat didn't come to school on Wednesday or Thursday. Cast Iron Kat's girls were unusually subdued, and Mr. Pierce was not sympathetic. I began to see him in a much different light and was less and less enamored of him since he decided to spend the rest of his life with another woman. I vowed never to go the extra mile to impress him. I felt nothing special when he asked me to please help Miss Morehead get a passing grade in his class. I gave him a simple nod, knowing full well I wouldn't go near Cast Iron Kat any time soon.

On Friday, I planned to fill my weekly appointment to read to my captive audience at Miss Lipstick's. Nothing pressing was happening at home, except Jerome's constant harassment. Mr. Curtis and the others even slowed their drinking to an extent to listen and understand what I read to them. Their favorite stories were about underdogs who came out on top and ordinary black folk triumphing over The Man. It brought me immense pleasure to see the light in their eyes, which was normally no brighter than a flicker. They listened attentively, and I read on and on. Miss Lipstick was usually keen on a good story, but she was conspicuously missing. She was feeling poorly again, her smoker's cough penetrating the solid wood of the door.

Dr. Sally was called in to pay Miss Lipstick a visit because she couldn't get out of bed. Dr. Sally was a distinguished-looking, older black gentleman with a salt-and-pepper afro and intelligent eyes peering out from behind a pair of wire rimmed glasses. He carried a polished but well-used black bag at his side and carried himself with an air of importance, but not arrogance.

Dr. Sally's arrival was significant to me, but it didn't seem to make a difference to anyone else. Johnny whined about his shot; the Williams brothers argued over whose beer tasted better, although they drank the same brand; and Phyllis was there entertaining a small contingent of men in the kitchen. I thought an occasion such as this would produce some movement in Root Charlie. It did not. When Dr. Sally entered Miss Lipstick's room, no one else seemed anxious about it.

Phyllis ended her show abruptly. "Hey, Phyllis, where you going?" The men in the kitchen were visibly upset that she was leaving them. She looked over her shoulder and dipped. "That's how Phyllis do it, baby." The men actually applauded her. Her charismatic smile was as beguiling as ever. "What is it, doll?" she asked, throwing her arm around my shoulder.

"What's going on with Miss Lipstick? The doctor's never been here before." I was astounded at her lack of anguish.

"It's probably a routine check-up," Phyllis said, trying to be nonchalant, but addressing her comments to my shoes and not to my face. This slip gave her away.

"Phyllis, I'm not a child. Do you know something?" I had a childlike belief that Phyllis wouldn't lie to me.

"You're right, baby, you're right. You are not a child." Phyllis looked genuinely remorseful. "It's not my place to say anything. When the doctor leaves, why don't you ask Lipstick yourself?" That meant I'd never know what was going on. Phyllis cuddled me, which took the edge off my distress.

I was too upset to continue reading. I sat in a chair, in the middle of the carefree atmosphere, just outside Miss

Lipstick's room. I waited an hour for the doctor to emerge so I could interrogate him.

"Dr. Sally, how's Miss Lipstick?" I saw my reflection in his glasses, and I was looking out of sorts.

"How are you doing yourself, young lady?" Dr. Sally asked in his medical voice.

"I'm a little tired, but I want to know about Miss Lipstick."

"She's a tough old bird, that lady." He gave me a curt nod and headed toward the door.

"That's a *medical* diagnosis?" I asked. I meant no disrespect, but I couldn't suppress it.

Dr. Sally raised an eyebrow.

"I'm sorry," I apologized quickly.

"It's OK. I know you're concerned." Dr. Sally gave my hand a short squeeze. "When Lipstick's had a chance to rest, why don't you talk to her?"

Miss Lipstick was the President of the Closed-Mouth Club and I didn't expect to get much information out of her about her health, or anything, for that matter. It was easier to believe that she was fine. It was difficult getting information out of anybody else about Karla.

Dr. Sally, as he reached for the door, found his egress blocked. Johnny nearly tackled the man.

"Hey, doc. What this here?" Johnny pointed to something on his own neck. "What's that? It's been bothering me for a while. You got something in that black bag for me?"

Dr. Sally squinted at Johnny. Johnny craned his neck to give the doctor a better view, but Dr. Sally was rummaging through his bag. Johnny was excited as the doctor scribbled something on a prescription pad and ripped it off. He gave Johnny a couple of quick pats on the shoulder.

"You take care now," Dr. Sally said as he withdrew hastily. Johnny immediately brought the piece of paper to me. Since I started helping Mr. Curtis fill out some official papers one day, the flood gates were opened. I became the go-to person for writing letters, reading correspondence and explaining official documents. I was prepared to decipher a doctor's handwriting. When I read it, the tension I was feeling over Miss Lipstick crumbled and I laughed until I cried.

"What is it, gal? What he say I got?" Johnny asked, thoroughly intrigued. "Do I get to take pills for it?"

"No," I said between gulps of air. "It says soap and water." The whole house screamed with laughter. A ghost of a smile even passed over Root Charlie's face. Johnny joined in the laughter initially, but then manifested his displeasure at being the brunt of the joke by brandishing his middle finger. He left before he could get his shot of booze.

"She even laugh just like Karla," I heard Mr. Curtis say. "She was such a sweet girl." At the mention of Karla's name, Miss Lipstick should have popped her head out. She didn't this time. I took my cue from Johnny, and left.

I walked home with my arms loaded with books. I hesitated as I neared the pass. I would be easy pickings if Cast Iron Kat found me. It was after 6 p.m., and I was a mobile library. I tiptoed across the bridge, terrified that every creak would draw her out like a troll. Nothing happened. I made it safely to my room without incident.

I thought about Pastor Ricky constantly. I looked forward to going to church with him more than I realized. Maybe he was ready to surrender his crutch, drop the drink and pick up his cross all the way. I wanted to know who he really was under that S-curl and those sherbet-colored suits.

Momma was in one of her beer-induced comas. I saw and smelled evidence that Jerome had been there. He'd left his special brand of funk on everything and the floor was littered as usual with the trappings of their favorite pastime. I found a small blanket and lay it over Momma, more for my sake than hers. She liked to lounge around in just a T-shirt and panties. Tonight, she wore the T-shirt only. I let exhaustion take me deep into my best dreams.

I spent much of Saturday in my room, going through my closet trying to decide what to wear on Sunday. My choices weren't difficult. I had three dresses. One was that old mauve thing, now moth-eaten, too short and too tight. The second was my dance dress, still ripped up the side because I didn't know how to sew. The last one was a hideous lacy purple thing that looked like someone sewed a bunch of grape-colored doilies together. I was leaning toward the moth dress, but decency dictated the doily dress. Besides, I wanted to impress Pastor Ricky and his father. I was full of curiosity about that introduction.

Since my impromptu excommunication from the church five years earlier, my religious experiences were confined to an hour of Reverend Billy Graham on Sunday mornings, before the cartoons. I could see Reverend Graham's passion; I just couldn't feel it. As I got older, that hour turned into thirty minutes, then ten, then nothing.

I was supposed to meet Pastor Ricky that Sunday at the front of St. Luke Pentecostal Church at 10:45 a.m. for the 11:00 service. There were bigger, smaller, and more extravagant churches in Quincy, but there was none more prestigious in the black community than St. Luke's. There was no black church more steeped in tradition or hobbled by its own rigid rules. One may enter its hallowed halls seeking love, forgiveness, and redemption, but only if one is dressed properly — which meant for the ladies, skirts to the knees, and for the gentlemen, coat and tie. Attitudes must be checked in the lobby and one may receive salvation, but only if one sat quietly through a three-hour service.

My doily dress didn't make any great fashion statements, but at least it didn't garner me any scornful looks. In my book, that made it appropriate for the occasion. I remembered St. Luke as a beautiful regal church made of red brick. As I reminisced, 11:00 loomed near.

I watched a procession of beautiful, elderly black women with white hair, blue hair, and black wigs adorned by magnificent and ridiculous church hats, pass slowly and carefully onto the steps on the arms of elderly men who were only slightly younger. Pastor Ricky was nowhere in sight. I wasn't sure I wanted to go in alone. I saw very few girls my age entering, and there was an age chasm in the men folk — I saw no one between the ages of 6 and 45, only older and younger.

"Pastor Ricky, where are you?" I asked myself aloud. In answer to my question, I heard directly behind me.

"Jasmine."

A smile broke out involuntarily across my face. I spun around, ready to hurl myself at Pastor Ricky, I missed him so much, and found myself staring at a stranger with Pastor Ricky's eyes. He was dressed in a conservative brown suit and his signature S-curl was gone. In its place was a low-fro.

"Pastor Ricky?" I asked tentatively as I searched him up and down for some sign of the man I knew. "Are you in there?"

"It's me, Jasmine." It sounded like Pastor Ricky, but he was a ghost of his former self. Misery was sketched into the grooves of the new lines in his face. His eyes were empty, devoid of anything alive. He was pale and thin, his whole being receding into the conservative brown suit that just hung on his previously robust frame. His lips separated into what was supposed to be a smile, but ended in a grimace.

"Let's go in." We entered the foyer side by side. The white-haired deacon moved to block our entrance.

"You don't belong in here, Mr. Sullivan," the deacon said, his speech slow and deliberate. "Remember Ephesians 5:18, "And be not drunk with wine wherein is excess, but be filled with the spirit.""

"I came here to be filled with the spirit, Deacon Perkins," Pastor Ricky responded. "This is God's house, not yours, last I checked. He said I could come as I am and to suffer the little children to come unto him."

The deacon blinked his eyes quickly, but moved out of the way.

"We don't want no trouble," the deacon said as we passed by him.

Without turning around, Pastor Ricky answered, "You won't get no trouble, as long as you leave me alone."

I could hear the haughty heads whipping around as Pastor Ricky and I walked the aisle in search of an empty pew. There weren't many to choose from. The church was enormous, with three aisles of seats, and it was about three-quarters full. We selected a pew toward the back of the church in the middle aisle and sat down. Pastor Ricky spoke to everyone around us. One heavy-set lady and her mother, a single black man in his twilight years, and a group of women with clucking tongues who were whispering behind their white-gloved, Christian hands. Pastor Ricky threw up a hand toward the deacon board, who sat somber in a row of pews that were perpendicular to the pulpit. One geriatric grandmother who walked with a severe limp, much worse than Momma's, came over to give Pastor Ricky a hug.

"We sho' do miss you up there, Pastor," she said in shaky voice. "Cain't nobody deliver the word like you use to, Pastor."

"Thank you, Mother Ethel. How is that leg treating you?" Pastor Ricky asked.

"Praise God, I still got one good one left and it's doing fine." She returned to her seat as the music geared up.

The service started innocuously enough. The a cappella renderings of the hymns were tiresome, with one choir member singing too high and another singing a different song entirely. I searched the hymnal for "Hey, Charles," which went on for a good five minutes, but the closest I could find was "A Charge to Keep I Have." There were the announcements, and then a choir song, followed by the sick-and-shut-in list, and another choir song.

Pastor Ricky sat limply beside me, his eyes to heaven and his lips moving silently. After the benevolent offering, there was an announcement that a guest vocalist would join the choir in the next song. My eyes also rolled to heaven. It was already after noon and I needed to hear something to appease the guilt I felt over hurting Cast Iron Kat and to make me feel better about Miss Lipstick's health. St. Luke's had its Communion service on the last Sunday, and since it was the last Sunday in July, we probably wouldn't be dismissed until after four. I did not want to hear another song.

A pixie-sized woman with squiggly black curls covering her head sauntered down the aisle. She was dressed from head to toe in white, as were many of the ladies in the service. Her two-piece suit was stark against the burgundy carpet and the burgundy pulpit, but complemented the altar that was decked out in white lace. She took her place at the piano that had not been in use and fiddled around with the keys. She played a chord, opened her mouth, and a big, glorious voice came forth. Gymnastic notes poured from her throat, and even the choir was in harmony. The vocalist delivered a masterpiece of intricacy about God's unconditional love and infinite forgiveness that had me on my feet and Pastor Ricky on his knees, both of us crying. The entire congregation was up and moving with the rhythm and cadence of the music, our bodies surplus instruments. I sang along with the vocalist, my voice cracking, hitting notes that didn't exist, but I felt alive. When she finally wrapped up after several encores, I was breathless.

By the time the church settled down, it was time for the visitors to introduce themselves. Six other people stood up, gave honor to God, who was the head of their lives, said their names and the churches from which they hailed. I stood up slowly, nervously, never having spoken in front of a large group.

"I'm Fla Frye, from Quincy," I said haltingly. "This is my friend, Pastor Ricky."

Pastor Ricky wasn't looking at me, as I was expecting him to. His attention was riveted on a woman who sat next to the visitor from Two Egg, Florida. The woman was golden-skinned, impeccably dressed in a black-and-white suit, and was enjoying herself as much as I was. When I mentioned Pastor Ricky's name, she turned to stare at him as the entire church had. She leaned down and spoke to a child — a most cherubic little girl with long pigtails and bows all over her head. She looked about six years old, was the spitting image of the woman, and was dressed in a bright pink princess dress. The little girl was trying to say something, but the woman whispered something in her ear and she quieted down.

"That's a cute little girl over there, huh, Pastor Ricky?" Pastor Ricky ogled the woman and the child.

"Pastor Ricky," I said softly. He didn't answer. The silence lengthened, so I settled back in my seat to hear the sermon.

The young pastor began speaking slowly. He directed the congregation to a passage of Scripture, which I couldn't find without the help of the index.

"He who is without friends must show himself friendly," the pastor said. I squirmed in my seat. The pastor opened his mouth and Miss Lipstick's words spilled out, about reaching out to people who didn't seem to deserve it. The pastor peppered his sermon with "say Amen" and "yes, Lawd." He primed the pump, bringing most of the congregation to its feet and piercing my heart.

I was deeply moved. I prayed for Miss Lipstick and Pastor Ricky and all those people who made Miss Lipstick's their second home. The service concluded around 2:30 p.m., but there was still Communion. The pastor allowed a brief respite for his preparation of the elements. Some people left and others stood around to talk to each other. The well-dressed lady couldn't leave fast enough. She gathered up the pretty little girl and practically pushed her toward the door. Pastor Ricky was on her heels. I had to run to keep up with him.

"Where are you going, Pastor Ricky?" I pulled on his arm to make him remember I was still there.

"Hold on, Fla. I'll be right back." I had always been Jasmine to him. My real name didn't even sound right coming out of his mouth.

"Peggy, wait!" Pastor Ricky yelled at the woman. His behavior was beyond strange. The woman burst through the church doors, dragging the little girl behind her. I was too far away to hear what they were saying, but a drama unfolded before me. Pastor Ricky caught up with them and seemed to be pleading with the woman. She put her hand in his face, and then pointed at the little girl. The girl was reaching for Pastor Ricky, but the woman held her back. Pastor Ricky grabbed the little girl, lifted her off the ground and hugged her, the way he had hugged me on Colored Street. The woman tore the child from his arms. They attracted the attention of some of the men, several of whom had to be approaching sixty, who intervened. When they put their hands on Pastor Ricky, it motivated me to intervene. A small hand came out of nowhere restraining me.

"That ain't no place for a child," Mother Ethel admonished me. "Let them men folks handle that. You ain't got no business being with that man anyway. It wasn't right what he did."

I wasn't particularly raised with manners, like putting handles on the names of grown folks, saying please and thank you, and not disrespecting my elders, but I knew it was something I shouldn't do. So, feeling helpless, I suppressed the comment that rose to my lips and watched Pastor Ricky's predicament. Four men held him back while another picked up the woman's child and escorted her to her car. Pastor Ricky looked every bit a broken man. He could have shouted and screamed, he could have wailed on the four men, who combined were not as strong as he was, but he remained composed. The men released him when the woman drove off in her car with the little girl. Pastor Ricky came back and pried me out of Mother Ethel's clutches.

"Let me walk you home, Jasmine," Pastor Ricky said. He didn't seem conscious of the events that had just transpired.

"Pastor Ricky! What was that? Who was that lady and little girl?" I felt a familiar tremor in my lip. Pastor Ricky pretended none of it had happened. His voice was cheerful, resigned.

"In due time, sweet Jasmine. You will know all," he said.

"No! I'm tired of people telling me they'll tell me later or I'll find out later. I'm not a child. I want to know now, Pastor Ricky. Not later today or tomorrow. Don't put me off anymore. I'm your friend, and I want to help you. Please!" I stomped my foot, emphasizing my desire to be strong for him, as he had been for me, and I couldn't do that blubbering like a fool.

Pastor Ricky closed his eyes and combed my face with his hands, like he was trying to remember it's every contour, every line, it's every mole. "You do deserve to know everything. You have been a good friend to me and a balm to my aching heart. For that, I'll love you forever."

"You're talking like you're going somewhere. You're just going to see your daddy, right? Where does he live?" I asked.

He laughed at me. Not a happy laugh, but one full of despair.

"Jasmine, you are so . . . wonderfully naïve and beautiful of spirit," he began in his preaching voice.

"Stop preaching to me, Pastor Ricky." I wasn't going to let him stall me today. He laughed again. For the first time, I regretted that no one else was around. The remaining church members had gone back inside for Communion, and we were the only souls outside on the grounds. Pastor Ricky sat on the bottom step and patted the spot next to him.

"Come sit by me, Jasmine. This is where it all began." He draped his arm around my shoulders and drew me closer to him.

"I was in love once. It was the purest kind of love," Pastor Ricky said.

"You're talking about that lady." I relished a good love story.

"I'm talking about God. When He called me, I answered. He took me out of the classroom and put me in the pulpit. That was something, 'cause I loved teaching. Did you know I was an English professor at FAMU?"

"Something like that. I bet you were the best."

"Filthy rags, Jasmine, filthy rags. He gave me everything. A good wife who loved me and a beautiful little girl who meant everything to me." He paused for a long time. "Her name is Jasmine."

"I thought so," I said. It had to be. Whenever he said that name, every letter was saturated with adoration.

"Yes," he said quietly. "But I let evil defile that perfect love. Evil and lust and covetousness." He chewed up each word. His eyes were closed tightly, but he couldn't stop the flow of tears.

"I thought I could handle it. I was doing a good job, hiding it from everybody. I had been wrestling with this problem for most of my life and I thought I'd overcome it. Then, in my office one day, I was praying for someone. I laid the holy hands God gave me on someone." Pastor Ricky surveyed his hands as if they belonged to another. Tears fell with abandon. "I was praying and we were crying and I was holding him and holding him and a lust overtook me." He had to breathe. "And I wasn't holding him like a man of God, just a man. I frightened him and he screamed and I hit him in my panic. I hit him and I didn't know what I was doing." Pastor Ricky grabbed his throat. "The church hushed it up, but I was thrown out of the pulpit. I lost everything, Jasmine. Everything." His voice broke and he unburdened his emotional debris all over my doily dress.

"You always preach forgiveness, Pastor Ricky," I offered, feeling a bit timid. "God will forgive you."

"I know He will. My ex-wife will forgive me in time. I can't forgive myself for all the pain I caused. That's the hardest part. I hurt my baby. I've been living in shame, hiding myself in drink. You see a person who hates everything around them, you can believe they started with themselves."

"You're supposed to forgive people. Your ex-wife should have forgiven you by now," I said. My self-righteousness would not allow me to be sympathetic with the woman he described.

"It's not as easy as it seems, Jasmine. You don't understand what I put her through." A fresh rack of sobs tore through his body. I, a child, held the man, and I was the strong one.

"It's okay, Pastor Ricky. I love you, no matter what. And Miss Lipstick loves you and I know your little girl loves you." I sensed I needed to keep talking. So I talked while I rocked him in my suddenly grown up arms.

"And your daddy. He must love you. We're going to see him. Promise me you'll be okay," I begged. "You have to promise me."

Pastor Ricky laughed a little. "My father. Yes."

"Let's go now and talk to your daddy and then come back to Miss Lipstick's with me. Everybody misses you. I miss you so much," I prattled on.

"Jasmine, here." Pastor Ricky picked up his well-worn, dog-eared Bible that smelled of his underarms and old beers past, and gave it to me. He was never without it.

"It's your preaching Bible. You want me to keep it for you?" I asked, thoroughly disconcerted. Did he hear anything I just said?

"No. I want you to have it. Read it and pray for me," he said.

"Pastor Ricky, what are you going to do without it? I don't think I should have this. It's too special." I wanted to get it out of my hands.

"It would make me immensely happy if you would take this. OK?" His puffy eyes were unreadable. I decided to keep it as a favor to him. I planned to take good care of it when he was ready to retrieve it.

I wanted to stay with him and continue to comfort him in his grief, but Pastor Ricky insisted I leave. He had to see his father alone. I left, but reluctantly and with a heavy heart. It was 3:30 in the afternoon. I glanced back at him, sitting alone on the church steps, his face in his hands. He grew smaller as I got farther away, and I hoped against hope he was talking about going to see a flesh-and-blood father.

/CHAPTER XV/

My jellies were caked with dirt by the time I got to the pass. A light mist kissed my skin. My head, my heart, and the large Bible I carried were all weighing me down. I desperately needed to forgive someone in my life, and I didn't know how to go about making that happen. It didn't matter how she treated me — I knew I had to clear my conscience.

I sat down on a rock under the bridge and could see right up into the sky through the hole. I propped the Bible up on my knees and started cruising through random chapters, stopping to rubberneck the chapters featuring the red words of Jesus. Suddenly, I heard feet above me, and to my surprise, it was not the sky I could see through the hole, but the beautiful and melancholy face of Cast Iron Kat. Our eyes locked and words of forgiveness stuck in my throat. With the sun beaming down over her head, she looked angelic — an angel in a tube top and green hot pants, carrying her book bag, as usual.

I stared up at her until the sun seemed to drop into the trees. Cast Iron Kat came down and stood over me on my rock.

"I'm sorry." The words came from somewhere.

"What for?" Cast Iron Kat asked.

I shrugged. I couldn't articulate what for. "Everything, I guess."

She made a move that took me aback. She sat down next to me.

"What you reading?" she asked.

"The Bible," I said and closed it up. I didn't know if I would be using it as a shield, a sword, or both.

"Oh." She ran her fingers through the dirt at her feet. The tension between us was palpable and supremely awkward.

"You still reading those murder books?" she asked.

"Oh, yeah. I read Agatha Christie all the time." Cast Iron Kat amazed me. She remembered, or at least almost, a book I had been reading weeks ago. This was not the bully I knew.

"You like to read, don't you? I guess that's why you so smart." She said it without resentment this time.

"I guess," I replied, trying to sound modest.

"I could be smart, too. But people don't think I'm supposed to be smart 'cause of the way I look." Cast Iron Kat was being unusually candid with me, but I had to agree with that statement. "I read, too, just not as much as you. See." She parted the top of her book bag, what I had always believed was her arsenal of torture, and pulled out our enormous English literature book. It was square and wide and it also had that well-worn look of having been read often. I was duly impressed.

"You've been reading that big thing?" I asked.

"It's the only book I got at home. I try to read a little bit every chance I get, and I have to come down here to do it. There's lots of folks at my house," she explained.

"Wow," was all I could say. That upset Cast Iron Kat.

"See, people don't take you serious when you pretty. All they see is what's on the outside. They don't care if you got anything real on the inside. You real lucky you ain't pretty, Fla," she said.

"Thanks, I think."

"I mean, just 'cause a girl pretty, people like her for just that and people don't like her for only that reason. The people that like her want to be around her all the time, I guess thinking the pretty gon' rub off. And the men." She shook her head vigorously and sighed deeply. "They just want to get in my draws."

Cast Iron Kat started to cry, softly and pitifully. I felt bad. I felt really bad. She even cried pretty. Her nose just wrinkled up and perfect tears flowed down her high cheekbones. I wanted to comfort her, but deep down, I was one of those people who didn't like her. I was grateful that she bullied me as it gave me justification for despising her. I forced myself to realize what I had willfully ignored before — that girl was as beautiful inside as she was on the outside. It crossed my mind to ease my guilt by consoling her, but her next words changed that decision.

"They always touching me, like they got a right," she continued. She shuddered, as if feeling the thousands of hands and eyes that were constantly on her. "Even teachers look at me different. They don't think I know nothing. They treat me like I'm dumb. Like Mr. Pierce. When he be pushing you up in my face, it make me mad. I can be as smart as you. I want to be as smart as you. I feel like I wish I was more like you, Fla."

"Ugly but smart," I said sarcastically.

"Yeah. You got it easy." She stood up, and I scrutinized her closely. She was gorgeous from afar, but up close, she was breathtaking. There was a reason people were so smitten by her. I rather liked her as bully. I wouldn't have to confront the idea that she was probably a really nice person under all that physical perfection. It was a concept I had to learn to accept.

"You can be whatever you want, Kat," I said.

"My name is Katherine." She smiled at me, its warmth rivaling the setting sun.

"OK, Katherine. What do you want to be?" I expected her to name any number of the glamorous professions that required beauty like hers — model, actress, TV anchor.

"I want to be a zookeeper." She said it with a straight face — a sweet, serene face.

"Really?"

"Yeah. I love animals and I like books about animals. But looks like it ain't never gonna happen. So, I don't think about it much. I'm scared to dream about it. I'll probably end up like my sister — pretty but with six kids 'cause she got to have one for every man she meet. I don't want to end up a nothing, Fla."

Her words struck a resounding chord in me. I reached for her hand. "You won't. I'll help you. Let's start with English," I said.

She viewed my hand like I was offering her a lit stick of dynamite. "You mean it?"

"I mean it." When she took my hand, I knew I had a friend, my very first friend.

"You know I gotta pass them other tests or I'm gonna be left back again." We walked toward the projects together, our respective books in our hands. Katherine aired her concerns and I felt them for her.

"Then let's start studying today. I'll change and come to your house," I said.

"It's too many people at my house," Katherine said. "We won't be able to hear nothing."

"We can't do it at my house either." I couldn't say more, but she understood.

"Okay. Let's do it on the landing and the stairs at mine." Katherine's voice was upbeat and that made me feel good, until I got home.

Momma was propped in her permanent spot on the couch, her hand curled around a beer can. She liked Colt 45. I walked to the refrigerator to see if there was anything to eat. I saw instead a six-pack of those tall, silver cans and a lone one in the back nestled between a pack of molded cheese and half a jar of jelly. I reached in for the jelly, but I pulled out the beer instead. I hid the beer among the pages of the Bible and pretended to read while I walked to my room. Momma hardly noticed anything I ever did, but, I expected her to notice the beer can was being taken away the way Jesus felt virtue leaving his body when the woman with the issue of blood touched him out of the crowd.

I hustled to my room. I put the Bible under the bed where it joined the college manual. I studied the can of beer. What was it about the liquid in this cylinder that held such power over so many people? It was nice and cool in my hand, though. I remembered the helplessness I had been feeling lately and the urge to pop the tab was very strong, but I didn't want to keep Cast Iron Kat — I meant Katherine, waiting. I put the beer under my bed and changed.

As I walked out the door with my English literature text and one other book, Momma didn't ask where I was going so late in the evening. She was scouring the refrigerator.

"I had another beer in here. You seen it?"

"Jerome must have taken it!" I said, my pulse racing.

"Oh, yeah." If Jerome took it, it was all right with Momma.

I arrived at Katherine's apartment thirty minutes after we left the pass. She was right. Her apartment was crowded. There were chocolate-skinned children of various ages, from about two to nine, in various stages of filth, hanging around the door. The youngest child's diaper was sagging down to her knees. The boys were playing rough at the entrance. I could see grown men and women sandwiched inside the tiny space watching wrestling on a TV the size of a breadbox. Between the children and the adults yelling at the screen to put him in a chokehold, it was extremely noisy. A man with long dread locks and a pencil mustache, wearing a T-shirt and khaki shorts, came out to greet me. He ignored the children and leaned on the doorframe.

"Hey," he said too enthusiastically. "What's your name?" He looked at me the way Jerome did. I didn't think my appearance called for such a greeting. I was wearing an oversized T-shirt and a pair of jeans I had to pin up at my waist.

"Fla. Is Katherine here?" I yelled above the din. I pressed my book to my chest, hoping it would halt his x-ray eyes.

"Katherine. Ain't no Katherine here," he said, still gawking at me.

"She talking 'bout me, Daddy. Go back in there and watch wrestling." Katherine spoke to him as if he were an errant child. He turned his focus on her, the admiration for her unmistakable. Katherine had changed also, into a T-shirt that was a size too small and revealed the lower part of her flat belly. She had squeezed herself into some tight jeans. Her assets caught the attention of every man in the place.

"Who your fine friend here? Where y'all going, Kat?" he asked as he slid his arm around her shoulders. Katherine removed the arm and pushed him away.

"You don't need to know who she is. We going to study on the steps. Tell Valencia to get her kids in the house and change that baby diaper." She must have been immune to the unfatherly way her daddy devoured her with his eyes. He popped her on the butt and joined his company. Katherine rolled her eyes.

"Come on, Fla," she said to me.

"Can I come with y'all, Kat?" a four-year-old girl asked. She was a lovely child with wild, curly locks all over her head. She was the spitting image of someone I thought I held dear to me.

"Cast, Kat, Katherine," I began. It was a struggle to remember we were involved in a new dynamic somewhere between friends and enemies. In order to maintain whatever it was, I had to ask a question that was never far from my thoughts.

"What!" she barked. Her fierce response was the result of her pulling on the little girl, who was determined to have her way. I jumped nevertheless.

"Whose little girl is that?"

"This Shay Shay. She one of Valencia's kids. Who do she look like?" Her words, though not mocking, still teased me.

"She looks like Randy," I admitted.

"That's her daddy," said Katherine. "I know you like him and all, but he got babies with everybody."

This information didn't surprise me, but it burst my fantasy about Randy with finality. There was still one more question that needed an answer.

"Have you ever been with him? I mean, like . . .,"

"I know what you mean. And no, I ain't been with him. I don't go with everybody like people think. You think that about me?"

I shrugged my shoulders. Of course I did. It was easier to think that way to keep the dislike of her healthy and alive. "I guess 'cause of the way the boys are always following you and stuff. But I don't anymore. I promise."

She seemed to accept my apology. At the same time, she was prepared to swat Shay Shay on her behind.

"Go play, girl!" The little girl held her head down and walked away dejected. I felt bad for her.

"She can help us a little," I said.

"She just gon' be in the way. She ask too many questions!" Katherine was unrelenting.

"Well, a good student asks a lot of questions." Katherine's expression said touché, so she grabbed the little girl by the hand and dragged her down the stairs behind her.

"You sit here and be quiet, Shay Shay! OK!"

Shay Shay's eyes lit up. "OK. I won't say nothing."

Katherine and I spent the next three hours going through the textbook. Deep red indentations in our knees were visible where we held the book up. Little Shay Shay asked questions every other minute, but we got through the sections we would be tested on. I saw realization dawn in Katherine's eyes as she began to understand the material. I gave her the other book, a fictional tale about animals in the jungle. The gratitude that came out of that girl that day, I will remember the rest of my life.

When I was ready to leave, it was dark and the streetlights had come on.

"Want me to walk you home?" Katherine's daddy offered.

"She don't need you to do nothing! Leave her alone!" Katherine rebuked her father.

"Girl, you just as fine as your momma was. We had some good times." He chuckled softly, stroking his barely there mustache.

"You know my momma?" I asked.

"Your momma and her friend, Millie. They was some good time girls! We stayed in trouble. Ask Millie." He licked his lips in remembrance of those days.

"Millie is my momma," I corrected him.

"Millie ain't your momma, girl! You don't know who your momma is? Betty, come over here!" Katherine's father yelled to someone in the house. "This girl don't know who her momma is!"

"So," a disembodied voice answered. "You don't know who half your children is!"

"Go home, Fla," Katherine instructed me. "Ignore my daddy. He drunk and he don't know what he talking about. I'll see you at school tomorrow."

He may have been drunk, but his words lingered in my mind. I wasn't ready to find out if they were true or not.

/CHAPTER XVI/

Summer school would end in eight days, and I was excited to know what it felt like not to have an anvil hanging over my head. I floated into the classroom like a detached bird's feather, actually anticipating this new chapter in my relationship with Katherine. Her clique obviously was not informed that we'd called a truce. They bore down on me like locusts and hemmed me up in a corner the minute I stepped into Mr. Pierce's class.

"You don't do that to Kat," said Myra, the head follower. One of the girls relieved me of my weighty book bag while the other prepared me to become a punching bag. My body instinctively attempted to curl into a fetal position. I saw a flash of fist and nothing else.

"Leave her alone," I heard Katherine's voice say.

"We don't like what she did to you. Let us handle her for you." Myra was drooling.

"You ain't got to do nothing for me. I said leave the girl alone." Katherine raised her voice another octave.

The girls cleared out as Mr. Pierce came in.

"Ladies, take a seat." He hummed to himself and unloaded his bag of books. I sent Katherine a look of gratitude. She acknowledged with a nod. She took out her book and opened it to the section we were discussing that day. Katherine's hand shot up on many questions, and she answered most of them correctly.

"Miss Morehead, you are full of surprises today." I prayed he wouldn't mention my name. He would just ruin it.

"I been . . . I mean, I've been studying with Fla. She helped me a lot." Every mouth in the room fell open. I couldn't resist finding Myra's face and giving her a silent "nana nana na na."

"Well, I'm glad to hear that. Keep up the good work, Miss Morehead." This time, Katherine gave me a look of gratitude.

I would have had lunch with her and the crew, but they weren't ready to break bread with me yet. I was OK with that. What I wasn't OK with was the comment Katherine's father had made the day before.

Miss Lipstick wasn't feeling well again when I went by the house. Mr. Curtis was conspicuously absent, and Phyllis was a no-show. Without them, the house seemed empty. It was a light day — everyone must have been out doing their own thing.

I knocked tentatively on Miss Lipstick's door.

"Miss Lipstick, I'm here," I announced. "Can I come in?"

"No, baby. Lipstick need to sleep." Her voice was weaker than I'd ever heard it.

"Miss Lipstick, somebody told me that Millie ain't my momma." I heard scrambling inside the room and shuffling at the door. Miss Lipstick opened it with a flourish.

"Get in here!" she ordered.

I walked into her inner sanctum not knowing what I expected to find. It was a small room painted baby blue, and it had one window. Her favorite multi-colored dress hung on a closet door. A lone, overstuffed dresser was littered with old jewelry, packs of unopened cigarettes and at least three handfuls of crumpled bills. The bed, covered by a handmade quilt, was caved in around the center. The nightstand was adorned with three single cigarettes, a small red lamp, a sleeve of condoms, with which I'd become acquainted thanks to Momma's carelessness, and a square silver frame holding the picture of a young girl. The girl looked about eight, wore pigtails, and had a smile I had not seen in years.

I held up the picture and looked at Ms. Lipstick. She was looking at me.

"What do you want to know?" she asked, her arms folded.

"This is me in the picture. I don't remember wearing my hair like that, but . . ."

"What do you want to know, gal?" Miss Lipstick repeated. "Now, I'm tired. I need to rest." On the floor, beside her nightstand, were ten or so bottles of pills — blue bottles, red bottles, tall bottles, and fat bottles. The labels were turned away so I couldn't see what they were for. Momma took a lot of pills, too. I suspected she didn't need most of them.

"It's just that, people have been saying . . ." I was distracted by her mini-pharmacy. I thought she had a bad cough, but the presence of so much medicine meant there was something more.

"Miss Lipstick, what's wrong with you? Are you really, really sick?" Miss Lipstick crawled back into bed and reached for one of the cigarettes on the nightstand. She lit it, dragged, and coughed.

"Yeah, baby," she said between gasps. "Nothing for you to worry about, though. Is that what you wanted to ask me?"

"No. That picture. Pastor Ricky said ... and then Katherine's daddy said . . ." I could not organize my thoughts into any cohesive, literate form. I kept looking at the picture with the pigtails. Miss Lipstick's eyes followed mine. Thoughts tumbled over themselves in my head — unconnected thoughts and phrases. Something was there, in front of me, but the harder I looked, the less I saw. The pills and the pictures all fit into some cosmic jigsaw puzzle. I wasn't sure I had all the pieces.

"Hey, there Lipstick! How you doing?" Phyllis breezed in and brought a spiritual ointment with her. Miss Lipstick's coughing and gasping eased up a degree.

"Not good, Phyllis. Not good," Miss Lipstick wheezed out.

Phyllis turned her attention to me. "Come on, gorgeous. Lipstick needs her rest. Y'all can talk later." She ushered me out of the room and closed the door soundly behind us. The coughing continued.

"Phyllis, how sick is she?" I knew Miss Lipstick wanted to protect me from something. "She won't tell me anything."

"Real sick," Phyllis answered somberly.

"She could die?" I didn't want to know the answer to that question.

"We all gonna die, someday," Phyllis answered flippantly.

"You know what I mean, Phyllis." My tolerance level for the little girl treatment had been maxed out.

"It's like this, baby doll. Lipstick is tough and she ain't gonna let nothing beat her down. She's been through worse than this. A lot worse."

"You're saying she's gonna be all right?" I locked in on Phyllis's eyes. She looked around furtively. I could tell by the way she carefully chose her words that she wasn't telling me the whole truth.

"I'm saying, Lipstick will get up out of that bed if she have to."

"OK." I swallowed her bill of goods. The hug she gave me did not put me at ease. When we separated, she headed to the back porch while I went to the kitchen to get my book and a soda I had in the refrigerator. The soda was at the back of the refrigerator surrounded by a fortress of beer bottles, brown and cold and inviting. The soda receded further to the back and one of the bottles moved forward, inching toward my waiting hand. This time, I deliberately reached for the beer. I closed my fingers around it and fondled its long, cool, elegant neck. I took it and sneaked out of the house. My dormant beer gene had finally, fully awakened.

I slipped the beer up my shirt, which sent shivers through my entire body. I camouflaged the bulge with my book and bolted from the house. My heart pounded against my chest so hard and loud I thought it might cause the bottle to implode. I was not out of the sphere of danger, the one square mile encompassing Miss Lipstick's house. If she caught me with that beer, she would skin me alive. I kept checking over my shoulder, certain there were phantom footsteps behind me. At the end of the block, when it seemed prudent to make a dash for home, I saw a blue-and-white, City-of-Quincy issued, police car driving slowly behind me. Panic didn't set in until I turned a corner and the police car turned, too. I didn't commit any illegal acts that day, not if I didn't count being underage and drinking alcohol and stealing a beer from an unlicensed vendor. The adrenaline that only abject terror can produce surged through me, and I began to hyperventilate. The police car sped up a bit and pulled up at the curb alongside me. The officer at the wheel leaned forward. It was Officer Larry, the young policeman who old, drunken Mr. Curtis had body-slammed.

"Hey there, little lady," he said gaily, his black face shiny with perspiration. "Can I talk to you a minute?"

Miss Lipstick and the porch dwellers schooled me early on situations like this — never speak voluntarily to a Quincy cop because you'll be confessing to the murder of Jimmy Hoffa. The officer smiled at me pleasantly. He was quite good-looking and I probably would have ignored Miss Lipstick's sage advice if I hadn't seen Calvin Walters trying to conceal his large frame in the back seat. His eyes met mine briefly — they were vacant. Then he looked away.

"Stop for a minute. This won't take long," Officer Larry said as he got out of the car.

"What's this about?" I asked, frightened out of my mind.

"Just come over here. I want to ask you a few questions. No need to be scared." Officer Larry advanced toward me and I tore out. The beer bottle tumbled from underneath my shirt and exploded on the sidewalk, coating my library book with its contents. The wreckage I left behind was the least of my worries. I ran while I looked behind me. The muscles in my throat had tightened, and I couldn't scream. Officer Larry tried to catch me, yelling something about "don't run" as he increased his pace. He was gaining on me as I sprinted forward. Suddenly, I collided with a big, black tree that sprouted in the middle of the sidewalk and fell back on my adequately cushioned rump. When I looked up, I saw

Root Charlie blocking the sun. Phyllis stepped out from behind him.

"Come on in the house," she said. I curled up under her small arm and held her rigidly as we walked hurriedly back inside.

"Gal? What's going on out there?" Miss Lipstick was up and out of her room. She had settled into Mr. Curtis's corner.

I couldn't catch my breath, and before I could answer, Officer Larry burst in with Root Charlie on his heels.

"Call him off, Lipstick. I don't want no trouble," Officer Larry said, eyeing Root Charlie, who loomed far above the officer. Officer Larry had grasped his side arm.

"Why you bothering this girl?" Miss Lipstick demanded. Root Charlie didn't move from the officer's side. Officer Larry didn't take his eyes off Root Charlie.

"I just need to ask her about an incident involving personal property, that's all." Officer Larry said.

"What personal property? This girl don't mess with other people's stuff," Miss Lipstick said. I certainly didn't know what he was talking about.

"I have a complaint here from a Mr. Calvin Walters that she and Ricky Sullivan scratched up his Mercedes on Friday, July 9," Officer Larry read from a small notebook he'd pulled out of his pocket.

"Miss Lipstick, I didn't . . ." I started to defend myself.

"Hush, now, gal," Miss Lipstick admonished me. "I know you ain't done nothing." To the officer she said, "That's almost three weeks ago now. Why y'all just now coming with this mess? Where this Calvin Walters? Bring him in here."

At Miss Lipstick's command, Root Charlie headed toward the door.

"Let Larry bring him in, Charlie. Just hold on." Root Charlie obeyed. Officer Larry left the house for about five minutes. During that time, I tried to explain to Miss Lipstick about my encounter with Calvin Walters, but she didn't want to hear anything. I assumed she was still ticked off at me for meeting him behind her back.

When Calvin Walters finally entered Miss Lipstick's house, he did so quite reluctantly. Officer Larry was practically pulling him in by the sleeve.

"Lipstick," Mr. Walters addressed Miss Lipstick stiffly.

"Calvin," Miss Lipstick responded, bitterness and something I couldn't fathom dripping from her tongue. "What you want with her?"

Calvin Walters was afraid of Miss Lipstick, just like Momma was afraid of her. As big as he was, he was brought down to size just by the tone of Miss Lipstick's voice. He did not look at her, and he wouldn't even turn his body in my direction. He was like a child, standing in Miss Lipstick's presence with his hands shoved deep into his pockets. His dark blue suit was immaculate, complete with the handkerchief peeking out from the breast pocket. I would have found him quite the dashing father if he hadn't turned my stomach.

"Lipstick," Calvin Walters answered softly. "I wasn't planning on doing anything, but India was upset about the scratch. I was going to let it go." He spoke perfect English.

"India?" Miss Lipstick asked disdainfully.

"Somebody scratched up the side of my car and left a brick by the front wheel," he continued.

"So what's that got to do with her?" I stood there in the middle of the room, but they both spoke as if I wasn't there. "Why you bothering her?"

"She came to my office with Rick about three weeks ago. He was out of control. I couldn't find Ricky, but I knew where she would be." He jerked his head toward me. My mind flashed back to Pastor Ricky and that brick, but I kept my mouth closed and my ears open.

"She," Miss Lipstick said. "That ain't no she. You can't say it. That's your daughter, boy. Say it!" Miss Lipstick displayed more energy than she had in a few days. Her anger was driving her.

"Now, I don't want to keep going over this same old territory. There's no proof I'm the father. You know she was out there . . ."

Calvin Walters couldn't even finish the sentence before Root Charlie pinched his neck in a lobster-like hold. I missed Miss Lipstick's signal.

"You say one more word about . . ." Miss Lipstick paused and glanced over at me for the first time. "Ain't nobody got to prove nothing to you. Just look at this girl. You know she yours, you lying coward, you!" Miss Lipstick's redbone complexion was burning hot.

Officer Larry seemed confused about what to do. Calvin Walters cringed under Root Charlie's hold.

"Tell him to let him go, Lipstick!" he ordered Miss Lipstick. Her keen stare communicated a message to Calvin Walters, which he understood very well, and in turn, got him a reprieve from Root Charlie's grasp. It didn't, however, stop him from completing his mission to find out what happened to his vehicle.

"I'm not here for that. I just need to know from her if Rick messed up my car." Calvin Walters exhibited no warmth for me. I could have been any stranger off the street. He turned to Officer Larry. "I need you to do your job, sir. Go ahead and ask her."

"Officer Larry, you need to step outside a little while," Miss Lipstick said. "You got my word Root Charlie won't hurt him bad." She said that last word so softly I almost didn't hear it. Officer Larry seemed only too happy to grant her this request.

"Go in my room and bring me that box under my bed," Miss Lipstick told me. I did and crouched down under the bed. I found old, ratty slippers, dust-covered photo albums and a shoebox that was crumbling. I brought it to Miss Lipstick.

"I got a birth certificate in here that you need to sign," Miss Lipstick said matter-of-factly.

"I'm not signing anything," Calvin Walters said steadfastly.

"OK. You got a choice then. You either sign this birth certificate and start paying this gal some child support, fifteen years worth, or I go to your boss on your job and tell him what I know. You ain't always been an upstanding young man." Miss Lipstick pulled from a plastic sleeve a document that was perfectly preserved. She began rooting around in the box for a writing instrument as if there was no question he would sign.

"I'm not signing anything!" Calvin Walters repeated, his calm demeanor crumbling before me. He looked the way I felt when Officer Larry pulled up beside me — nauseous.

"You know I know people up there at the City Hall. How you think that boss man of yours gonna feel about one of his top money men not taking care of his children? If you can't take care of your personal stuff, how he supposed to believe you can take care of city stuff?"

"All right!" Calvin Walters fairly screamed. "All right. I'll sign the damn paper. But I don't want to hear nothing else about this from you."

"I'll shut up when you show me you set up the account for her and that it's good and gonna take care of her for the next few years." Miss Lipstick sported a sly grin. "Your daughter going to college. You know my banker. Set it up through him. When he tell me it's done, my lips closed about it forever. Don't try to fool me, Calvin. You'll regret it."

Calvin Walters snatched the birth certificate out of Miss Lipstick's hand, scribbled on it furiously, and stormed out of her house. He nearly slapped the screen door off its hinges.

"Oh, Calvin!" Miss Lipstick yelled out at him. "Tell India you couldn't find out who scratched the car! I don't want to hear about this no more, either!" Calvin Walters had disappeared down the street, but I'm sure he heard every word she said.

"Can I see that?" I asked Miss Lipstick about the birth certificate.

"Not yet!" She replaced the contents of the shoebox and put the top back on. She inched slowly back to her room — very, very slowly.

I sighed deeply. "Phyllis?"

"Don't ask me. I'm out of here." Phyllis was true to her word. I was left alone with Root Charlie, who'd moved back to his chair as quietly as a mouse.

"Did I do something wrong?" I asked myself a rhetorical question.

"Nope," Root Charlie muttered. His answer encouraged me to go on.

"Why do things keep happening to me?" I asked.

"'Cause you alive," Root Charlie said simply.

"How can I make the bad things stop?"

"You just die." Root Charlie said, and then closed his eyes. I firmly believed that beer I stole was the catalyst for that entire incident, but it only made me more determined to find out what other powers liquor possessed.

/CHAPTER XVII/

Conversation in my house was reduced to grunts and bodily noises. I clung to my anger at Momma and Jerome for their embarrassing behavior. I never had a boy show me any interest, and they'd run off the one I thought I wanted the most. I was still surprised that Randy could be so easily put off. I was also still reeling at being twice-rejected by Calvin Walters. I scrambled for anything to get me out of bed on those days.

I was a pale imitation of myself. I didn't know who I was anymore, or whose I was. I studied my reflection in the mirror. There was something dead behind my eyes. This was life? This was what I had to look forward to? Everywhere I turned, people were pushing me away. When I found a reason to get up in the morning, there were at least ten more campaigning for me to give up. If ever there was a time to drown my sorrows in something, this was it.

There was one reason, though, that gave me a glimmer of joy. Jerome had made himself scarce again the last few days. I assumed he had fallen victim to Momma's plan of smothering a man to death by the three-month point of their courtship. In every relationship Momma had gone through three phases — acceptance, when the man took everything she gave him and some things she hadn't; bargaining, when she begged him not to leave her; and denial, when she couldn't believe he'd left her. Those phases were as predictable as the fact that Momma would drink herself into oblivion on the first of the month. What was unpredictable, though, was that Jerome terminated the relationship three weeks ahead of schedule. It must have had something to do with one of their last arguments after they ran Randy off. It was so violent, their voices woke me up out of a sound sleep. All I heard was Momma pleading, "Don't do it, Jerome!" He retorted with something unintelligible about her giving him a gift.

After that, she became like a ghost and stumbled around the house like an insect in its death throes. I stayed out of Momma's way as much as possible during her mourning period, but after Jerome left, she acted like a woman unhinged. She burst into my room periodically through the morning and afternoon just to glare at me. Once I felt compelled to defend myself.

"I didn't do anything!" I said.

"Did I say you did something?" she snapped. She slammed the door, and then opened it again. "You still seeing that boy!"

"No." I wanted to tell her he would probably never want to see me either because of her.

"You better keep them legs close. If you get pregnant by anybody, I'll stomp you and that baby in the ground!" She slammed my door, then went to her room and slammed her door.

I didn't know where all that came from. It was my cue to get out and hide in the library. I grabbed my recent acquisitions and tiptoed to the front door. I wasn't quiet enough.

"Where you going?" Momma demanded. She'd seemed obsessed with my whereabouts lately. She had previously been disinterested in me, period.

"To the library. These books are due today." I looked inside the jacket cover of the book on top of the stack and discovered the books were due in two days, on Saturday, July 31. "I'll have to pay a fine if I don't get them back right away." I waited to see if any parental instructions would follow. Since there were none, I left with my arms full of books.

I took a slight detour to Miss Lipstick's house. On my way, I thought about Pastor Ricky. I wanted to visit him but I didn't know where he lived. I felt a tugging in my spirit I couldn't explain. Usually, when I conjured him up, he showed up shortly thereafter.

As I neared Miss Lipstick's house, I saw Phyllis running toward me. A smile automatically came to my face.

"Phyllis," I said, still smiling. Phyllis was out of breath.

"Hey, gorgeous," she said between great gulps of air.

"I was just coming to Miss Lipstick's. Have you seen Pastor Ricky lately?" Phyllis seemed to know everything.

Phyllis didn't answer me. A weird expression I couldn't read covered her face. I ventured a guess.

"Is something wrong with him?" She still didn't answer.

"Phyllis, what's wrong with Pastor Ricky?" My heart sank. Phyllis put a hand on my shoulder and squeezed.

"Sweetie, ain't no pretty way to tell you this." Her eyes misted up. "Pastor Ricky dead."

Every book in my arms fell to my feet. I didn't feel the pain in my toes until much later.

"Are you OK?" I heard Phyllis ask. She positioned herself at my side, as if she expected me to keel over. I had no answer for her this time. I didn't know what I was feeling. My whole body was on pause.

"What happened?" a disembodied voice asked.

"He stepped in front of a train this morning," she said softly.

"My train?"

"What's that, baby? If you want to cry, it's OK. I know you loved him." Phyllis' voice sounded like it was in a jar.

"But that was my train." A giant wall rose up in my psyche, insulating me from this tragic news. Pastor Ricky wasn't dead. He took my train, and he left me just like all the others. Worse yet, he destroyed the image of the train that was supposed to take me away from this miserable life. He stole my train.

"He stole my train," I kept saying. Phyllis was definitely worried. She took me by the shoulders and shook me hard.

"You gotta come back to me, now. Pastor Ricky is gone, honey. He didn't take no train. The train took him."

"Nooo," I wailed. "He's gone. But who's gonna call me Jasmine? I was his Jasmine, his black Jasmine. He said so." I put my palm to my forehead, as the wall came crashing down like thunder, leaving an incredible pain in its wake.

In a dream-like state, I watched Phyllis pick up my books. She was holding on to me.

"I want to see him. When's the funeral?"

Phyllis stopped. "Uh, sweetie. There ain't gonna be no funeral, just a memorial. You don't need to go anyway. Just remember him like he was." She clutched my arm firmly. After that, she must have walked me home. I didn't remember walking with her. I didn't remember going inside the apartment. I didn't remember removing that can of beer from where I'd stored it under my bed not long ago.

My memory returned when I began choking on that warm beer after I turned it vertical down my throat. It tasted weird. I retrieved three more cold ones from the fridge. I didn't care if Momma got upset and I wasn't afraid of what she'd do to me. She must have been somewhere scouring back alleys looking for Jerome because she was not at home.

The guilt that lay on me as a result of Pastor Ricky's death was like a concrete blanket. If I doused myself pretty good, maybe I could slide out from underneath it. So, I drank. The second can was cool going down. The buzz was slight at first. By the third cold one, I believed I could fly. In my dreams, I did. I swooped in and tried to rescue Pastor Ricky before the train obliterated him. I tried several times, from different angles, but I always dropped him. I couldn't save him. The next morning, I was soaked from a combination of tears and spilled beer. Pastor Ricky's Bible was open upside down on my chest, some of the pages wet. I sniffed my shirt — it was soaked with vomit.

Like a hollow, mechanical robot, I left my bed, but I ran to the bathroom. My equilibrium was off and I banged into the walls in the hallway. I threw up again, all over myself and the toilet. My head felt like it was stuffed with cotton.

My stomach was boiling. My vision was hazy. I managed to draw myself a bath and dumped half a bottle of bubble bath into the steaming, hot water. I teetered on the edge of the tub and watched the water rise. I removed my clothes with great difficulty and plopped myself into the suds, splashing water everywhere.

The hot water was calming and soothed my aching body. My mind was still cloudy with frenzied thoughts that bounced around my head unchecked. It hit me again that Pastor Ricky was gone. But he shouldn't have been. I still had his Bible. Didn't he promise me that he'd come back for it?

I slid down in the tub until the water level was just below my chin. "Pastor Ricky, how could you?" I asked the fly on the wall. How could he ruin my romantic image of the train? How could he leave me like that? Who was going to call me Jasmine?

I sank a little lower in the tub. The back of my hair was wet. Who would miss me? Just a little water over my mouth and nose, and I'd be out of my misery like Pastor Ricky. No one would miss me, I told myself, as more of my face was covered by water.

"I need to come in there, Fla!" Momma said, beating on the door like a maniac. I choked and coughed, nearly swallowing a mouthful of water. "What you doing in there?" she asked.

"Nothing," I spluttered. "Nothing."

"Come outta there! Some girl name Katherine came over here!" Momma yelled through the door. Her voice and the mention of Katherine cut through the drunken haze and made me realize what I was doing. I stayed in the tub until the water became cold and my skin the texture of a raisin. The smells of my drinking binge reminded me of Momma's parties. I was disgusted with myself.

I sat around the house all day in a zombie-like state, with Momma ranting and raving about Jerome and cussing about her missing beer. I understood why she slept so much. That beer took a lot out of me. It didn't erase the pain of losing Pastor Ricky or the guilty knowledge that I was responsible for his death. I could have done something different. I could have said something different. I never should have left him. Maybe I should have drunk more.

"You drunk my beer!" Momma accused me. "It had to be you. You better put my stuff back. I don't care how you get it. Ask Lipstick for it, whatever. You know I don't play that!"

I was too far gone to allow her anger to affect me. Getting out of the house seemed like a good idea, though. Going to Miss Lipstick's in the shape I was in, was not. I would try to find Katherine.

I held on to the railing outside for dear life. My footsteps were not as steady as I would have liked them to be. It was late in the afternoon, but still very hot. The sun drummed into me and heightened my loss of control. Katherine lived perhaps two minutes away from me. It took me all of ten minutes to get over there. Her little nieces and nephews were outside playing in the dirt and recognized me immediately. God bless the pure hearts of children — I looked the same to them.

"Kat, that girl here!" one little boy yelled at the top of his lungs. I stood still, afraid I would fall over on the children.

Katherine came out of the apartment and down the stairs. I was good and drunk, but I didn't think the hallucinations would be so strong. Katherine glided down the stairs, gracefully like a swan, resplendent in a purple blouse that almost covered her entire upper body, and a pair of white capris that left her a little room to breathe. Her hair was down and hung loose around her shoulders. I reached out to touch it, and it was as fine as silk.

"That you, Katherine?" I couldn't believe my hung-over eyes.

"That you, Fla?" Katherine asked. I didn't check out my ensemble before I left the house, but I was sure I was a wreck.

"Mm, hm," I responded. Suddenly, a large belch formed in my body and I released it with no warning. Even though I had scrubbed myself mercilessly, the air around me revealed my secret shame.

"What happened to you, girl?" She sniffed hard and pinched her nose. "Ooh, you stink! You smell like you fell in a beer keg. Come on." She turned me away from the children and marched me toward the pass. She had to hold me up most of the way. We found a dry spot on the embankment, in the same place a lifetime ago where she'd thrown my Agatha Christie book.

"I'm like Mr. Pierce now. What's going on with you and don't tell me nothing." Her tone was serious. I couldn't speak.

"You drunk as a skunk, Fla. That ain't like you."

"So you know me now," I lashed out. "You don't know me like you think you do. If I want to take a little drink, I can. I'm grown." I could hear Johnny's voice coming out of my throat, but I was powerless to stop it.

"I'm just trying to help you, girl," Katherine said. She couldn't hide the hurt. "You don't need to talk to me like that."

"You don't know what I'm going through. You can't judge me." I couldn't stand myself, I was so ornery, but I had stripped myself of all dignity.

"You ain't the only one going through stuff, Fla. But if you start this drinking, you gon' end up like them people at my house and the ones hanging out in the street." Katherine searched my face. "You got what it takes to get outta here and do something with your life. People looking up to you."

"What for?" I wanted to lie down right there in the dirt I was so tired. "I ain't no different than the rest of y'all. I wanna stay right here in Quincy and work at TG&Y and have babies and . . . and."

A mean expression covered Katherine's face. "That's what you think the rest of us want? That's not what I want. I want to go to college. I want to be something. But you got the best chance of all of us and you just want to throw it away 'cause life ain't perfect."

"You want what I got," I said to her. "Then take it. And I'll take what you got. I want to be pretty and popular and stupid so nobody will expect so much from me. Who do you think you are to tell me that junk!"

Katherine reared back as if I'd slapped her. "I thought I was your friend." She stood up. "I guess I was wrong." I was alone for a while before I even noticed. It would be even longer before I realized what I had done to my friend.

The sun was dropping in the sky. I contemplated again going to Miss Lipstick's, but I still had enough sense to stay away from there. I decided to go in the opposite direction of her home and take a leisurely stroll through town to clear my head. One run-down home after another lined the streets. People sat out on their porches and waved at me. Regardless of how hard their lives seemed to be, they were always hospitable and friendly. I walked further uptown to the courthouse square, where the entire block was the local courthouse. It was an enormous square building, constructed of yellow bricks with grand turrets on the top. I circled the block a couple of times, believing I was sober enough to function as my old self. It had grown dark and I was just a few yards away from the courthouse when headlights illuminated the night. A car that was spitting and spluttering pulled up next to me.

"Hey, girl. Where you been?" It was Randy. I'd know his voice anywhere.

"Hey, Randy," I said. I leaned against the driver's side door of his car, which rattled violently and shook me like a baby's toy.

"Oh, Fla. Get in, girl." He jerked his head toward the seat next to him.

I slid into the passenger's side of the car. Although the car was obviously something he pieced together from other car parts, the inside was immaculate and shined up like a new showroom vehicle. His pride in it was evident.

"So, where you going this time of night?" he asked in a suave manner.

"Huh?" I asked. I could barely hear him over the loud engine.

Randy raised his voice above the noise. "I said where you going?"

"Oh, nowhere." I said. The shaking and the stirring inside the car were creating a storm in my stomach.

"You wanna go somewhere and park?" he asked.

"Uh, uh. Can you just take me home? I don't feel so good." The storm was rising.

"Come on, girl. You know you want to. I'll take you home after." I didn't know where I was, but he did apparently. He parked in a vacant lot and turned off the car. My ears were ringing. He reached over to grab my neck and I pulled away from him.

"This ain't gonna hurt, know what I'm saying?" Randy said. He reached for me again. This time, he tried to maneuver himself so that he could get his arm around my waist. I struggled with him and tried to get out of the car.

"Randy, you better stop!" I screamed. "I don't feel good." I tried to warn him. The telltale sign of a grade "A" retching was upon me before I could do anything about it. That storm rose up out of my belly and all over Randy and his spic and span interior. The remnants of my last meal and what was left of those four beers splashed him like a geyser. He recoiled in disgust.

"Oh, God! Girl, you just puked all over my car!" He showed me no sympathy whatsoever. "You got to get out."

"I told you I didn't feel good," I said when I was able to speak. "Can you take me home?"

"Hell no. Get out!" He jumped out of the car, ran around to my side and opened the door. As I stepped out, I threw up once more, causing Randy to dance in the parking lot.

"Ooh, that's nasty. Hurry up and get out!"

"Randy, I don't know where I am," I cried. "Please take me home."

"Shoot! Shoot!" he yelled. "This just ain't my night." He ran his hands through his beautiful hair. "Dang. I'll take you home, but you can't throw up in my car no more."

"I'll try, but I can't control it," I said.

"You better try." Randy groaned again and stared at his once spotless interior. He went to the trunk, pulled out some dirty towels, wiped himself down, and shoved them in my hands.

"Before I take you anywhere, you gotta clean this up. Dang, girl!" I wiped up as much of the sludge as I could, but the sour smell nearly inspired another episode. I turned my head in time to miss the inside of the car, but I didn't miss the side of the car. Randy couldn't take it.

"Gimme that!" he said as he snatched the towels from me. He wiped the seat viciously. He went to the trunk and found some old rags. He used those to clean the side of the car. When he was done, he barked at me to get in the car, his once handsome face deformed by fury.

Randy finally took me home. He drove in silence and wouldn't even look at me. He would probably never look at me again. I'm pretty sure he broke some speeding laws that night because I made it home in record time. I was extremely weak after that episode, but I managed to thank Randy with what strength I had left. He pealed off without another word to me.

The weekend passed by in a blur. I was firmly entrenched in a melancholy state of mind, nursing my little collection of hurts. The guilt, the rejection, the stress, and the feelings of abandonment, were weeds in my garden of despair and I watered them generously with beer from momma's stash. Monday morning came and I didn't know when. I dressed myself without much care, but miraculously put together a reasonable outfit consisting of a pair of jeans and a wrinkled, black T-shirt. Pastor Ricky's Bible and the train's distant whistle mocked me. I shoved the Bible back under the bed and turned a deaf ear to the train.

I reached the school twenty minutes late and staggered to my seat. All eyes were on me, and usually that would frazzle my nerves. I just didn't care what anybody was thinking right then, including Mr. Pierce.

"Thank you for joining us, Miss Frye," he said, which brought a low rumble of laughter from the class — everyone except Katherine. She looked right through me, and that added another layer of guilt. I put my head on my desk and tried to forget everything. The only thing that brought a glimmer of light to my dark mood that day was the sheer joy on Katherine's face as she gave intelligent, succinct and accurate observations about the writers we were discussing that day. Mr. Pierce's face lit up and Katherine's clique looked stupefied.

In the cafeteria after class, I tried to get Katherine's ~~attention, but her protective group would not let me near~~ her.

"Katherine, can I talk to you?" My brain was still throbbing from the weekend.

"No," she answered.

"Get away from her," said Myra, pushing me with each word. Katherine did nothing to stop her. I tried to go around Myra, but she was good at blocking me.

"She don't want to talk to you. Now get gone." I didn't want to give Myra any more excuses to put her hands on me. I gave up and left.

I dreaded the trip to Miss Lipstick's. I was sure she would be concerned about me and I didn't want to add anything that might affect her fragile health. It took me much longer than usual to make the journey to her house. When I opened the door, Phyllis was waiting with her arms open wide. I didn't want to be held. Phyllis was stunned and seemed a little hurt.

"Gorgeous, how you making it?" she asked. "You been crying all weekend, you poor baby. Look at them red eyes." As she rubbed my back, I wondered if she knew.

"I'm OK." My response was short because I didn't have the energy to say more.

"If you need to talk, you know, about what happened, I'm here," Phyllis offered.

"OK." I put my book bag down and made my way to the kitchen sink. I ran hot water over my hands until it was too hot to bear. Behind me, I heard Miss Lipstick's door swing open. Miss Lipstick rarely left her room anymore. The air in the house had never been pure. Whenever she took a breath, it brought on a fit of painful-sounding coughs.

"Gal, there wasn't nothing you could do to save Pastor Ricky," Miss Lipstick said. The woman had the power to read my mind. I just hoped her sense of smell was a little off. "You couldn't have said nothing different, did nothing different. God don't consult nobody when he ready to take his children." She shut the door.

I flopped down in the chair at the kitchen table and replayed her words over and over in my mind. Phyllis was ready to be my sounding board.

"It's like she doesn't feel anything. I thought she liked Pastor Ricky," I said.

"Believe me, baby, she feeling everything you feel a hundred times over. She been through this before," Phyllis said.

"When? Her husband?" I asked.

"With Karla," somebody piped up from the floor.

"Shut up, Leonard!" Phyllis hissed.

"It's true," Leonard continued despite the warning. "We didn't think Miss Lipstick was gonna make it. Ain't that right, y'all." No one else wanted to corroborate his story. I gave Phyllis an inquisitive look.

"Yeah, Miss Lipstick lost her daughter, but that was a long time ago. She ain't been doing so good, but she still feel bad about Pastor Ricky." Phyllis spoke to me in a soft, soothing voice. She took a dishtowel and dried my wet hands. "I'll finish these. Why don't you go on home? Rest up. I'll tell Lipstick later."

I followed Phyllis's advice. The punishing effects of my reckless binge were beginning to wear off. My bed clung to me as if I had never mistreated it. It bore the stains and the scent of my first drink and my first hangover. Just thinking about another beer should have launched me into a catatonic state, but it didn't. It was that feeling of nothingness, a vacation from the pain, if only for a few hours, that made me want to try again. After all, the folks at Miss Lipstick's house had been doing it for years, and they kept coming back. There was a reason they kept coming back. Momma was parked in front of the refrigerator and I was too exhausted to go around her. I folded myself into my bed and I slept.

During my rapid-eye-movement cycle, I felt someone shaking me. I thought I was dreaming. My eyes opened gradually and an apparition that looked and smelled like Momma was sitting on the side of my bed. I barely remember the conversation.

"Fla, Fla," she kept saying. "Wake up."

"Momma, what is it?" I said sleepily.

"Fla, I gotta tell you something," Momma said.

"What?" I was irritated that she had disturbed my slumber. I didn't dream anymore.

"Don't go through the pass no more," Momma whispered.

"Huh?"

"Don't go through the pass," she repeated.

"OK," I said. I felt her lift off my bed and close my door quietly. Her words evaporated into the night air.

/CHAPTER XVIII/

"I got an appointment at the Social Security office and you have to come with me," Momma said that morning.

"We just went to your review in May and the next one is supposed to be in August," I said. "And your appointment is always on a Wednesday, not a Tuesday."

"Them people said they want you and me to come up there today at 3:30!" she yelled at me. "You saying you know better than them Social Security people?"

"No. It's just that I have to go to the bank for Miss Lipstick at 4:00. I'll just tell her about the appointment."

"You ain't got to tell her nothing. Don't think I ain't seen that stuff she be giving you. Just 'cause she buying you watches and books and other junk don't make her nothing to you. You better be here at 3:30! That's all I got to say!" Her face was glued to the set, but she wasn't watching. *All in the Family* was her favorite show and nothing tickled her more than Archie Bunker's racist mouth.

"Do you have my birth certificate?" I blurted out. Momma nearly fell off the sofa.

"Hell no! What you asking for? You don't need it." Her teeth were tripping all over her lips. She couldn't say no fast enough.

"Mr. Pierce said I could go to this program next summer and he needs my birth certificate. Is it because Calvin didn't sign it? Miss Lipstick got him to sign it the other day," I said.

"She what! That don't make no difference. You ain't going nowhere! Don't be asking for that nonsense." Momma was more agitated than ever. She constantly asked me where I was going, even if it was just to my room. She was behaving like a certifiable nut case. I still couldn't fathom the talk we had the night before. I was convinced she was beyond drunk — she was smashed.

As I was leaving the apartment, I was shocked to find myself bumping into Jerome. His putrid, onion-saturated breath alerted me that he was not on speaking terms with a toothbrush. The short time he'd been away was like paradise, and now it had come to an abrupt end. I pressed myself against the wall to let his carcass pass by. He didn't move, but Momma was up and ready to accept him back into her nest.

From the door, Jerome said, "You know why I'm here. I ain't staying unless I get it."

"Go on to school, Fla," Momma said, in a rare display of parental instruction. "Jerome, don't."

I scooted out as quickly as my legs would carry me, but the front door remained ajar. "You can have anything else," I heard Momma pleading with Jerome. Letting him back into her life was like a dog returning to its vomit. I wanted her to stop capitulating and just banish him from our lives. Why didn't she just give him what he was asking for so he would leave us alone?

At school, I felt the old me returning, but Katherine still refused to talk to me. Although we were both stars that day and Mr. Pierce treated us like we walked on water, we couldn't share it with each other and it was my fault.

"We can study for tomorrow's test at my house today, if you want." I tried offering an olive branch to make amends. "I have to go with my momma to her appointment at 3:30, but I should be back around 4:30." She was ignoring me, but I continued talking. "I'm real sorry, Katherine. I didn't mean those things. I hope we can still be friends."

Myra laughed out loud. Katherine wouldn't look at me. I gave myself credit for trying. It was nice having a friend, even if it was only for a short while. I missed her already.

Outside, the sky was overcast as I walked to Miss Lipstick's. The weatherman had been lying all week about rain. It was dry and hot, and we certainly needed it.

The crowd at Miss Lipstick's was thinning because most of them were old enough to feel the impending weather in their bones. They didn't like to drink during rainstorms. They thought God might strike them down with a bottle in their hands.

Phyllis greeted me as usual with a warm hug. "How you doing, precious?" she asked.

"I'm doing fine, Phyllis," I said. I wanted to put her at ease.

"You sure?" she demanded.

"I'm sure." She peered into my eyes looking for any signs of deception. Finding none, she said, "All right. I believe you."

I spotted a batch of damp towels that needed to be washed. I grabbed an armload when Phyllis came up behind me.

"You never told me about your kiss, gorgeous," she said. "You holding out on me. I know handsome kissed you, didn't he?"

That kiss seemed like it had happened a million years ago. At Phyllis' question, I recalled it as if it happened the day before. My eyes closed and I willed the memory to fade away — the memory of Randy's lip-bruising kiss and the image of him leaving me. I opened my eyes and saw Phyllis with a wide grin on her face.

"Somebody been kissed!" Phyllis teased me in the kitchen. "How was it, girl?"

I couldn't readily find the words to describe the experience so that Phyllis would be happy. "Oh my God," was all I said.

She slapped me on the back. "My girl! Hey Lipstick, your girl been kissed! When you gonna . . ."

"Phyllis, watch yo' mouth!" I heard Miss Lipstick say. Her voice sounded weak.

"I'm just playin' with the girl. Calm down." She put her hands with the stubby nails on my face and squeezed it. She leaned over and placed a soft kiss on my forehead.

"My girl." She pinched my cheek and walked out to the porch. I glanced at the new watch Miss Lipstick bought me. The hands were inching toward 3 o'clock. I had to finish up and get going. I normally rapped on Miss Lipstick's door to let her know I was leaving, but I heard loud, deep snoring coming from the room. I saw no need to disturb her.

At quitting time, I noticed the clouds were much darker and hanging heavy in the sky. The weatherman's predictions had finally caught up with the weather. I swear, the minute my foot left the porch, rain pellets began dropping on my head. A little water didn't bother me, though.

"You got to go home now!" Phyllis bellowed from the porch.

"Yeah! Momma has an appointment. I'll run." I yelled back. I was preparing to sprint when Phyllis called me again.

"You left your book, gorgeous! Come back and get it." Phyllis met me halfway down the sidewalk and passed me the latest book I'd been reading to the group. It was *The Count of Monte Cristo*. The clouds chose that precise moment to open up and give me a midday shower. I had nothing to cover my head except the book. Alexandre Dumas wouldn't mind, as the book was already in sad condition. Mrs. McCullough would be OK with it, too.

I hoped the appointment could be rescheduled because I wasn't going to make it home by 3:30. The rain was coming down with such force my visibility was zero. I had to seek refuge under the bridge, which was no match for the rain that was now coming down in a steady torrent. I fairly dove into that spot under the bridge where it hadn't turned to mud yet. I settled in to wait out the rain and became reacquainted with the story.

"What you reading?" I heard outside of my little refuge. The onions and the stink made the hairs on my neck salute. Jerome reached out and snatched the book out of my hand.

"Ah. The Count of Mountain Crisco by Alex-an-dree Dumb Ass. I read that. It's pretty good." If I were not paralyzed by fear, I could have gotten a pretty good chuckle out of Jerome's woeful lack of education. I was deep in the cut of the bridge and Jerome's wide load blocked my only means of exit. He was soaking wet, the water in his nappy hair beading up.

"Girl, let me in there. It's cold out here." Jerome wrapped his arms around himself to illustrate his point.

To my horror, he began insinuating himself into my space.

"You can have the whole spot. I'm going home." I tried to move past him. He put a hand out.

"That ain't necessary. We'll just sit here 'til the rain stop, snuggle a little to keep warm." The nasty smile pasted on his filthy countenance was not a good sign.

All the alarm bells went off, and I made a second attempt at getting past him. Jerome anticipated the maneuver. He grabbed me by the waist and thrust himself backwards from a crouching position. We tumbled over each other onto the molehill of a muddy embankment, where we landed with Jerome's full weight on top of me.

"Get off me!" I screamed. I wiggled underneath him. That excited him more. He held my arms flush to the ground and began kissing me all over my face and neck. I moved my head rapidly from side to side, trying to dodge a full lip kiss. I wanted to hold my breath because Jerome's stench was overpowering, but if I didn't breathe, I couldn't scream.

"Stop moving!" Jerome said through gritted teeth. "I'm getting what I want today." He pinned my arms together with one hand and put his other hand around my neck. He began to squeeze. "You wanna breathe? Stop fighting me."

My eyes were as big as saucers. My short life had been dull save for the last few weeks. I kind of wanted to be around to see how it ended, but not this way.

Jerome pressed harder into me and I could feel his arousal. If only I could throw up at will. The more I squirmed, the tighter he gripped my neck. Panic had filled my gut. If I didn't find some measure of control, I was going to choke out.

Although I was terrified, I knew I had to act fast. I didn't want to be tomorrow's headlines. I wanted to call out for help — Miss Lipstick, Pastor Ricky, Root Charlie — but I had no voice. There was only one person who could save me now, and that was me.

I suddenly recalled Phyllis' words, about how people behave when they're about to get something they'd been wanting for a long time. "They lose their minds a little bit," she'd said. I was ready to give Jerome exactly what he was asking for. I moved my head rapidly from side to side, making it harder for him to kiss me. He loosened his grip enough for me to take some life-saving breaths.

"Jerome," I whispered. "I'll do it. I'll do it."

"Hm," he answered. His voice was muffled because his face was buried in my neck. Beer and wine and some other libation emanated from his skin.

"Let me take my pants off." My backside was wet with mud. My hair was vertical on my head and my face was puffy from crying. I could have been wearing a paper bag on my head. Jerome didn't care.

"Huh?" He bolted straight up and looked at me quizzically.

"You gotta get off me so we can do this." I put on what I thought was a come-hither look.

"OK." Jerome said. "Hurrup, too. I been waiting for this for soooo long." He was drooling and panting like a rabid dog. His tongue was hanging out of his mouth. It was a revolting sight, but I pretended it turned me on. As soon as he moved, I got on my knees and I began fiddling with the buttons on my jeans. So many buttons and hands that were shaking like a fan made progress slow.

"I gotta stand up, OK," I said seductively. He sat there on his knees, his eyes never moving above my waist.

I crouched down slightly, and then brought my knee up hard under Jerome's chin. While he grabbed his face, I fell backwards but flipped over and attempted to climb back to my feet. But they abandoned me. I landed hard on my face. My front matched my back. I scrambled to get up again but Jerome had recovered. My voice had returned also, and I screamed as loudly as I could. My desperate pleas were washed away in the wind.

Jerome flailed his arms at me and I kicked him everywhere he was soft — his gut, his thighs, his groin area. The last kick made a solid connection. I tried to drive my foot up into his ribs. Jerome let out the wail of a wounded animal. That should have bought me at least five minutes, I thought. I slipped and slid back up to the bridge, ignoring the chill in my bones and the dirt in my mouth.

Jerome was like the bad dreams I was constantly having. Something big and horrible would be chasing me, would be right at my heels, and no matter how fast I ran or how skillfully I flew, I couldn't get away from it. I couldn't get away from Jerome. Somehow, he managed to massage his injured body parts and reach out with a rubber arm to grab my leg. With amazing strength, he pulled me right back down under him.

Jerome's anger must have usurped his pain because he rose up and raised his fist. I instinctively covered my face and braced for impact. In my fantasies, somebody would have jumped on Jerome and pulled him off me. This was no fantasy and it was no movie. The only thing that came was Jerome's fist full force into my face. The strike was quick and powerful. My jaw exploded from the inside and blood filled my mouth. I began to drift out of my body, but I couldn't let go. My ears were clogged, so I was spared the barrage of obscenities coming out of Jerome. His face was so twisted, I didn't recognize him as the lazy sleazebag who liked to lie under my momma. He was transformed into something much more evil.

My throat was sore from screaming and I was beginning to lose the energy to fight. I deflected the punches and jabs as best I could. Jerome sat back on his haunches and did his best to knock my lights out. I covered my face again and waited for another onslaught of punches, but they never came. A piercing scream popped my ears, but the scream didn't come from me.

I uncovered my face and saw Jerome was fighting off someone who was beating him about the head and neck with a heavy object. It was Katherine, and she was wielding that English Lit textbook like no sword a Samurai ever held. She delivered several practiced blows to Jerome's torso before he was able to wrench it away from her. Katherine was ready for him. She must have watched wrestling with her father — she put her powerful arms around Jerome's neck and clinched. Jerome was able to peel Katherine's arms off his neck, but she was prepared to fight. Katherine pummeled him with the only other lethal weapon she possessed — her hands. Jerome was beginning to match her punch for punch. That's when my adrenaline kicked in. I was reinvigorated enough to join Katherine in a mission to send Jerome to heaven, because we beat the hell out of him that day. He cried like a child, begging and pleading for us to stop.

We didn't stop until we were exhausted. We got up and shared a silent agreement that we had completed our mission. We left Jerome, semi-conscious but face up in the mud. He looked like a beached whale with his soaked shirt rolled up over his hairy belly, his mouth wide open, and his arms flung east and west.

"Let's go, Fla, before he wake up!" Katherine grabbed my hand with an urgency and we ran toward town. I stopped on a dime and dropped Katherine's hand.

"Why you stopping? We going to tell somebody." Katherine was frantic.

"No. I can't tell nobody about this. I can't." It was still raining. I was soaked and trembling furiously from the cold. I also looked like I was covered in chocolate cake batter.

"Why not? You should see your face, Fla. He messed you up and somebody need to mess him up." Katherine was angry. "How did he know you would be down here anyway?"

That was a question I couldn't answer — a question I didn't want to answer.

"Promise me you won't say anything about this, Kat," I begged. "I can take care of myself."

"But, Fla . . .,"

"Promise me, Kat." I took her hand and squeezed it. "As my friend. Please."

Katherine looked as distressed as I felt. Eventually, she gave in.

"Okay. All right." We turned back toward the pass to see if Jerome was still there. He had not moved. The longer I witnessed that human abomination, the more I wanted to do the backstroke in an Olympic size pool of liquor. Then I heard the tittering. It was low and soft, and gradually got louder. I searched for the source of the noise. It was Katherine.

"What's so funny?" I asked. It was sickening that she'd find any hilarity in this situation.

"Look at him," she said, pointing at Jerome. He did look idiotic, splayed out in the mud with rainwater filling his mouth. He was pathetic and wretched. It was laughable that I used to be afraid of him. So, I joined Katherine in a cathartic laughter that had my abdominal muscles contracting. We were bent over, slapping our knees and filling that space with the sounds of two friends sharing a cleansing moment. The harder we laughed, the less I thought about drinking. With our arms around each other, our bodies rocking joyously, the pressure of the last few weeks was released somewhat. We came down from our high, wiping our eyes, although the rain was indistinguishable from the tears.

"I need to get my book," Katherine said, still chuckling. We spotted it in a puddle and it was damaged beyond repair.

"Don't worry about it. You can have mine. I'll get it to you." We shared a look that wrapped up thank you and I'm sorry all in one.

"You still have to tell somebody. You gotta take care of yourself, Fla," Katherine said.

"I will."

Jerome began to stir, so Katherine and I ran home together, laughing. Bits and pieces of the debris I'd been rolling in followed me. I didn't stop until I was in the apartment. The instant I was inside, all those bad feelings tried to creep back into me. The sadness, the despair, and the misery were like hungry infants whining to be fed. Momma was gone, so I went to the refrigerator, found every beer that was inside, and poured them all down the sink.

When I went into the bathroom, I scanned my face in the mirror. My reflection wasn't as hideous as I thought it would be. My jaw was swollen. My left eye was black. My arms were bruised around my elbows. I was covered with tiny cuts, but I was alive. I soaked my aching body in the tub until the hot soapy water turned to cold scummy water. Then, I heard the front door open. Shortly thereafter, Momma started beating on the bathroom door.

"Where Jerome at?" she asked.

I refused to cry. I could not cry. The moisture on my face was the steam from the hot water.

"You ain't seen Jerome?" Momma continued to ask.

"No!" The word burst from me involuntarily. "Leave me alone!" Her voice to me was like the annoying scrape of fingernails on a chalkboard.

"Fla! Open this door!" She shook the door hard. She wouldn't get in, not with a hamper full of clothes pushed up against the door, not with a heart full of hatred growing in my chest. I tried not to wonder if the appointment was real.

/CHAPTER XIX/

I hunkered down in my room and embarked on an impromptu fast. I didn't want to see my Momma's face and thanks to Jerome, even the thought of beer made me want to purge. I denied myself the exposure of the sun, as my self-imposed solitude would last until my bruised and battered face healed. I would not see daylight until no one could tell I had been beaten. Momma yelled at me, cursed at me, and threatened me to come out, but nothing short of an earthquake would evict me from that room.

Katherine paid me a visit on Wednesday afternoon. "Fla, let me in," she said after rapping lightly on my door.

"I want to be alone," I said after a long pause. I couldn't bear to behold her pretty face when mine was so deformed.

"We need to talk," she said with firmness in her voice.

"No we don't," I said rudely. She didn't deserve that, especially since she saved my life twice in one day. "Maybe later. Not right now. OK?"

"OK." Katherine was silent for a moment, but she had not walked away. "You coming for the last day of school tomorrow?" she asked. "Mr. Pierce asked about you."

School was the furthest thing from my mind. I wasn't sure I wanted to leave the house ever again. "You didn't tell him!" I panicked.

"No, I didn't say nothing," she answered. "I just told him you been sick. So, you coming?" she asked again.

"Maybe."

I was bored sitting in my room hour after hour. I had not picked up a book in days. I felt my brain shrinking from lack of use. Finally, my appearance was acceptable to me — the swelling in my jaw had decreased and my black eye looked like ordinary bags. Nobody paid much attention to my face anyway.

On Thursday morning, my path converged with Katherine's just outside the main entrance of the projects.

"Fla, I thought you was never coming out of that house," Katherine said, her voice full of concern. "How are you feeling?"

"Better," I answered.

"You look better," she said." Did you tell your momma yet?"

"No. And I'm not going to tell her. I'm not telling anybody!" I said vehemently. "You promised me you wouldn't tell anybody."

"You can't keep that to yourself," Katherine said. "You got to let it out. It do things to you."

"I have to learn how to take care of myself because I'm going to be on my own soon. I can't keep running to people to help me or rescue me. I have to grow up." My voice cracked but I swallowed hard. I would not allow myself to cry. "You still promise?" There was a haunting echo to those words.

"I promise," Katherine said yet again.

I had been accustomed to her face balled up in anger, and what I came to learn was jealousy, when she looked at me. Now, it was etched with concern and looked kindly upon me. It wasn't real to me until just that moment — honest, true and soul-knitting. I ignored the bounds of decency and high school etiquette, and threw my arms around the beautiful former bully, who was now, simply, my beautiful friend.

"I don't think I said right out before," I said, trying to edit my emotions, "but thank you, Kat. Thank you so much. If you hadn't come by when you did . . .," I swallowed the enormous lump in my throat.

Katherine also ignored our former positions in the high school hierarchy, and returned my hug. "It's OK, Fla. You helped me, too. Look at it as me returning the favor."

"Kat, what you doing? Why you hugging her?" Myra's voice caused me to stiffen. Katherine and I both turned to confront her, and Myra looked absolutely betrayed.

"None of your business, Myra. I do what I want," she answered Myra.

"I don't believe this. Wait 'til I tell the other girls," Myra said, apparently not accustomed to having Katherine address her in that manner. "Maybe you forgot how this girl is a smart aleck and a bookworm and a teacher's pet and she be making fun of you and calling you dumb," Myra said. "You forgot about all that."

Katherine's shoulders tensed up. I saw that some of her hardness had returned. Was I about to lose the friend I had so desperately needed?

"Look, Myra. If you took the time to get to know her, you would see she real nice and she smart because she want to be, not because she showing off. You could be smart, too, if you want to be, if you tried hard enough. So, stop taking what's wrong with you out on her. I ain't gon' have it. She my friend, and you better leave her alone."

It was a good thing Katherine's hand never left my shoulders, because I would have fallen over like a rotten tree in a hurricane. I thought my heart would burst open.

"You don't like that girl, Kat!" Myra continued. "You used to say . . .,"

"Shut up, Myra!" Myra recognized that tone. She closed her mouth and walked off in a huff.

Even with an asset like a stable friendship, I still wasn't doing a very good job of handling my problem. I was only halfway functional in class. I slept a lot. I gave incorrect answers to questions I'd answered correctly before. Mr. Pierce pointed out the changes in me.

"Miss Frye, you're despondent, you're subdued, and your work quality has deteriorated. Fortunately, you did so well in the beginning, you've still got the highest grade in the class. Your work of late wasn't Fla anymore." I used to dissolve when Mr. Pierce trained his beautiful brown eyes on me. It did nothing for me this time, even with him in kissing distance.

"I'm just not feeling well. Can I put my head down for a while?" I asked.

"Do you need to go home? I could call your mother and you can leave early," Mr. Pierce suggested. "It is the last day."

"No!" I shrieked. Mr. Pierce stepped back. "No," I said a little softer. "I'll be OK."

"All right, Miss Frye. Let me know if you need to go home. I'll release you early." He recommenced his teaching.

"Miss Morehead, I'm very pleased to see that you overcame your initial weakness, young lady. I've never been happier to give anybody a B-, which is enough to send you on to the 11th grade." Katherine beamed at him. I believe Mr. Pierce stumbled a bit. She squinted her eyes at me, a visual warning to speak up about what happened. I waggled my head at her, a signal that I would not.

My behavior was worse at Miss Lipstick's. I made sure there was no trace of the incident in my face, as many of her customers were familiar with the wreckage of beatings. I avoided Phyllis as much as I could.

"Hey gorgeous, we missed you around here." When she embraced me, I went cold in her arms.

"What's the matter with you?" Phyllis asked, eyeing me skeptically. "Girl, your momma came by here that day it rained. She was acting the plumb fool looking for you. You know anything about that?"

I was afraid to speak, so I shook my head.

"You can't talk? Cat got your tongue?" Phyllis joked. I gave her a wan smile.

"I'm just tired," I lied. "I had a long week."

"Doing what? Beating rocks with your face?" I thought Phyllis was still joking. My hand flew to my jaw, giving myself away a bit.

"I know a beat-up face when I see one. Something happened to you?" Phyllis had shifted into maternal overdrive.

"No, I just fell on the steps at my house. That's all." I moved away from her rapidly to stop the questions. "I need to finish these dishes." I turned my back to Phyllis, but she didn't go far. One or two glasses slipped from my hand because I was nervous. The clattering against the porcelain sink was earsplitting. The last glass fell to the floor and shattered completely, cutting my hand and bringing Miss Lipstick to my side. She made me sit down while she rummaged through her ancient drawers for a serviceable bandage. She held my hand awkwardly, as if tenderness and intimacy were outside her field of expertise. What she was good at was sensing that my pain was not the result of my broken skin, but a very deeply broken heart.

"What's wrong, gal?" she asked while she opened the bandage. She was breathing heavily.

"Nothing," I mumbled, trying to sound nonchalant.

"You ain't a good liar, gal. I can see right through you." She fumbled with the bandage, her arthritic hands making it difficult to place the adhesive side on the wound. After she was successful, she held onto my hand.

"I miss Pastor Ricky," I said. That was the truth, but it wasn't the whole truth. I had to get Miss Lipstick off the scent. "Why do people have to die?"

"Baby, if I could answer that, I would sell it instead of moonshine," she said. "Pastor Ricky was hurting something awful. It was too deep for anybody to help him. Like I said before, you couldn't have said or did nothing different to change that." My hand was quivering, and I did not look her in the face. "I'll tell you something, though. You made his last days real good ones. I heard you was all he talked about."

"Really?" I asked. My throat was quivering.

"Really." Miss Lipstick held my hand tighter. "What else?"

"Ma'am?" I tried to sound confused.

"That ain't all that's bothering you, baby. I can tell." She found my eyes and I could not hide anymore.

"Miss Lipstick, you been in Quincy a long time, right?" I asked. My eyes were downcast and I couldn't fight the tidal wave rushing up behind them.

"Too long."

"So you know my momma pretty good?" My shoulders were heaving.

"I know all your people." The trembling in my body transferred to hers. Her thin arms were jiggling.

"Can you tell me something? Why my momma hate me?" My lips shuddered and I knew I was beyond being able to stop the waterworks that were already spilling from my eyes.

Miss Lipstick reached over with her open hand to wipe away the tears running down my face. Her calloused palms were rough on my skin, but I didn't care, because the gentleness of the gesture broke the dam. She drew me into her deflated bosom. The scent of smoke and Vicks vapor rub stung my nose, but I held on tight. It was like squeezing a large, bag of leaves she was so weak. Everything I'd been holding back for weeks poured out — my father's rejection, Mr. Pierce's wedding, Randy's behavior, Pastor Ricky's dying, Jerome's attack, and something else I could not put a name to. For all those things, I bawled like a hungry infant in Miss Lipstick's arms.

"Y'all get out of here. Everybody out," she said to the room full of spectators. They moved too slowly, so all Miss Lipstick had to say was, "Root Charlie." The place emptied in seconds.

"She don't hate you, baby. She hate herself. " She lifted my blubbering face from her chest. "Why you asking?"

I was speechless. I was unable to construct a single intelligible word. I allowed myself to grieve and Miss Lipstick absorbed it all. Tears streamed down my face and onto my neck, and dampened the collar of Miss Lipstick's housedress. Miss Lipstick allowed Phyllis to remain, who busied herself wiping my face and mouth.

"Tell me what happened now. Somebody do something to you?" Miss Lipstick was growing impatient. She stroked and tapped my back, as if I would burp the answer to her question. Anger was creeping into her tone.

After the initial wave of grief had passed, I was composed enough to launch into the delicate tale of how I was violated.

"Jerome attacked me," I said, giving the abbreviated version. Just thinking about it made me nauseous and I was already beginning to feel another wave of weeping.

"What did he do?" Miss Lipstick carefully enunciated each word, digging her nails into my wrist at each syllable. Phyllis gently pried her hands away and assumed the position of hand holder.

"The other day, when it was raining, I had to hide under the bridge," I recounted. The agony of the memory was as painful as the original injury. "He . . . he." It was so difficult to go on, but Phyllis knelt down next to me. "He kissed me on my neck and he tried to r-r-rape me and I fought him, then he beat me." Fresh tears rolled out while I hiccupped and sniffed. Miss Lipstick was incensed. She paced back and forth from the living room to the kitchen. I heard Root Charlie cracking his knuckles. It was like firecrackers exploding.

"I need my cigarettes," Miss Lipstick declared.

"Lipstick!" Phyllis said. "Come on, now. That's not gonna help nothing." Phyllis had her gaze fixed on me. "He just tried, baby girl?" she asked with bated breath. When I nodded my head, she sighed with relief.

"But we got him back. We got him back good," I said, perking up a bit. "Katherine showed up and we beat him up."

Miss Lipstick was livid. She seemed to make up her mind about something when she stopped in the middle of the floor. Root Charlie was getting up before she opened her mouth.

"Root Charlie!" she hollered as if he was in a well, her voice extra high. "Get on the job! Get him and bring him here." As she headed toward her room, I saw that her eyes were not dry, either.

I had no love loss for Jerome, but Miss Lipstick's reputation for making people disappear, or at least, parts of their bodies, flashed in my mind.

"Miss Lipstick, I don't want to be no caged bird," I sobbed. I saw Root Charlie in his corner flexing his fists.

"What you talking about?" she asked, perturbed.

"You're not gonna kill him?" I asked. I didn't want any blood on my hands. "Please don't kill him."

"When he leaves here, baby, he won't be dead. But I promise you, he'll wish he was."

Phyllis tended to my internal and external wounds for the next few hours. Miss Lipstick wouldn't let me go home. She fed me, and Phyllis entertained me. I was afraid to ask Phyllis what was going to happen next. She kept the atmosphere too jovial, as if she was avoiding the discussion as well.

The hour was getting late. Root Charlie was gone a long time and Miss Lipstick was scarce. Phyllis was advised to take off. I was very anxious and on pins and needles. I missed my books, which had never made it back to the library. I secretly hoped and prayed Root Charlie couldn't find Jerome, but I believed Root Charlie could find the man in the moon.

Around 10:00 p.m., Root Charlie's deuce and a quarter came to a screeching halt outside Miss Lipstick's house. Miss Lipstick stomped out of her room and took me by the arm.

"Stay in here. Don't come out 'til I tell you." She pushed me in and slammed the door in my face.

I didn't know what real power was until that night. I learned later that when Miss Lipstick summoned Jerome, Root Charlie found him out in that nearly condemned home where Momma and I had picked him up. Because of Root Charlie's imposing presence and Miss Lipstick's reputation, Jerome wasn't able to hide for long. His own friends gave him up. Root Charlie thereafter delivered him to Miss Lipstick's house without delay.

I cracked the door open a sliver to see for myself what events would transpire. Whatever punishment they would levy against Jerome that night, I would be a witness to it. Root Charlie had Jerome in that four-fingered grasp that even brought tears to my eyes. He threw Jerome down at Miss Lipstick's feet where he sprawled out over the floor like a lumpy rug. Jerome grimaced and groaned, but he couldn't pull off the tough act. Miss Lipstick sat on the couch at an angle that allowed me to see her cool, calm demeanor. She was smoking again.

"Jerome, Jerome? What happened to you, boy?" Jerome climbed to his feet, huffing all the while. When he looked around, possibly looking for an avenue of escape or someone to rescue him, his face was a picture of the afflicted — a recent black eye, a split lip and a deep gash on the side of his head that was still oozing thick, red blood. Root Charlie reattached his hands to Jerome's throat in a strangulation hold. Jerome couldn't answer Miss Lipstick with Root Charlie crushing his wind pipe, so Miss Lipstick snapped her fingers and Root Charlie released him. Jerome took great big gulps of air before he responded.

"This gang of boys beat me up. Big boys. About six or seven of 'em. They robbed me for my money and beat me down," Jerome lied.

"Yeah, you don't say?" Miss Lipstick looked like she was suppressing a smile. "That there is Root Charlie's work. What you talking about?"

"Ma'am?" Jerome said. He shifted his feet from side to side in the pee pee dance. He was sweating like a hog at the slaughter. I almost felt sorry for him. Almost.

"You heard anything about somebody messing with Millie's girl? You know Millie," Miss Lipstick said. Her voice was very controlled.

"Oh, you mean Flaw?"

Miss Lipstick winced at Jerome's botched pronunciation of my name. Jerome was wringing his hands and rubbing his turkey neck. His entire three hundred pound frame quivered. He drew in excessive amounts of air, as if he thought they might be the last he'd ever take. "Somebody bothered her?"

"Yeah. Somebody put his hands on her and beat her. What somebody didn't know is what that gal means to me and nobody put they hands on what's mine." Miss Lipstick's face betrayed none of the fury she expressed earlier. She was again poised, smoking her cigarette like she was reacquainting with an old friend. "You see how I can't just let that slide, Jerome. You understand." Miss Lipstick's eyes moved over to Root Charlie. Jerome dropped to his knees, causing the floor under him to buckle.

"Miss Lipstick, I'm sorry," he said. "I'm sorry. I don't know what came over me. I was drunk. I didn't know what I was doing. What you gonna do to me, Miss Lipstick? I'm so sorry. I'll say sorry to Flaw, Flea, to the girl. I'll do whatever you want me to do. What you want me to do, Miss Lipstick?" Jerome groveled. He was talking fast and begging hard.

I hoped Miss Lipstick wouldn't have any mercy on him. He didn't have any mercy on me when he punched me in my face. I ran my tongue over the inside of my mouth. It had not completely healed.

Jerome's supplication continued uninhibited. "I know some things, Miss Lipstick. I can help you out. Whatever you want me to do, Miss Lipstick, I'll do it. What you want me to do?"

"Can you undo what you did to my girl?" Miss Lipstick asked in a hushed tone. Jerome cried into the meaty hands he'd put around my throat. He was so pathetic. Miss Lipstick hadn't laid a hand on him yet, but the anticipation was nerve-wracking.

What occurred next left me dumbfounded. An emotion I could not name crossed Root Charlie's face. He stared at Miss Lipstick, waiting for a green light, but she told him, "I got this one, Charlie." Root Charlie took his post behind Jerome. He reached down and lifted the slobbering, fat man back to his feet. He then moved him a couple of inches away from Miss Lipstick's face. Suddenly, she reached out, with both hands, and grabbed Jerome's family jewels. Miss Lipstick had some reserved strength because that little woman's grip made Jerome's eyes bulge out of his head and a horrific scream escape his mouth, followed by a series of high-pitched squeals.

While Miss Lipstick yanked and pulled as if she was trying to twist them off, she spewed a litany of offensive, indecent, and crude phrases that Jerome's howling couldn't drown out and that burned my ears.

"If you ever touch her or even look at her wrong, I'll find out," was the hygienic version of what Miss Lipstick said next. "You know I will. If you do, I'll take this, cut it off, and plant it in my back yard with the others. Do you understand me, boy?" Jerome grunted in agreement.

The whole bizarre scene was hilarious to me. I hit the floor, beating it silently, trying to stifle the laughter. The corner of the shoebox under Miss Lipstick's bed caught my attention. I took advantage of the opportunity to sneak a peek at my birth certificate. I dragged out the box, opened it, and found the document. I unfolded it, spread it out in my lap, and skimmed over it. What I read confused me more than ever. The line for the mother's name was blank. Calvin Walters had signed in the father's place. The only other blanks that were filled out were the date and time of my birth, and the state.

When I heard Jerome thanking God for Miss Lipstick, I knew the execution phase of his punishment was complete. I quickly replaced the birth certificate and shoved the box back under the bed. Miss Lipstick entered the room, her appearance haggard. Her eyes darted from the bed to my face. She knew I'd been snooping.

"Found what you was looking for?" she asked as she crawled into bed.

"Why do you have my birth certificate anyway, Miss Lipstick? Shouldn't my Momma have that?" I asked.

"She should."

"Why is her name missing on it?" I asked.

"Baby, you got a right to know all that. I just can't tell you right now. I'm tired. Jerome won't be messing with you no more . . ." She rolled over and closed her eyes.

"But . . ." I started.

"It's too late for you to go home. Stay here tonight." Miss Lipstick was out after that. I went into the living room to find Root Charlie and Jerome gone. Only a pool of what I hoped was sweat remained where he'd been standing. I decided to bed down with Miss Lipstick for the night. I had no idea what the next day would bring.

/CHAPTER XX/

I overslept Friday morning. When I finally awoke at 9:30, Miss Lipstick was not next to me. The scent of real eggs and crisp bacon brought me to my feet. In the kitchen, Phyllis was cooking up a storm.

"Hey, Phyllis. I didn't know you cooked, too."

"Well, good morning to you, too, sunshine," she said sarcastically.

"Oh, good morning." My manners were atrocious.

"Don't you know there ain't nothing Phyllis can't do." My stomach appreciated the genuine fare. I ate enough for three people.

"Where's Miss Lipstick?" I finally got around to asking after my fourth cup of hand-squeezed, non-concentrated, orange juice.

"She had something to take care of this morning. She said not to wake you up." Phyllis avoided my eyes the way she did when she was reluctant to tell me the truth or protecting me from it.

"What's really going on, Phyllis?"

"Let Miss Lipstick handle things," she said. "You want some more eggs? For a little thing, you sure can put it away."

"What things? I thought she handled things last night with Jerome." Bits of the toast I was nibbling on were flying out of my mouth.

"She went to talk to your Momma, baby. She left about fifteen minutes ago."

To my knowledge, Miss Lipstick had not left her house in weeks due to her poor health. If she went out, it had to be important. I wolfed down the last bit of toast and bolted before Phyllis could stop me. She chased me down the sidewalk yelling for me to come back. I couldn't stop.

I reached the projects in record time. A small crowd had gathered at the foot of the steps leading to the apartment. Root Charlie sat stoic in the driver's seat of his deuce and a quarter, parked with abandon on the sidewalk. The neighborhood children surrounded the car, touching it and sitting on it. I climbed the stairs two at a time.

The door was open and a heated exchange was already taking place. I slid as close to the door as I could without being seen.

"Ain't nobody gonna give a child to no old, broke-down whore," Momma said angrily.

"Broke-down whore? Girl, I'm the master whore!" Miss Lipstick bragged. "I been under some of the finest men in this county and a few in the next. They come looking for Lipstick, you hear me! You don't know what men'll do to have they cake and eat it, too. Some men can only handle a slice, but others can open a bakery. When Lipstick call, they answer. Don't think I can't get what I want."

"Well, you can't have her." Momma retorted loudly.

"You ain't taking care of her," Miss Lipstick said with her usual calm. "How did that boy know where she would be and when? He ain't no genius and he ain't no mind reader."

"I didn't have nothing t-t-to do with that," Momma said, beginning to stutter.

"That's mighty funny, considering you came by the house looking for her. You ain't done that the whole time she been working for me," Miss Lipstick pointed out.

"I had an appointment. She was supposed to be at your house," Momma said, trying her best to deflect the accusations.

"That don't wash with me, Millie. You ain't holding up your end of the bargain. I told you what would happen if you didn't keep your promise." Miss Lipstick said.

"You know what, Lipstick," Momma said. "I'm sick of this promise. I never should have told Karla I would do something like this."

That tidbit of information nearly caused me to interrupt. I held back.

"You need to crawl up out of your own mess and think about that child. I tell you what," Miss Lipstick continued. "You let another man touch her like that, you got my word all they gonna find of you is that pin in your leg. You got me?"

"I'm not scared of you, Lipstick." Momma lied brazenly.

"You a fool not to be. If it wasn't for Karla, you'd be long gone by now, missy," said Miss Lipstick.

"You ain't never gonna forgive me, are you?" Momma asked.

"Millie, you ain't never said you was sorry." I heard footsteps coming to the door, but I didn't move. Miss Lipstick displayed no surprise when she saw me. Her skin appeared grayish in the sunlight. She wore a dress I'd never seen before — a long, black one, with red roses on it. On her feet were white flats. A newer black wig graced her head. She had aged another twenty years since the night before. She walked by me and waved down to Root Charlie. The giant man opened his door, sending the neighborhood children scurrying away. He climbed the stairs as I did and assisted Miss Lipstick down and to the car.

I was guarded as I crossed the threshold into the apartment. Momma may have said she wasn't afraid of Miss Lipstick, but her mug told a different story. She was on her knees, slobbering. Her hair was standing straight up on her head and matted in the back, the way it looked when she got up out of bed. She was in her customary T-shirt and panties. Her crutch was across the room.

My mind couldn't process all that I had just heard. I was in shut-down mode and the questions that should have cropped up all over the place were put in pause. Karla's name alone should have sent me into a psychic overload. I was staring at momma, or this woman I thought was my momma.

"What you looking at?" Momma screamed at me.

"What happened?" I asked.

"Like you don't know." She struggled to get up, so I tried to help by getting her crutch.

"Put it down!" Momma yelled. "I don't need no help from you."

"I'm gonna change clothes," I said. I needed to remove myself from the vicinity of this powder keg.

"I don't care what you do. I hope you happy. Lipstick done run off Jerome. Now I ain't got nobody!" She started to cry again. I didn't know what to do. I went to my room and closed the door. I planned to spend the day at the library to give Momma a chance to cool down. I searched all over and couldn't find a single book.

"Momma, where are my books?" I asked.

"Check the bathroom. If I ain't happy, you ain't gone be happy neither!" she said, staring me down with her hands on her hips. I should have known her statement was a prelude to disaster.

I approached the bathroom cautiously, the faint smell of smoke entering my nostrils. I threw the door open and encountered a traumatic sight. Every book I had in my possession, including the borrowed library books, had been torched beyond recognition and then drowned. Their charred remains floated on the surface of the water. The plastic tub had melted and warped. Ironically, the only two books to survive the senseless destruction were the books Momma could not get to under my bed — Pastor Ricky's Bible and Mr. Pierce's college manual.

This was the final straw. I marched into the living room with my battle face on, ready to unleash some long overdue teenage rebellion. I could not suppress the hatred that radiated from me and flowed in waves toward Momma. A girl shouldn't feel that way about her mother. She waited for me, pouring one beer after another down her throat, with impunity.

"Why would you do something like that?" I screamed. "What did I ever do to you?"

Her reaction was anything but kind. "You were born and I got stuck with you," Momma sneered.

"You don't have to be stuck with me anymore," I said. Buoyed by my newfound independence, I proceeded to manifest in words what I'd been feeling in my heart for years. "I hate you! I wish you were dead!"

"I'm already dead, girl," was Momma's parting shot.

In my inept attempt to hurt Momma, I blurted out, "I'm moving in with Miss Lipstick."

"Go on. I don't care." Momma's words started to slur.

"She ain't nobody to look up to. You know what she is? Men pay her to . . ."

I curtailed her sentence. "You don't think I know that? I'm not naïve," I murmured.

"There you go again with them big words," she said. Momma was past the point of being drunk. She was highly intoxicated.

"At least she doesn't have to pay men to be with her," I shot back. My arrow had found its target. Momma swung at me and I ducked. She threw herself on the floor.

"You don't know nothing!" she spat in my face. Her high yellow complexion deepened to an unattractive burgundy. "She killed her own child. Yeah! Wanna look up to her now. And you wanna know what else? She your grandma. That's right. You come from a bunch of . . ."

I didn't hear the rest. I was out the door, down the street and turning the corner before she could put a period on that sentence.

/CHAPTER XXI/

I burst into Miss Lipstick's house like one of Quincy's finest. It was business as usual. A multitude of people filled Miss Lipstick's house to capacity, both inside and on the porch. I dispensed with my usual pleasantries and got right down to business.

"Where is Miss Lipstick? I need to talk to her right now!" I said to anybody who was listening. The door to her bedroom opened and Dr. Sally emerged. He shook his head sadly. I pivoted to confront Root Charlie. That hulking figure of a man was no longer distant and preoccupied; his baby face features exhibited genuine distress.

"Dr. Sally?" My pride, or perhaps arrogance, had elevated me to an irrational being. Dr. Sally's presence extracted sanity.

"I'm sorry, baby. She doesn't have long. If you need to talk to her, you have to calm down. She can't handle all this drama."

"What's wrong with her, doctor? Can you tell me?"

"It's cancer, my dear," he said resolutely.

My heart dropped to my stomach. I was in danger of losing my wits, and my breakfast, if I didn't get it together. I received silent approval from Dr. Sally to go in. I cracked the door open a fraction, and the first thing to meet me was the scent of sickness and decay. The ten bottles on the floor had tripled in number and there were enough medical supplies to stock a small pharmacy. Then, Phyllis rushed at me. She wasn't her usual optimistic, energetic self, but just a strained outline. She gave me a superficial smile, not the disarming grin that could light up a dark room.

"This ain't a good time, precious," she muttered.

"Miss Lipstick?" I said softly. Miss Lipstick's face was turned away from me, toward the lone window. Even in a prostrate position, with covers up to her chin, she appeared shrunken and feeble. Her hair had been neatly corn rowed, most likely Phyllis' work, but there was more scalp than hair. Her skin hung loosely around her face and neck. The moles on her face seemed to have grown and leapt off her body. I couldn't move from the spot.

"She need to rest," said Phyllis, a steeliness entering her tone.

Miss Lipstick turned her head slowly, and in voice barely above a whisper, she said, "No, you leave, Phyllis. I have to talk to my baby."

Phyllis was reluctant to go, but she obeyed Miss Lipstick's wishes. Miss Lipstick patted the side of her bed. "Come sit here by me."

It was the longest three steps of my life. Miss Lipstick's breathing was labored. When she exhaled, it seemed like an eternity before she inhaled again. I didn't want to stress her, but I needed answers.

"I have to know, Miss Lipstick. Are you my grandma?" She bobbed her head up and down. "Then Momma isn't . . . She isn't . . ." I could not construct a lucid thought from the disjointed string of words coming out of me.

"That's right baby, Millie is not your Momma," Miss Lipstick summarized for me. "Not the one that birthed you."

I had a million and one questions and I didn't know in which order to ask them. I plunged ahead. "Who is Karla? Tell me about her."

Miss Lipstick cried and I joined her.

"Karla was a wonderful child. The best any mother could hope for. She was good and kind, just like you, baby." She put her narration on pause to sit up in the bed. Every position seemed uncomfortable. I should have let her rest, like the doctor ordered, but my boundless curiosity was finally being satisfied. "Lord, she was smart. Brought home report cards with nothing but 'A's on it. Just like you. And she loved to read, too. I was so proud of her. God knows I loved that child. I didn't want to do nothing to hurt her." Miss Lipstick stopped and closed her eyes. I imagined she was meditating on her daughter's face.

"What happened to Karla?" I prompted her.

"What I do for a living made Karla turn against me when she got up in age. She was doing real good in school and was supposed to go to college. To spite me, she got wild and did things unspeakable. But she changed when she got pregnant with you. She stopped drinking and all that other stuff."

"Momma said you killed her," I stated. "I didn't believe her because she was drunk."

"In a way, she was right." Miss Lipstick shuddered. "We were getting back right with each other, you know. She was studying to go to college and everything. Then, one day, her best friend came by and took her for a ride. They got into an accident and Karla got hurt real bad. Real bad." Miss Lipstick seemed imprisoned by the memory, so I caressed the dry, peeling skin on her forearm to let her know she was not alone.

"She went into labor because of the accident, and they took her to the emergency room. But there was a problem." Miss Lipstick's voice was weak and hoarse. "The doctors gave her a choice. And she decided before I could get there." Fresh tears coated her face.

"What did she do?" I was enthralled and couldn't sit still. Our wet eyes met and she squeezed my hand tighter.

"They could save her or they could save the baby. She told them to save the baby."

The magnitude of what Miss Lipstick told me rattled me to my core. I grieved for a mother I never knew, but who had given me everything. All those heroes in my fantasies and dreams were embodied in one real person, my mother — my real mother. I thought about all that I had missed, all that I could have been, the life I could have had, and I grieved for her anew.

Miss Lipstick and I held each other and wept in unison. "Baby, don't cry so much," she said as she stroked my hair. "When you look in the mirror, you looking at your momma and she was beautiful. Get that basket out of that closet over there."

I disentangled myself from her embrace and went to the closet. I found the basket behind a moth-eaten wardrobe. It was heavy and covered by an old towel. I brought the basket to Miss Lipstick and pulled the towel back. Inside, there were all sorts of trinkets and small boxes.

"You know what this is?" Miss Lipstick asked and smiled.

"No, ma'am," I replied.

"These are your birthday presents. Fifteen of them. I gave you some of them already." She rifled through the box, pulling out box after box.

"The radio and the watch?" I asked.

"That's right. But this is what I wanted you to see." Miss Lipstick lifted out all the boxes and a flat piece of cardboard. Underneath that was a long, flat object wrapped in another towel. She removed the towel to reveal a beautiful, glass picture frame with a silver-gilded edge and slots for three pictures. Two of the slots were already filled. The first picture was of that little girl in pigtails whom I had seen earlier and thought was me.

"I can't believe I didn't figure it out before," I said. "So this was Karla." She was beautiful, as Miss Lipstick had described. We shared the same smile. I scanned the next picture, which absolutely took my breath away. It was Karla and she was in a hospital bed. She was oblivious to the camera because she was cradling an infant in her arms, kissing tiny cheeks.

"Me?" I brought the picture to my chest, so my heart could beat against it.

"She died not long after I took that picture," Miss Lipstick said. "I was able to see her hold you and love on you. She loved you something awful." She traced her finger over the face of the little girl in the first picture. "This other place is for your college picture."

The thought of my real momma loving me enlivened me, but saddened me, also. Something still didn't make sense to me.

"Why didn't you raise me? How did I end up with Momma, I mean Millie?" The mention of her fraudulent name was distasteful.

"I couldn't, baby." Miss Lipstick shrugged her shoulders. "I was too old and I couldn't bring no baby around this place." She hesitated. "And, I was scared you wouldn't love me."

"You, Miss Lipstick?" It was too incredible to associate Miss Lipstick's name with the word fear. "I didn't think you were afraid of anything."

"Believe it, honey. I was scared you might turn away from me like Karla did, and I couldn't lose you. You all I got left of my baby. That's why I had Millie bring you around here every few years so I could love on you, too. I couldn't do it no more when you got older. I just didn't want you to know, so I did for you what I could, even if you never saw fit to love me."

"But I do love you, Miss Lipstick. I mean, Grandma. Can I call you Grandma?"

"You don't know how long I been waiting to hear that." We shed a fresh batch of tears, but this time, there was more joy. Miss Lipstick's grip had loosened up. Her strength was waning and it was time for her to rest.

I massaged my throbbing temples. The roller coaster of emotions was over stimulating my brain. "So I wasn't dreaming that time I came over here and played with your moles. I knew it was you kissing on me. Momma never did anything like that."

She nodded. "I remember that. I remember every one of your visits." She continued to nod, her chin resting on her chest for several seconds before she brought her head up again.

"I'm leaving so you can rest now, Grandma." The word melted in my mouth like butter.

"Hold on, baby," Miss Lipstick squeaked. She held her head up, but her eyes were closed. "You have to do two things for me. You have to go to college. It's what Karla wanted."

The business with college would not go away. I could not reject out of hand the request of a dead mother and a dying grandmother.

"I'm scared. I don't want to leave Quincy," I said sheepishly.

"I understand you scared. But you can lay down and let fear beat you or you can stand up and fight it." Miss Lipstick's neck muscles strained as she spoke, but she continued her lecture. "These people in my house — every one of 'em laid down, and stayed down. When they got up, they still needed help, that crutch we talked about. If you can make yourself forget about that fear, you don't have to deal with it. And you put it off 'til you can't get rid of the crutch. A few tried to get up like Phyllis and Pastor Ricky. I even let it beat me. Being scared kept me away from you too long."

I couldn't argue with that logic, but it added another layer to the dilemma I'd been struggling with all summer. I started to get up again.

"What's the other thing?" I asked.

"Giving you up to somebody else was a hard thing to do. Everything I done was for your best." She was drifting away from me. "I know you ain't been getting along so well with Millie, but I need you to try to make up with her."

Before I could protest, she fell asleep.

Phyllis peeked in on Miss Lipstick, and then pulled me out to the porch. I could not relax enough to sit down, and I was too tired to stand up, so I leaned against the porch post, exhausted and mentally pillaged.

"Why didn't anybody tell me this before?" I asked Phyllis angrily.

"It wasn't nobody's place to tell you nothing until Lipstick was ready for you to know," she replied.

"But all those years Millie mistreated me and let her boyfriends mess with me and made me go all over the place getting her beers, I could have been here. That's not fair," I preached.

"I can't answer for how Millie treated you, but I can tell you how Lipstick always cared for you," Phyllis said. "She might not have been able to put her arms around you every day like she wanted, but she always made sure you was gonna be OK after she was gone."

"I don't want to talk about that," I said. Losing my grandmother when I'd just found her wasn't right.

"You have to face it, precious," Phyllis said as she gathered my face in her hands. "Why you think you just now coming over here? Lipstick could have brought you over here years ago. You know why?"

I answered in the negative.

"Because, Lipstick knew she was dying even before you started working for her." Phyllis let this information sink in before going on. "She wanted to spend as much time as she could with her baby's baby. And she wanted to make sure you had the money you need to go to college. That's why you been seeing folks coming and going all summer bringing in money. She cut off everybody tab and made them pay up because she was building up your account. She wouldn't even let me get a taste on credit." Phyllis's sincere smile returned. "You gonna be all right, gorgeous."

"What about all that money Momma, I mean Millie, was getting every month? Do you know anything about that?" I asked.

"That was Lipstick, too. Millie was supposed to be taking care of you with that," Phyllis responded.

"See, Phyllis. She didn't know anything about being a mother. I would have been better off letting Johnny raise me." We chuckled about that ridiculous notion.

"Listen, precious. You don't know everything that happened back then. You got to cut Millie some slack," Phyllis advised me.

"No. I hate her. I never want to see her again," I said with conviction.

"Don't say that. You have to remember, she hurting, too," Phyllis said.

"I don't care about her. I'll just come and live with Miss Lipstick."

"You know you can't do that right now."

"I'm not going home," I said stubbornly.

I did not return home, and school was over. I spent the next couple of weeks reveling in my newfound relationship with my grandmother and, on occasion, my friend, Katherine. I rarely left my grandmother's bedside. I administered her medicines until they offered her no relief from the suffering. I fed her soft foods until her appetite abandoned her. I poured water down her parched throat until she began coughing up spoonfuls. When she could talk, we talked about Karla. When she wanted to discuss college, I clammed up.

Miss Lipstick had some good days, but disproportionately, they were bad. On the worst days, I read to her. She'd bought me a collection of Agatha Christie's works and several others of my favorite authors. I sat Indian-style on the floor and read with all the energy and enthusiasm I could muster, willing my healthy vibes to invade her body. Some days, she had to scold me to get out of her face and get myself something to eat.

On one of Miss Lipstick's better days, Katherine dropped by to visit me. It was about 10:00 in the morning on that Thursday. I was reluctant to leave but Phyllis told me to get out of the house.

"Go on and spend some time with your friend. I got Miss Lipstick," she said. Spending time with Katherine was just the healing balm my bruised soul needed. Miss Lipstick made sure my pockets were never empty. One day, she ordered Root Charlie to drive Katherine and me to the mall in Tallahassee where we shopped for hours. I bought myself a whole new wardrobe — two snazzy, multi-colored dresses, some new denim jeans, and pants and tops that matched from name brand stores where I didn't get change back from a five dollar bill. I bought three pairs of shoes — some real sneakers, a pair of black open-toed, strappy high heels, and some sensible brown flats. I treated Katherine to some new outfits as well. She chose an orange blouse, a green blouse, a pair of jeans and a pair of black slacks.

"I never had clothes that covered up everything," Katherine said. She could have chosen a brown paper bag and it would have looked good on her. Her new clothes didn't cover up everything, though. Her inner beauty shone clear through the thickest material.

Before we left the mall, I bought a present for Miss Lipstick. It was a bottle of perfume called Jasmine.

Miss Lipstick also insisted we stop at a friend's hair salon. I had my hair permed by a professional. It was cut and styled with that Farrah flip I loved so much, with the feathering at the forehead. Even I thought it was becoming to me. Katherine, on the other hand, only needed her hair washed. It was still shiny and wavy and slicked back on her head. She wore it loose around her shoulders. Everybody in the salon complimented her on it, and nobody touched her.

We wore our new outfits and new hair-dos to the library that day. "We'll be back soon. We're just going to the library." I was sure I said an hour.

Katherine and I sojourned through the city. I had not been back through the pass since the attack. The trauma was still too fresh.

"I'm glad you found out Miss Lipstick is your grandma," Katherine said. "That's real cool."

"It is cool. It's just so much fun being with her, even though she's really sick," I shared with her.

"That's good." Katherine broached the next subject cautiously. "What about your momma? You ain't been home in a while."

"Oh, more good news. She ain't my momma, just like your daddy said," I said with mock cheerfulness.

"You just gonna leave her?" Katherine asked. "She might not be your real momma, but she the only momma you got."

"I got Miss Lipstick now. I don't need her," I said with certainty.

"OK. Whatever you say. I almost forgot, though. Mr. Pierce axed me to ax you if you still wanted to do that Upward Bound thing."

"Asked, Katherine," I found myself correcting her. "Say asked."

"Asked," Katherine said, over exaggerating the word and rolling her eyes. "Guess what? He asked me to do it, too. So you gotta do it!" She was so excited. I couldn't say no, not right then.

Mrs. McCullough gave me a warm hug when I entered the library. She still hugged me even after I told her that I'd had a little accident with the books. I insisted this time, that she take some compensation for the damaged books. I also asked if she could order a replacement English Literature book on my tab since Mr. Pierce said Katherine had to buy a new textbook. After all, Katherine wouldn't need the tenth grade text anymore— she'd be reading eleventh grade material in the coming weeks.

Katherine and I had such a good time with Mrs. Mac, the time had flown by. When we left, we stopped at the ice cream shop to get sundaes, but in honor of Pastor Ricky, I called mine a Saturdae. As we rounded the curb to Miss Lipstick's house, I could feel that something was wrong. There were multitudes of people standing outside in the yard. As I got closer, I saw that the porch had also exceeded its maximum capacity. I dropped my ice cream at somebody's feet and tunneled my way through the house. I tried to get into her room, but somebody tugged on the back of my shirt. I spun around and looked up to see Root Charlie with tears in his eyes. I absolutely knew then.

"Noooo!" I screamed. "Nooo. I said I'd be right back!" I was hysterical, jumping up and down in the middle of the floor. Phyllis came out of the room and I could see behind her that the bed was empty. "Phyllis, no. Please tell me she's not gone."

Phyllis could only shake her head. Her eyes were puffy. Her mouth quivered. She tried to console me, but I was beyond consolation. I started kicking and screaming and beating the walls. I became too much for Phyllis to handle. I let grief overtake me and I wallowed in it. Several people, including Mr. Curtis and Johnny, had to clear out of the house to give me room to express it physically.

"That was my grandma. She can't be gone. She can't be gone. Why, God, why!" I wailed. "I got nobody else to love me. They're all gone. Who's going to love me now?" I asked piteously.

"You got a whole room full of people who love you, precious," Phyllis said in her most soothing voice. "Every one of us love you, baby. You ain't alone, and you still got your momma."

I still fought the invisible forces that stole my grandmother from me. She left me that day, for good, on August 18. Suddenly, I was scooped up in a vice-like embrace. Root Charlie picked me up as if I were a rag doll, and brought me to his wall of a chest. He held me tight while I squirmed. He held me until I could fight no more. He held me until his tears mixed with mine. He held me into the night, while others around us prepared to bury my loving grandmother.

They would lay my grandmother, Miss Lipstick, to rest on Saturday, August 21. She didn't want a church funeral. She wanted a simple burial at the gravesite, and had asked to be laid next to her daughter, my mother, Karla, at the Cottrell Cemetery. I slept in her bed at her house, soaking the sheets and pillows I had washed many times over. I woke up the day of the funeral, the Saturday after she passed away, and it seemed the air was a little less pure, the birds sang just a little less, and the sun was not as bright.

Among those who came to pay their respects to Miss Lipstick were several men of diverse races in dark suits and shades who skulked about the outer circle of the mourners. Root Charlie looked tall and handsome in his shirt and tie. Mr. Curtis looked sober and dignified in his suit. Even Johnny was upright and silent during the service. Phyllis was neatly dressed in a black skirt and top, and Katherine was resplendent in a black top and jeans. I wore a simple, black A-line dress that Miss Lipstick had Phyllis purchase for me two weeks before she died.

I think I cried enough tears that day for everyone out there. After the funeral director made his speech about this concluding the services for Miss Beatrice "Lipstick" Miller, the crowd began to disperse. Most of them headed back to Miss Lipstick's house, now mine, to take part in the repast.

Mr. Curtis stood next to me, and I leaned into his shoulder.

"What am I going to do now, Mr. Curtis?" I asked, tears spilling all over my dress and my nose running.

Mr. Curtis took a handkerchief out of his breast pocket and gave it to me. Then his clear eyes met mine and he said, "You got to pull yourself out of her grave and find something to live the rest of your life for." Those words had a familiar, haunting echo.

"I don't know if I can." Katherine came back to my side and rubbed my back.

A figure in black lingered after most of the others had left. I recognized her immediately and began to walk in the opposite direction.

"Fla, wait. Can I talk to you?" Millie asked. She was wearing a bra. It was the least she could do in honor of Miss Lipstick. Her face was flawless and her eyes glistened under very light make up. She didn't have her crutch.

"I don't want to hear anything you have to say," I said as I continued walking. "Let's go, Katherine."

"Fla, please." I'd never heard that word from Millie in my whole life. I slowed my steps but I did not stop.

"Fla, meet her halfway. Come on," Katherine said. "You know that's what your grandma wanted." I wished she hadn't brought that up, but I owed it to Miss Lipstick.

"What?" I said rudely.

"I don't know where to begin," she said.

"I don't have all day," I said.

"Karla was a good friend to me. I called her Mimi because it just seemed right. She was the best friend a girl could have. We hung out together. We got in trouble together. We did everything together. Then she got pregnant."

I let Millie talk. As soon as she was done, I wouldn't have to listen to her anymore.

"Mimi was always smart in school. I knew she would go places. She stopped hanging out with me and started studying for college. All she could talk about was that baby. Baby Jasmine this and Baby Jasmine that. She didn't have time for me anymore."

"Wait," I said. I thought I'd heard wrong. "She was going to name me Jasmine?"

"Yeah," Millie replied. "Me and Karla was in high school with Ricky, Pastor Ricky. Karla loved the name Jasmine and Ricky liked it, too. So, when he had a little girl with his wife, I wasn't surprised he named her Jasmine."

"How did I end up with the name Fla?" I asked bitterly.

Millie shrugged her shoulders. "Karla begged me to take care of you. I couldn't say no. She was dying. Then, Miss Lipstick made me go through with it. It all happened so fast, we all forgot about the birth certificate. I was still hurt over Karla and just named you after the only thing I saw on the birth certificate. That was the state."

"I don't believe you," I said.

"It's true," Millie went on. "I honestly couldn't think of Jasmine and I just never bothered to get it changed. "Anyway," Millie resumed her painful story. "I asked Mimi to go for a ride with me in that Honda, and we got into an accident." She began twisting her hands. "I was drunk, Fla. I lost control of the car and hit a pole. Messed up my leg real bad. If it hadn't been for me, she would still be here." Millie's voice was filled with anguish, but I felt no pity for her. I was enraged and exploded.

"You killed my Momma, and you had the nerve to say Miss Lipstick killed her! I hate you! I wish you had died instead of my momma."

"Fla," Millie said. "Don't you get it? I am dead. I died in that accident, too. I live with the guilt every day. I loved Karla. She was a good person and smart and she was going places. I always saw that in you."

"Then why do you hate me? Why did you treat me so bad? All those times Jerome was bothering me and messing with me, you didn't stop him!" I was furious and wounded. "Ever since I got home after Jerome attacked me, I believed you set me up for that." I could barely finish the sentence. "Why did you let him hurt me like that?" I asked. "He hurt me real bad, Momma." I didn't mean for "momma" slip out.

"I'm sorry, Fla. I'm so sorry. I tried to stop him, but he wouldn't. I came over to Lipstick's that day to get you, but you were already gone. Ask Phyllis. I wish I could make it up to you, but I can't," Millie sobbed.

"You're sorry because you won't be getting those checks anymore. I'm even getting money from my daddy. And Miss Lipstick, I mean my grandma was smart enough to buy toilet paper stock all these years and I get that money, too. So, see, I don't need you." I spat at her. "You'll have to get your own beers from now on."

"That ain't it. I promise. I need you to forgive me, Fla. Give me another chance." Her eyes pleaded with me.

"You killed my momma, treated me like garbage for years, and you want me to forgive you!" I yelled. "I don't think so." I left her in the graveyard, a sobbing, wet mess on the ground.

I became an adult a little earlier than I'd planned. I had no mother, no father, and now no grandmother. They'd all left me. I was an orphan. On whose doorstep would I rest? I was thankful for Katherine. Her shoulder was on permanent loan to me. If it weren't for her and Phyllis, I might have joined my mother and grandmother.

"What are you gonna do with yourself?" Katherine asked me. "You can't live with me and you know you can't be in Miss Lipstick's house."

"I can take care of myself," I said.

"You said that before." She was quiet for a moment. "You need somebody to look after you."

"I got Phyllis."

"But you told me Phyllis was going back into rehab so she could get her baby back," Katherine reminded me.

"Yes, but she can have two babies, right?" I was hopeful.

"That would be a lot on her," Katherine said, making good sense.

"I suppose. It wouldn't be fair to her."

"So, there's only one other place you can go."

"I'd rather live in the streets," I said angrily.

"You don't mean that, Jasmine." My new name sounded good to my ears, but what Katherine was suggesting was like vinegar on my tongue.

"You have to forgive her. Isn't that what Pastor Ricky would have wanted? Didn't you tell me he was all about forgiveness?" Katherine was good at reminding me of my own words.

"But look where forgiveness got him."

"That's because he didn't forgive the one person who needed it the most. Himself." Katherine would have made a great counselor, or preacher herself. "Who in your life needs forgiveness right now?"

"That's not fair, Katherine. You know what she did to me."

Katherine shrugged her shoulders. "A lot of stuff has been done to a lot of people. You can dwell on it the rest of your life like a crutch, or you can throw it away and start over. Have a real good life for a change."

I wanted to slap Katherine. Everything she said was right, but what I wanted to hear was that Millie was wrong and deserved to live out the rest of her days in utter misery. She was also right that I couldn't continue to stay at my grandmother's house. Although it would be mine when I became legal, I couldn't live there without Phyllis, who was determined to do everything necessary to get Vishay back. I had a lot of decisions to make.

My tenth grade year loomed on the horizon. Normally, I would have been excited, but I was still in the midst of my grief. Since Katherine was moving on to the eleventh grade, we wouldn't be sharing the same classes. Although we had become inseparable, I still wished we could also be in the same grade.

Miss Lipstick's was never again the same. Johnny made his way to Miss Rutha looking for shots. I saw Eugene from time to time around town, but he never darkened the doorstep. Root Charlie arrived every morning and sat in his corner, apparently waiting for somebody to tell him to get on the job. Katherine came over to walk with me to the school to give Mr. Pierce our birth certificates.

"Look at it, Kat," I said. I opened up my birth certificate and proudly read the baby's name on it. "Jasmine Miller." It rolled off my tongue. "That's me. Jasmine."

"You want to come by my house later?" Katherine asked.

"Yes," I answered. "But let's stop by Millie's place first."

"You're going back?" She was excited.

"She asked me to come back. She said she wanted to talk to me about my momma. I guess that's as good a place to start as any."

The end

About the Author

Felicia S.W. Thomas is a freelance writer currently living in her native Quincy, Florida, with her husband and three children. She holds a B.S. in Journalism and a law degree. She has written many short stories, plays, and other creative works, but *80 Proof Lives* is her first published novel.

Contact her at:
feliciathomas917@hotmail.com,
www.feliciaswthomas.com, and on Facebook.

CPSIA information can be obtained at www.ICGtesting.com
Printed in the USA

240468LV00004B/2/P